A Lo

Eternity

JANICE K. BRASWELL

OakTara

WATERFORD, VIRGINIA

A Love for Eternity

Published in the U.S. by:
OakTara Publishers
P.O. Box 8
Waterford, VA 20197

Visit OakTara at **www.oaktara.com**

Cover design by Muses9 Design
Cover image young girl © iStockphoto.com/Igor Balasanov

Copyright © 2009 by Janice K. Braswell. All rights reserved.

Joshua 24:15 (p. 29) and Proverbs 22:6 (p. 222, with author change of "train" to "raise") are taken from the *New American Standard Bible®,* copyright © 1960, 1962, 1963, 1968, 1971, 1972, 1973, 1975, 1977, 1995 by The Lockman Foundation. Used by permission.

Psalm 37:4 (p. 74), Matthew 11:28 (pp. 75, 255), John 6:47 (p. 76), Jeremiah 1:5, the concept (p. 76), Deuteronomy 6 (p. 230), Matthew 11:28 (p. 255) are taken from the HOLY BIBLE, NEW INTERNATIONAL VERSION®. NIV®. Copyright © 1973, 1978, 1984 by International Bible Society. Used by permission of Zondervan. All rights reserved.

Isaiah 40:11 (p. 188) is taken from the King James Version of the Bible.

John 14:1-4 (p. 252) is taken from the *Holy Bible,* New Living Translation, second edition, copyright © 1996, 2004. Used by permission of Tyndale House Publishers, Inc., Carol Stream, Illinois 60188. All rights reserved.

ISBN: 978-1-60290-218-3

A Love for Eternity is a work of fiction. References to real people, events, establishments, organizations, or locales are intended only to provide a sense of authenticity and are used fictitiously. All other characters, incidents, and dialogue are drawn from the author's imagination.

To My Husband, Karl

You truly epitomize what a partner should be in a marriage.
No matter what dream I have wanted to pursue,
you never questioned it, but gave me your unconditional support
even though most times that meant taking up the slack at home.
We have weathered all kinds of storms only to come out stronger.
I thank God for you in my life.

To My Children, April, Ken, Dustin, & Cody
& My Grandchildren, Jake, Luke, & Van

Each one of you has enriched my life beyond measure.

To Wanda, My Mother

If there is an ideal mother-daughter relationship, then I hit the jackpot.
Simple words could never convey how proud I am of you.
Thank you for supporting me when you didn't always agree
and for loving me when I wasn't always lovable.
While our family has gone through trials,
your loyalty has never faltered.

For Jim

I've heard all the quotes about what makes a man a father,
and I have something to add.
For a man to love his wife beyond measure,
to love her children as his own and invest emotionally in his family,
that makes a father. Thank you for being my father.

Acknowledgment

To Ramona, Jeff, and the entire OakTara staff, for taking a chance on a first-time author.

Prologue

Jayden strolled leisurely down the sidewalk with her cap and gown under her arm. Twelve long years of school had come to an end tonight as she'd walked across the stage and accepted her diploma. It should have been one of the memorable times in her life, yet it was hard to be happy when the only two guests she invited for the ceremony didn't show up.

The sun was starting to set, but the festivities were well underway. For once she wanted to be a part of them. In all the years she'd lived in the small west Texas town of Odessa, Jayden had been considered an outsider. "If you ain't born here, then you ain't a true Odessan," she was once told.

She was startled when a line of cars passed her, their occupants hooting and hollering.

Family and friends were gathered all over town tonight in honor of their graduate. The aroma of outdoor grilling filled the air, a reminder to Jayden that she hadn't eaten all day. Off in the distance, a Mariachi band played loud enough to break a city ordinance; however, no one would complain. The chaos was expected. Graduation from high school was a rite of passage.

Today was Jayden Arman's emancipation. No longer would she be someone's meal ticket or a case number in an overburdened foster care system. It was a new beginning. No matter how uncertain her future was, it had to be better than the last ten years of her life. That should be reason enough to celebrate. Yet when she walked away tonight, she'd be leaving behind the one person in this world who gave meaning to her life: five-year-old Emma.

One

The wooden planks creaked as Jayden sat down on the front porch. A cool breeze washed over her. She pulled her lime green gingham dress over her knees. It wasn't the semi-formal attire most of the girls wore for the big event, but that didn't matter. The resale shop price fit her pocketbook.

Unclipping the long silver barrette, her hair cascaded to her shoulders. There was no doubt that she was her mother's daughter with her auburn hair, ivory cream complexion, and hazel eyes. Quite unlike her father's dark Mediterranean features.

Not a day went by that Jayden didn't wish she could turn back the clock and not carry the stigma of "foster child."

Jayden sighed. *Daddy, I wish you hadn't taken away our choices.* She wiped away tears before they streaked down her cheeks. She glanced at the unopened gift. It was from Jonathan Baxter, youth minister at the church where Emma attended Sunday school. She assumed he was invited to the graduation by the group of seniors from church, but when he saw her he immediately came over.

"I wanted you to have this." Jonathan handed her what was obviously a book wrapped in comic strip paper and a picture he had taken of her crossing the stage.

Over the last several months she had developed a wonderful relationship with Jonathan Baxter. He possessed all the charm of a born leader. He had charisma, was articulate when he spoke, and presented himself with such confidence. He was the epitome of style. His chestnut-colored hair touched the top of his shirt collar and was way too long for the older generation who considered anyone without a crew-cut a rabble-rouser. His eyes were the color of driftwood. A neatly trimmed beard lined his chiseled jaw line with a hint of aftershave that was enough to arouse one's sense of smell. Never one to dress conservatively, he looked more like a movie star in a pullover shirt, sports jacket, and casual slacks.

Jayden reflected on the time she met him....

It was in the spring on a Sunday morning, a time when the earth woke from winter hibernation spreading new wealth across the land, a time when the West Texas sun spared its desert inhabitants from the scorching sun.

The Sunday routine rarely varied. Jayden took Emma to Bible class and waited out front for her. It was the one time of the week Emma was able to socialize with other five-year-olds and the one time of the week Jayden had an entire hour of heavenly solitude. Jayden loved this stage of childhood. It was a most precious age, an age when the young minds of children were untainted by society's skewed views of right and wrong, a time free from prejudice and free from casting judgment on others. A child didn't notice the color of one's skin or dwell on handicaps. It was a time of unconditional acceptance.

The particular Sunday when she met Jonathan, she assumed her usual place on the bench at the south end of the church, waiting for Emma to burst through the doors with a slew of papers. Jayden had settled into a comfortable position and leaned her head backwards, her face tilted toward the sky. Between the tranquil surroundings and the sunrays bathing her flesh in a sedating sea of warmth, Jayden found it difficult to remain awake. With her eyes closed she started to nod off when suddenly she heard a man's voice.

She bolted up and cupped her hand over her brow to shield against the sun's harsh glare. A nice-looking young man sat at the other end of the bench.

"Pardon me. I didn't hear what you said," Jayden asked.

"I said, 'It's nice to see you again.'"

"I'm sorry, but you must have me confused with someone else."

"I don't think so. I've seen you here several times on a Sunday morning. You leave when a little blonde girl comes out. Your sister?"

"Yes."

"That's interesting," Jonathan said.

"How's that?" Jayden looked puzzled.

"I don't know; I guess that's what you call filler. You know, when you don't know what else to say. I guess I should introduce myself." Jonathan stuck out his hand. "My name is Jonathan Baxter, and I'm the youth pastor of this church. Would you and your sister be my guest for church service today?"

"Thanks, but as soon as Emma gets out, I need to go home and fix her lunch."

"See, that's the beauty of it all. After the service some of our best Southern cooks in the congregation have conjured up a potluck. I've seen it; there's enough food to feed an army." He smiled, as if to convince her. "And with all that aside, it would really help me out if both of you were there," he said, hoping to persuade her.

"How is it that by attending church service I would be helping you out?"

"For starters, today is the first time I've opened the service. All eyes will be gaping at the young pastor, waiting for that little slip-up."

"Isn't that rather judgmental of the congregation?"

"Maybe, but this congregation knows their stuff. They don't nor do they deserve to be led by a pastor who doesn't know his as well."

"You want me to critique something I'm not even familiar with? How would I know if you were doing it right? No thanks, I'll pass. I'm not a Jesus follower or a born-again Christian or whatever the term is."

"Yet you sit out here every Sunday."

"Only to bring Emma to class because that's what SHE loves to do."

"If that's truly your only reason, then maybe you would allow me the opportunity to share with you."

"I don't understand."

"There is so much I would like to share with you," Jonathan said quietly.

Jayden was normally uncomfortable with this topic, but she was curious to see what Jonathan would say.

"For instance, the way you say 'Jesus follower' with such disdain tells me that you don't know Him personally. And I don't judge you for that. Unfortunately, a lot of people, even some in the church, don't know Him. You see, going to church every Sunday, knowing all the songs, even knowing the books of the Bible, doesn't necessarily mean that you have met Jesus in your heart. Many people miss it."

"I'm happy with the way things are."

"But if they could be better?"

"Things are the way they are." Jayden only wished that she could erase her past. "You think my life would be better if I walked into that building?" She pointed in the direction of the chapel.

"No, just entering inside a church building won't change you. There's a lot more to it than that."

Jayden saw Emma running towards her, papers flapping in the wind. "Thank you for your company, Reverend, but I'd better run along."

"Please call me Jonathan."

"All right, Jonathan. I'd better be going and, by the looks of things, so should you." Jayden looked over at the groups of people walking inside the front doors of the chapel.

"I'll see you next week." Jonathan brushed a strand of Emma's hair away from her face.

"Well, I'll be here, the Lord willing."

Jonathan smiled.

Jayden stopped in her tracks, realizing what she had just said. "It's a figure of speech—like a filler…."

Thinking back on that day and the ones that followed, Jayden realized that Jonathan was the only true friend she had ever had. It would be hard to leave her best friend behind. When she'd told him she was leaving, he seemed genuinely saddened by it. Her promise to him was that they wouldn't lose touch.

Two

Jayden gripped the door handle and took a deep breath. *Here we go.*

She walked in and closed the door, then stood in the hallway. Tilly was where she usually could be found—asleep in front of the television. A cigarette hung from her lips with ashes falling onto her lap, and a shot glass of whiskey rested in her hand.

Jayden thought about the first time she'd met the people she lived with. It was right after her mother's funeral....

The social worker pulled in front of the most neglected home on the block. It was the eyesore of the neighborhood. The home of Douglas and Tilly Jenson.

"Here you go—one little girl and a paper bag with a few clothes in it and a box," the social worker said as she handed Jayden over to an unfriendly looking man and woman.

"What's in the box?" Mrs. Jenson asked.

"Don't rightfully know," the social worker said. "Maybe family stuff."

Douglas Jenson glared at Jayden through bloodshot eyes. He wore a sweat-stained sleeveless undershirt and his beer belly hung over his boxers. "Hey! When do we get a check for her? We don't do this charity work for nothing."

"Now, you know things like this take time, Mr. Jenson. She came over here on an emergency situation, so none of the paperwork is complete."

As soon as the social worker drove off, Douglas turned to Jayden. He threw his head back and guzzled down a beer, then crushed the can in his bare hands. It was a moment he seemed very proud of.

"You be a good girl and we'll get along just fine," he said.

"Yes, sir," she said in a tearful voice.

"Now don't start that sniffling, or I'll give you something to cry about."

"Oh, you big bully, leave the girl alone." Tilly swatted her husband on the shoulder. "Come with me, girly girl, and I'll fix you something to eat."

But Douglas achieved what he was hoping for. From that day on, Jayden tried to avoid him at all cost. Yet there were times in the night, when his wife was passed out from the drink, that he searched for her....

Above all else the memory of Douglas was better kept locked in the deep recesses of Jayden's mind. It was safer when she didn't allow them to float to the conscious level.

Douglas could unleash a slew of vulgarities in one of his drunken rampages faster than you could blink an eye, chipping away any shred of self-esteem. The stench of alcohol reached Jayden many times before he did.

"Shh, don't want to wake Emma now, do we?" he would whisper. Jayden became adept at stepping outside herself until it was over.

How could Tilly not know? Or did she?

It was an unforgivable act that she never spoke to anyone about. Jayden chose to remain silent. She wasn't about to chance being removed from the home and potentially separated from Emma. From the moment Jayden looked into Emma's eyes, the two of them had a soul bond.

But that was all in the past now. With Douglas' death two years earlier, she had nothing to fear. He was no longer a threat to Emma. He would never be able to destroy the life of another child.

Blaming Tilly for not protecting them was useless. Tilly had her own demons to battle. Emotionally bankrupt, most days she preferred the companionship of a bottle of Jack Daniels.

Today you're moving on with the present, finally able to set down roots and make a life.

"Is that you, girly girl?" Tilly called out in her deep, raspy smoker's voice.

"Yes, Tilly, it's me."

"Come on in here and let me take a good look at you. The little graduate. Go ahead, put on your black robe, and let me see how adorable you look." Tilly's speech was slurred from the effects of alcohol. "How was it?"

"How was what, Tilly? My graduation? If you'd come, you would know." Ordinarily, Jayden wasn't so bold, but for years she had held her tongue, trying not to rock the boat.

Tilly looked down at the ground; she was never one to confront issues.

Jayden sat on the couch next to her. "Tilly, I'm sorry if I'm being short with you, but if it hadn't been for Reverend Baxter, there wouldn't have been anyone there for me. He at least captured the moment with this picture," she said, holding it up for Tilly to see without touching it.

"Oh, big deal, girly girl," Tilly said. "I didn't even graduate high school, and you got that diploma of yours to frame. Now let me see."

Tilly reached for the picture. Grudgingly, Jayden handed it over.

"Well, looky here; very nice. You know Emma talks to me all the time when you're at school. You don't know what she tells me, do you?" Tilly looked smug.

"I don't know what you mean."

"She tells me this man talks to you every Sunday when she's in class."

"Is there a point to this?" Jayden asked.

"I don't know; is there?"

"I have nothing to hide. The man's name is Jonathan Baxter. He's a youth minister for the First Congregational Church."

"Youth minister? What does he want to do—save you from yourself?" Tilly's humor was more accusatory.

"No, he's a nice guy who likes to talk with people. That's all there is to that."

"Well, I got a little piece of advice for you. Take it or leave it." Tilly was having difficulty forming her words.

"Go ahead." Jayden couldn't wait to hear Tilly's profound statement.

"I can tell you this. I know what they do in those places. Once the doors close, that's when the brainwashing starts. That's what it is, you know. They get in your head and tell you things that can make you crazy if you listen to them." Tilly took a long drag on her cigarette. A flash of red-hot ash fell to the floor.

"I didn't know you knew so much about what goes on inside church," Jayden said.

"Oh, I know more than you think I do, missy. They can put on their Sunday best and act like goody two-shoes, but they're sinners the rest of the week. I've seen a couple of so-called church-going men. Well, heck, I've sat right next to them on a bar stool. Hypocrites, the whole lot of them."

"Jonathan says we're all imperfect." Jayden knew better than to get into a debate with Tilly, especially after she'd been drinking. Instead, she decided to spend what time she had left with Emma, so she walked away.

"Hey, where you going? I want to talk to you," Tilly called out to Jayden. "I have a question! How come you're home so early? You should be at one of those graduation parties. You need to get a little wild—you know, let your hair down."

"I'm not interested in a party. That's the last place I want to be tonight. I want to spend the evening with Emma before I leave."

Tilly pursed her dry, cracked lips and blew a chain of smoke rings. "That always thrills Emma when I do that."

"I'm going to go say good-bye to Emma. I'm disappointed and hurt tonight. If we keep talking, we'll just get into a fight, and I don't have the energy for it."

"Oh, for heaven's sake, will you stop it already? After all, there will be bigger and better things in life. I told you, if you remember correctly, that we might not come. If Emma hadn't carried on from the moment you left, maybe I could have managed. You know I can't handle that commotion. It's my nerves. And don't you think it was unreasonable of you to expect a five-year-old to sit still and pay attention for that long?" Tilly rationalized. "Anyway, don't ruin my surprise." With a flick of her wrist, Tilly whirled the envelope in the air as though she were playing with a Frisbee.

"What's this?" Jayden asked, only mildly interested.

"What do you think it is? A graduation gift, silly. Well, come on, open it."

Jayden slid a finger under the sealed flap, pulling out a handwritten letter. A check fell to the floor. Twenty-five dollars. "Tilly, I didn't need you to give me a gift."

"Just read," Tilly insisted.

Dear Jayden:
Today is a very special day. Your future is what you make of it. I have to admit I'm probably a little jealous of the opportunities that lie ahead for you. When you turned eighteen last October, the State of Texas no longer considered you a minor, so the monthly support checks stopped. I could have turned you out, but I couldn't imagine putting that kind of pressure on you before you finished school. I kept thinking, *How would I feel if you were my real daughter?*

Real daughter. How many times have I heard that? Jayden wondered.

What I'm trying to say is that I'm guilty of being an old softy. Without a dime of support from the State, I have allowed you to stay here, supporting us on my widow's pension. And you can't imagine how expensive it is to raise children.

Jayden lowered the letter and raised an eyebrow.
"Okay, I know you worked some, but don't ruin the moment." Tilly said. "Read on."
Jayden continued reading.

I could have prorated your stay here, but my heart said something different. I want you to know I'm not expecting any type of repayment.

Jayden dropped the letter down by her side, staring at Tilly in total disbelief. "No repayment expected?"

Tilly grinned from ear to ear with her tobacco-stained teeth. "That's right. I won't accept one red cent from you."

The urge to crumple the letter and throw it in the trash was tempting, but Jayden had to put her feelings aside and think of Emma. She had to keep things on an even keel for the child's sake.

"Well, don't just stand there with your jaw hanging open. Give me some feedback. What do you think?"

"What do I think?" Jayden asked. "To tell you the truth, I can't find the words to convey what I'm thinking."

"Never mind, the look on your face says it all. I know you're appreciative, so just go on and get your things ready; that is, if you still insist on leaving tonight. For the life of me, I don't understand why you're in such an all-fired hurry. We could work out a payment plan for you to stay on. Heaven knows, I could use the extra income, not to mention help with Emma," Tilly offered.

Staying on to be with Emma was a temptation, but Jayden knew if she remained, she would die a slow death. There were too many unpleasant memories within these walls. A fresh start was what she needed for survival. Jayden thanked her for the offer but politely declined.

"Suit yourself," Tilly said with an attitude, "and be quiet when you go in the room. Emma is sound asleep, and I sure don't want you waking her up. Goodness knows, the child drove me nuts while you were gone."

Jayden's worst fears were about to come true. Emma would be surviving on Tilly's mothering skills, which were short of nothing.

"Why is Emma in bed so early? It's not her bedtime!" Jayden asked, then winced inwardly. She didn't want to provoke an argument.

"You'd think she was your kid instead of a foster sister the way you worry over her. To answer your question, she wouldn't stop acting up, so I said to her, 'Emma Marie, go lie down on your bed this minute.' Lo and behold, I went in to check on her not more than fifteen minutes later and she was in there sawing logs. Have to admit the quiet was wonderful." Tilly was winded just by explaining.

Jayden shook her head, tiptoeing into the same room the girls had shared for the last five years. She walked over to the pint-sized preschooler. Emma was sprawled across the bed, an arm and leg dangling over the side. She looked so angelic. Flecks of spun gold weaved throughout her flaxen curls, glistening in the dusky light.

Where did the time go? It seems just like yesterday you came into my life. You were so small and helpless.

Jayden sat next to Emma. The long, floppy ear of Emma's favorite stuffed animal, the one Jayden had given to her at Christmas, was clutched in her fist. Jayden tucked Emma's arm under her comforter. A pang of guilt tore at her gut when she thought of how exasperated she had become with Emma earlier in the day. And for what? The child wasn't doing anything different than she usually did—twirling around the room until she became so dizzy she fell into everything, all the while laughing hysterically. It was a game to her....

"Emma, stop being a pest!" Jayden had scolded her. "I need you to do me a favor, okay? Go play somewhere else so I can finish packing my suitcase."

"Where you going, Jay?" Emma asked, giggling, wildly flinging herself on the mattress, trying to touch her feet to the ceiling.

"That's great, Emma. I was afraid I wouldn't have an opportunity to explain for the hundredth time why I'm leaving."

Immediately Jayden regretted her sarcasm. How could she expect a five-year-old to understand the situation when she didn't fully comprehend it herself?

"I'm sorry, honey," Jayden apologized. "Come over here and sit next to me." With as much patience as she could find, Jayden explained to Emma again why she was leaving. "I'm all grown up now, and it's time to start a life of my own. Do you understand, Emma?"

"I'll go with you," the child protested.

Jayden picked her up and cuddled her, nuzzling her face into Emma's tender flesh, her sweet innocence filling her senses. "Do you know how loved you are?"

Emma squirmed. "This much," she said, her arms stretched out as wide as she could.

"Bigger than that," Jayden teased.

"Bigger than the world."

They played this game every night before bedtime.

"More than life itself," Jayden fought hard to remain composed. This could be the last time they did this for a long time....

Now Emma slept. The silence was deafening. There was no

incessant chatter or heartwarming laughter. *How am I going to do this? How can I leave you behind?*

When she leaned over to kiss her cheek, she noticed Emma's favorite book, the children's Bible, on the nightstand. Every night, without exception, she read a chapter from it, sometimes the same story over and over again until it was committed to memory. Jayden's favorite chapter lay open, which so happened to be Emma's favorite because it was pictures only.

Jesus sat on a hillside while dozens of children gathered around him. "I'm his little girl, too, right, Jay?" Emma asked each time she saw it. Explaining to a five-year-old that the whole "Jesus loves all the little children" was only a make-believe story would have crushed Emma. Jayden would never allow that to happen.

Still, it was propaganda instilled into the minds of the young. The myth of an all-powerful being, a supernatural force. It didn't make sense praying to open air. As far as Jayden was concerned, it was a religious crutch. Yet she would never steal Emma's joy. All too soon Emma would learn what Jayden was forced to realize at an early age: Trust in no one but yourself. And "Trust in no one" was exactly the motto Jayden lived by.

Jayden turned her thoughts back to the sleeping child. Emma's long curls wound around Jayden's finger. "It wasn't supposed to be this way, sweetheart," she whispered in her ear. "You were supposed to leave first."

With the number of childless couples desperate to adopt, it was highly unusual for an infant to remain available for long. When Jayden entered foster care at the age of eight, she knew she wasn't a prime candidate for adoption. And that was fine with her—no, preferable. She would still be living with her real father now if the State of Texas hadn't severed their relationship. But in her heart she knew one day they would be reunited.

However, Emma was no one's child. She would have been ideal for adoption, that is, if she'd had come into this world perfect. But born three months premature to a heroin-addicted mother, Emma's frail body was twisted and contorted with agonizing pain from the effects of drug withdrawal. The tiny infant cried around the clock, unnerving the most seasoned nurse.

She was deprived of human touch for the first four months of her life. Instead she was imprisoned inside the sterile atmosphere of a Plexiglas chamber, probed and prodded by medical personnel like a human pin cushion. The prognosis for her future was bleak. Down syndrome was the least of her problems.

No matter how desperate a person wanted to become a parent, a life sentence as a permanent caregiver wasn't inviting. Yet the moment Jayden laid eyes on Emma the day she came to live at the Jensons', she was committed to serve as Emma's surrogate mother for the next five years, foregoing her own wants and needs.

"I'll come back soon, sweetheart. I promise," she whispered in a tearful voice. Picking up her suitcase and a small cardboard box, Jayden made her way down the hallway, hoping to make it a quick good-bye. She stood for a minute in the entryway, watching Tilly's head bobbing back and forth as she dozed off, then tried to catch herself. A thick haze of cigarette smoke formed a rancid halo around her.

Jayden knew that if she didn't walk out the front door quickly, harsh words would be exchanged, and that would only make it worse for Emma. "Tilly, I'm leaving now. Is there anything you might need?"

"Like?"

"Like anything I can tell you about Emma?"

"You tell *me* about that child?" By the tone in Tilly's voice, Jayden knew she didn't phrase that right. "Who do you think you are, missy?" I've been raising kids since you were still in diapers. How dare you insinuate you know more about that child than I do!" Tilly tried to steady herself as she stood.

"Let me help you to bed before I leave." Jayden was accustomed to the routine.

"Go away!" Tilly said, swinging her arm in front of her, accidentally knocking over a bottle of whiskey. "Whoops! What a waste of a good drink." She picked up the bottle, sprinkling what was left on her tongue.

Jayden knew from past experience it was better to let her sleep it off. "Good-bye." Jayden's hand was on the doorknob.

"Wait one minute. Before you leave, I have a request."

Jayden waited.

"It would be a great favor to me if you wouldn't call here to speak to Emma. Instead, you can speak directly to me."

The line of communication is further severed.

"I don't understand, but I guess you have your reasons."

"Yes I do, but I'm thinking about Emma. I mean, she won't understand if she talks to you on the phone and then you don't come to see her. Who will comfort her then?"

Jayden was surprised by Tilly's words, because they had discussed her plans.

"So you see who worries more about that child—you or me?" Tilly's voice was shaking.

"First of all," Jayden reiterated, "I plan to see Emma every chance I get; and second, you'll need to be the one to comfort her when I'm not here."

Tilly's expression turned stone cold. "You will only come here to visit if I say you can, and with that attitude, I don't think that's likely to happen," she snapped, taking the upper hand.

"I'm sorry. Yes, of course that's what I meant to say. I will only come here if you allow it." Legally, Jayden knew she didn't have a leg to stand on, so she had to choose her words carefully.

"Look, Jayden, call me whenever you wish, and I'll call you with important news on Emma; that is, as soon as you find a place and give me your number."

Talking back wasn't worth losing any privileges to visit Emma.

"Okay, when I get my own place, I'll let you know you right away."

"Good, now that's settled." A sigh of relief escaped from Tilly's lips. "Let me get Mrs. Campbell to stay with Emma so I can drive you to the bus terminal."

"Thank you, but it's probably better for Emma when she wakes up to see a familiar face."

"Suit yourself, but you can at least wait inside until the taxi gets here, if you want. I'm going to bed to get a little shut eye in case the little monster wakes up."

Jayden cringed at Tilly's referenced to Emma as a "little monster."

"You know, Jayden, there's something I've been meaning to say to you."

What next?

"You've been a good little mother to Emma, but you've also created a difficult situation for anyone who watches her."

"How's that?" Jayden asked, annoyed with the amateur psychoanalysis.

"Well, for one thing, you've spoiled that child to the point that all she wants is for you to care for her."

Jayden's first thought was to tell Tilly the exact truth. *If you'd stay sober for any length of time to help with Emma, maybe you wouldn't find her so difficult.* But she thought better of it and held her tongue.

"I know life wasn't always good here. Douglas, God rest his soul, could be difficult at times."

Difficult. That's how she would describe his actions—difficult? "Tilly, it's in the past and needs to stay there. It's pointless to dredge up what we can't change," Jayden said.

"No, no. I think it's important for you to know how I feel before you leave," Tilly said, teetering back and forth. "I know you think I should have done more to protect you, and you may be right. But you have to understand: I wasn't capable of standing up to him. I never could. I just wasn't strong. Not like you. I guess what I'm asking you to do is to forgive me."

Tilly started to sob. However, that wasn't unusual. When she drank, crying jags followed.

"It's fine. You did your best, but now my concern is for Emma."

Tilly appeared relieved that Jayden had let her off easy. "Don't you waste one more minute worrying over that child. Taking good care of her will be my little way of repaying you for all the nice things I should have done years ago.... Enough of all this. Do you have everything?"

As far as Jayden was concerned, she didn't have everything she needed. She was leaving without Emma, and there wasn't anything she could do about it. "I suppose. But if I've forgotten anything I'll get it when I come back for a visit."

"Well, it's better to make sure you have it in the first place. Who knows? I might get a bee in my bonnet and decide to do some spring cleaning. I don't want to throw out anything that's yours. I see you have all of your mother's things." Tilly pointed to the cardboard box.

"I have everything."

Jayden waited until she heard Tilly shut her bedroom door before she walked out of the house. The wind chimes resonated in the evening breeze. The cabbie jumped out of the taxi, popped open the trunk, grabbed her suitcase, and tossed it in.

She took one last look at the house. One last look at the night light burning in the room where Emma slept.

Today was the emancipation of Jayden Darlene Arman, yet it was bittersweet. Today she was leaving behind the one person who gave meaning to her life…Emma.

Three

Jayden placed as much distance as possible between her and the next person on the bus. Her stomach felt queasy. She removed a small complimentary pillow from the overhead bin, folded it in half, and tucked it under her head. Sleep was definitely out of the question. The best she could hope for was to rest her eyes.

Between Odessa and San Antonio, there was virtually nothing except a stretch of two-lane, desert highway with only the occasional headlights from a passing car cutting through the midnight sky. Not a place one would want to experience a mechanical breakdown. She removed her journal out of the satchel and decided to write.

June 2, 1977
Today I'm free. Yet in the long scheme of things, what does that actually mean? True, I'm free from the Jensons and free from all case workers. I can live my life as I see fit. Yet with that freedom comes a price. Tonight, when I walked out the door, I left Emma behind. Not out of choice. There were no choices where she was concerned. I worry what will happen when she wakes and I'm not there. Funny, the other day I was thinking of something I heard once. "It's better to have loved than never to have loved at all." That was spoken by someone who never had to leave his heart behind.

The bus driver dimmed the inside cabin lights. There was a loud snort followed by heavy nasal breathing coming from the elderly gentlemen in the seat directly in front of her. She envied anyone who could manage to sleep among strangers. Strangers, for all she knew, could be fugitives on the run. Her eyes burned and teared from exhaustion as she fought to stay awake, though she was gradually losing the battle. The rhythmic whirling of the Greyhound bus's pistons lulled her to sleep with only the occasional bump in the road stirring her.

Within minutes, Jayden's mental and physical state slipped deeper and deeper through the stages of sleep until the ultimate level was achieved. The level where there are no inhibitions. Where past and present memories are free to roam in the subconscious.

An obscure recurrent dream started again. It was always the same. Jayden was there, but not as a physical being; instead she was a weightless floating witness capable of seeing everything at once....

A young girl lay in bed with the blankets drawn up to her chin. Her long hair was draped on top of the covering. Her fingers were laced together across her chest. Nothing was familiar to Jayden except for the man who entered the child's room. It was her father. He sat on the edge of the girl's bed and pressed his cheek to hers. Jayden felt the bristles of his unshaven face against the child's tender flesh. His deep masculine voice said, "Happy birthday, dear eight-year-old" softly in her ear.

Taking her by the hand, he led her into another section of the house. They entered a large room void of furnishings with the exception of a banquet table covered in a bright yellow paper liner. In the center of the table was a chocolate cake with eight lit candles.

He coaxed the child closer to the table. A recording of children singing "Happy Birthday!" was heard, but no one was in the room but her father and Jayden. The girl drew in a deep breath, filling her lungs, then blew as hard as she could.

"Yeah! I got 'em all!"

The child looked around the room, then realized she was alone. Her father had vanished. She began to tremble in fear.

"Where are you?" the little girl screamed.

A small hole in the wall started to open up and spread across the wall. Within seconds the hole had become so large an adult could crawl through. Inside the opening there was complete darkness.

The child peered inside the opening, tracing the outer edges of the entrance with her fingers. Distant sounds of a woman's cries echoed from the depths of blackness. The voice was very familiar to Jayden. The woman's cries became loud and more urgent. The child stepped back; her father suddenly appeared behind the little girl with open arms. "Don't be afraid. I'm here," she heard him say.

"A woman is crying," the girl said.

"Don't be frightened," he reassured her. Her father walked over to the makeshift doorway and put one foot inside and then the other.

"No! Don't leave me alone! I'm coming with you," the girl yelled.

But by then he was completely inside. Now only his face was visible. "You can't come with me; they won't let you," he said.

Suddenly Jayden herself took the place of the young girl in the dream. The more she struggled to reach her father, the more difficult it was to move her legs. Her extremities felt embedded in cement.

"Help me!" she cried out.

He looked back at her one last time. "Don't try to follow me. There's nothing I can do for you now." Her father held up handcuffed wrists and slowly backed inside the hole until she could no longer see him.

"Please, Daddy, don't leave me here by myself."

Slowly the hole closed up until it was nothing more than a pinpoint.

Jayden moaned and cried out, "Daddy! No! Wait, please don't go...."

"Miss...Miss..."

Jayden heard the voice but wasn't ready to leave her dream and her father behind.

"Miss, are you all right?" the man asked again.

"All right?" Her eyes opened partially.

The elderly man's face was inches from hers. "You cried out in your sleep. Are you sick?" He looked worried.

Embarrassed, not knowing what she may have uttered in her sleep, Jayden sat up and cleared her throat. "No, I'm fine, I guess. Just a little overtired."

"It shouldn't be much longer now." He turned to face the front, tucking something under his neck.

Jayden stared out the window into the night. She tried to put together the pieces of the puzzle that orphaned her. Why was the dream always the same, and was the crying woman her mother? There were speculations as to the cause of her mother's death. Rumors were that she died by the hands of her father, but Jayden wouldn't allow herself to believe that. She remembered him as a compassionate, loving man. Nonetheless, the jury was convinced there was enough evidence to convict him of first-degree murder, sentencing him to twenty years in the state penitentiary.

Jayden remembered her mother as a fragile woman. Most of the time she was bedridden, unable to care for herself. Jayden's father said she was *melancholy*, a gentle term for what she now knew was severe depression. Looking back, Jayden believed the sedatives, more than the illness itself, were probably responsible for her zombie-like state.

Although she loved both of them, her heart went out to her father. For all practical purposes, he was a single parent. As far back as she could remember, he was sole caretaker while working a full-time job. Sadly now, she struggled to see their faces in her mind or recall their voices.

The dream was significant to her. There was reference to her eighth birthday, the day her childhood was banished, the day she lost her identity.

Jayden shifted in her seat trying to get comfortable. It would be several hours before she reached what she hoped would become her new home. She thought back over the details of putting together the pieces of the puzzle on that fatal day. The librarian had been very helpful....

"October 1966! Whew!" the librarian said, "Quite some time ago. We'll need to look this up on the microfiche. The library doesn't keep newspapers or magazines lying around. Fire hazard, you know. Here we go—all the back issues in October 1966. All you need to do is turn this wheel this way to move forward and the opposite way to move backward, okay?"

Jayden waited until the woman left so she could be alone. She didn't want to share what she was looking for with anyone.

She turned the handle until she came upon the date of October 19, 1966, her eighth birthday. No mention of the incident. Just ads, a little local news, and that was it. Turning the wheel forward to the next day, Jayden stopped. There it was, on the front page, the lead story: "Man accused of murdering his wife in home during daughter's birthday party." There was a picture of her father, being led by two officers into a squad car. Another picture of the coroner removing a body from their old house, the body of her mother. Why couldn't she remember that? At that very minute, her mother's death seemed more real than ever.

"No, Daddy! Tell me you didn't do it," she cried under her breath. Page 4-C, the obituary. A picture of her mother. Jayden was listed as surviving daughter and something peculiar…a Jacob Lucas Stamen and Joseph Cain Stamen as surviving sons. Sons? Her brothers? It had to be a mistake; she didn't have brothers; she was an only child…or was she?

That was when Jayden remembered a box wrapped in twine that came with her the night she arrived at the Jensons'. When she returned from the library, Jayden immediately went to the hallway and pulled the cord that dangled from the ceiling. A ladder extended that led upstairs to the attic. Only a minimal amount of daylight sifted through the small attic window. There wasn't one item up there that didn't have a thick layer of dust on it.

It had been years since she had seen the cardboard box. Most of the articles in the attic were in boxes with the exception of a few odds and ends and some old furniture. She shuffled through the disarray and was about to give up when out of the corner of her eye, she saw what she had been looking for.

There was a cardboard box with thin twine curled around it. "That's it." She hoisted the box on her shoulder and took it straight to her bedroom. With the door closed she spilled the contents on the bed. Maybe here she would find a clue. There was a dried corsage pressed between wax paper, a yellowing envelope, a velvet drawstring bag that held a gold chain and half of a coin pendant, and a large burgundy vinyl covered yearbook, *The Fighting Wolverines*. Jayden flipped through the pages searching for her mother.

Finally, there it was. Darlene Elizabeth Stamen. *Stamen.* So that was her maiden name. Jayden had never known that until tonight. The table of contents listed everyone by last name followed by the first name. She searched down the list to the *S*s…Sanderson, Savedra, Sellers, and Stamen. Her mother was listed on several pages. It was like looking into a mirror when she saw her picture; however, her mother was breathtaking and Jayden had always considered herself plain.

The next page was a picture of her mother in a strapless chiffon evening gown arm in arm with a handsome young man decked out in a tuxedo, who looked mesmerized by her. The page was entitled *Prom Night, April 15, 1951, "Dancing the Night Away with Darlene Stamen and Jay Breckenridge."*

Jayden turned to the front of the yearbook, again looking up the *B's* until she found Breckenridge. There were several pages of him in various sporting activities. In one photo, her mother was pictured on the sideline wearing a letter jacket. *Probably Jay's.* He was listed as the all-star quarterback for the high school.

When she turned to the last page, Jayden froze. She couldn't believe her eyes. The heading said, "A tribute to Jay, January 9, 1933—April 18, 1951." Three days after prom, he was killed.

She took a close look at his picture and noticed something glittering around his neck. It was a gold chain hung with some type of pendant attached on it. Jayden picked up the gold chain that she emptied from the velvet bag. The inscription on her half of the coin said, "Two hearts." That was it. She looked back at the picture of Jay. He must have had the other half of the coin to complete the verse.

There was a list of his accomplishments and tributes from fellow students with their favorite memories of him. Her mother had written a passage at the very end.

> My beloved Jay,
> My life will no longer be the same. I have lost my one true love, never again to share with anyone else what we had. How will I go on? I know if you were here right now, you'd say: 'Get over it, kid; there's still a lot of living to do.' I will treasure what we had and what we shared. No one can take that away from me. Your legacy will live on in our child.
> Love, Darlene

Jayden couldn't begin to imagine the devastation her mother must have gone through. She felt as though she was prying into her mother's private belongings. Jayden put each item carefully back into the box, then noticed a folded parchment paper stuck under a flap of the cardboard. She hadn't seen it there when she emptied out the contents.

It was a birth certificate...not hers. *Born this day December 31, 1951, twin sons born to mother Darlene Elizabeth Stamen.* She listed the father as...*no, it couldn't be*...Jay Breckenridge.

Jayden looked down at the envelope that was on the bed. It was postmarked Sun City, Arizona, December 19, 1958. The return address was Martha Stamen, 871 E. Riverside. Arizona. *Martha Stamen...my grandmother?* Jayden's hands trembled as she read the letter.

Darlene:
I received your letter today. I can't say I was surprised; you were never good at keeping your word. So you're married now. You have an infant.

I must admit I do think the name Jayden a bit unusual. Definitely not biblical. I can only guess you named her after that boy, Jay. Why on earth you would do such a thing, I won't pretend to know. I'm much too old to try and figure out why you do the things you do.

My son, your son Jacob, is a wonderful little boy. He will be starting the second grade this year. Very obedient; never a problem. He does as he is told without the continual argument I remember you burdened your father and me with.

You've asked if you may come for a visit with your new husband and infant daughter. Why would you think I want to meet them? We have severed our ties. I no longer speak of you to anyone. It is better this way. I don't mean to be cruel, but I have no desire to meet with you or your family.

Jacob doesn't know you exist. If you care for him like you say, respect our agreement. Why would you want to upset him now? It would only be for selfish reasons. For the sake of your husband and child, move forward and stop looking back.

Yes, I did try contacting the orphanage where your other offspring was placed. I felt it was my Christian duty to check on his progress. You remember how small and frail he was at birth with his seizures and all; well, it would have been too much for me to deal with at my age. Even in all of your selfishness, you should be pleased to hear he thrived. To my knowledge, he was never placed with a family. I will check on his progress when I can.

About Jacob's gift, it's a bit odd. Why you want a little boy to have a necklace is something I can't figure. I noticed it's half of a coin with part of a verse written across it. I'm assuming you hold the other half of the coin completing the rest of the verse. I will put it away for safekeeping; however, you know I don't believe in people adorning their bodies with jewelry. How trashy.

I'm not completely heartless. I have enclosed a picture of Jacob. It must be kept between us. Your father would become very angry if he knew I was corresponding with you.

Martha Stamen

Jayden reached over and picked up the necklace. Her mother had sent Jay's chain to her son Jacob to have. Jayden put the necklace around her neck and fastened the clasp. She reached for the pictures her grandmother had sent.

One was of a gangly boy with a crewcut and large eyes, her eyes, and a harsh-looking woman, her grandmother. The back of the picture said, "Jacob age six, first grade, 1958." Something about her grandmother seemed so familiar. Then Jayden remembered it was from her mother's funeral. Jayden reminisced about that day....

A police car pulled alongside the curb. Two officers stepped out and opened the back door. One of the officers helped a man out of the back of the vehicle. Jayden's heart jumped. "Daddy!" she screamed. No matter how hard she struggled to free herself, she couldn't break free of the hold the caseworker had on her.

"You stay right here, little missy," the social service woman said.

The guests were aghast that he was allowed to come near his wife's burial plot. The officers kept her father at a distance but close enough so he could hear the funeral. Jayden couldn't take her eyes off him. It was obvious he was in shock. His head remained bowed, and from where she stood it appeared that he was sobbing.

When the graveside service ended, the officer led her father back to the squad car.

"Good riddance to bad rubbish," the case worker mumbled as they watched the squad car pull away.

"That's my daddy!"

"I know, sweetheart, and no one's blaming you for that."

A few of her mother's acquaintances lingered around afterwards to discuss the news report as the cause of her mother's death. "Murder, isn't that dreadful?" one of the women said, oblivious that Jayden was within earshot. "You never know when the person you live with will snap just like that." The woman slid her finger across her neck, imitating cutting her throat.

Jayden noticed an elderly woman and young boy coming towards her. Something about the woman made Jayden uneasy. Her features were severe, and deep crevices ran the length of her face. The woman's gray, brittle hair was pulled back against the nape of her neck, pinned into a tight bun. Puffy dark circles surrounded her eyes. The woman held onto the young man's hand as she knelt on the wet ground. Jayden was now face to face with her. "You look just like your mother," she said with tears in her eyes. "Would you mind if I hug you?"

"No thank you," Jayden said, not intentionally meaning to be rude but more interested in the boy. There was something in his eyes that seemed familiar.

The caseworker nudged Jayden. "Don't be rude, child; the woman is giving you her condolences."

The strength of the elderly woman surprised Jayden. She pinned Jayden's arms to her side when she embraced her. Without warning, the woman burst into a loud, gut-wrenching sob. "God forgive me," she cried. "I did love your mother."

The boy reached out for the woman's hand and helped her to her feet. "It's time to go. I'm sorry for your loss." As they walked away, the young man's arm went around the elderly woman's waist....

Jayden stared down at the letter. "Why didn't you tell me you were my grandmother when you held me? Why? Why!" she cried out, not caring who in the house heard her.

Sometime later, after learning where her father was incarcerated, Jayden wrote to the prison warden requesting permission to visit. It was granted by the warden but declined by her father, followed by a letter of explanation. A brief letter with powerful words. Words that ripped at her heart.

Jayden:

I understand you want to visit me. My first question would be, "Why?" Why would you come to see a man accused of taking the life of your mother and robbing you of your childhood? If you don't have any better sense than to ask to see me, then I must make that decision for you. The answer is no. I don't want you at a place like this, nor do I think it is a good idea for you to see me...ever.

You are hanging onto a dream, a dream where your father is a hero who will come to your rescue. I can't help you. Go on with your life and make better decisions than I did. I may not be a praying man, but I will ask God to watch over you.

Jeffrey

Jeffrey. He didn't even sign it, *Dad*. Jayden felt such sadness. She sat up in her seat, not wanting to think about her past any longer. Now all her energy would be focused on what lay ahead. There was Emma and her brothers to think about. Where to begin the search was the question.

Jayden pulled out of her jeans pocket an apartment rental ad from the San Antonio newspaper. It was the only place she could afford. It was only fifty dollars a month, and all meals were included. Eight hours later, the bus pulled into the San Antonio terminal. She collected her suitcase and box. Tonight she would stay in a motel. Tomorrow, Jayden would find a place to call home.

Four

At one time, Edna Sullivan's boarding home was alive with proper, single young women transitioning from a parent's home to semi-independence. Today, the red-brick building was just one step ahead of landing in the hands of a demolition crew. Most of the other buildings in the area had already succumbed to the decay of the downtown area. Jayden avoided the large cracks in the cement walkway while she tried to get to the front porch. She noticed the rusted frame of an old swing glider, now lying in a crumbled heap, its weathered canvas top nothing more than bare threads.

A long, diagonal crack ran the length of the window pane, waiting for a minor tap to send glass spraying into every direction. Strands of intricately woven silk, evidence of a spider's hard labor, hung from the eaves.

With the heel of her hand, Jayden knocked on the front door, avoiding the splintered wood. After several attempts and no response, she started to leave, when a heavy-set matronly woman, possibly in her sixties, peered out from the window shades before she opened the door.

"Yes, dear, may I help you?"

"Ms. Sullivan?"

"Yes, I'm Ms. Sullivan. What can I do for you?"

"I'm Jayden Arman. We spoke on the phone about the room you have for rent?"

"We surely did," the woman said. "But before we go on let's get one thing straight. My mother-in-law was Ms. Sullivan, not me. I'm still a spring chicken, or at least I feel young at heart." She had an infectious laugh. Wiping her hands on the apron tied around her waist, she added, "You can call me Edna."

"All right, Edna." The women shook hands.

"I apologize for not tidying up a bit, but I thought you were coming out tomorrow," Edna said, motioning for her to come inside.

"That was the plan, but things kind of changed. I arrived late night and stayed over at the Wagon Wheel."

"Gracious me, I thought that old place had closed down some years back."

Jayden grinned. "I thought it was extremely reasonable; now I know why."

The women laughed.

"If you're not ready to show the room, I can come back later," Jayden offered, hoping Edna wouldn't turn her away.

"No, dear, it's fine. If you don't mind a messy place, come on in."

"I don't mind at all." Jayden felt an instant comfortable rapport with the woman. "I wanted to get over here as soon as possible before you rented the room out."

"Land's sake, honey! Look around. Do you really think someone will be busting down my door to move in here? Come on in," she said, holding the door open. "Have a look around before you get too excited; it's probably not what you're expecting."

Jayden stepped inside, her eyes adjusting from the bright outdoor light to the dimly lit room. A powerful, musky scent hung in the air; it was the kind of odor you would expect in damp basements. A grand, cherry wood staircase led to the second floor.

The only time she had seen anything so magnificent was in the classic movie, *Gone with the Wind*. To the left of the staircase was a large archway leading to the main area. Crushed red velvet curtains, much too heavy for the curtain rods they hung on, blocked all the natural light creating a macabre effect. Eclectic furnishings filled every corner. A fading wallpaper design, covering the plaster walls, was now cracking and peeling off in layers.

"Well, you want to run now or later?" Edna teased.

"I don't want to run at all," Jayden said. "It's perfect."

"Yeah, well, you haven't seen your room yet." Edna led the way up the staircase. When the two women reached the top, Edna pushed open the door, anxiously watching Jayden's face for a reaction. "Tah dah," Edna said, stretching out her arms like a game show host presenting the first place prize to the winning contestant.

"Let me give you a tour, madam."

Jayden couldn't believe her eyes. The room was a stark contrast to the downstairs area. Vibrant shades of sunflower yellow splashed across the walls, radiating warmth from every angle. The honeysuckle bush in the garden below the window lent a flowery aroma to the room. Pushed up against a wall was an oversized sleigh-bed wrapped in a yellow chenille spread and covered in every shape and size of pillow imaginable. A crème colored rug partially covered the buffed wooden floor planks.

However, it was the caned-back rocker with its fine craftsmanship that caught her eye. She sat the suitcase down and walked over to it, her fingers lightly tracing the engraved wood.

"Handmade by my grandfather," Edna commented proudly.

"It's incredible."

Attached to the back of the rocker was a white cotton pillow with a Bible verse embroidered across the bottom. "My mother made that for me as a wedding present some forty-five years back," Edna boasted.

Jayden admired the painstaking hours of intricate workmanship that went into every stitch. Her own mother would never see her joining hands in marriage, she realized sadly. *"As for me and my house, we will serve the Lord. Joshua 24:15,"* Jayden read aloud.

"You know that verse?"

"No, not really. I don't know much about the Bible."

"Oh, honey, I didn't mean to put you on the spot. The verse is from the Old Testament. I know you haven't had time to give it much thought, just getting into town and all, but once you settle in, I'd be pleased as punch to take you to a Sunday service at my church. There are a lot of young people your age there."

Jayden cleared her throat. "I don't go to church…much. Guess I have a hard time believing that someone from above watches over us."

"I didn't mean to suggest—"

Jayden didn't give Edna a chance to finish her sentence. "No apology is necessary."

Edna shook her head. "No, honey, I wasn't going to apologize. I know young people these days get their heads full of that Darwin mumbo-jumbo amongst other stuff. It's a shame, trying to explain everything from a scientific approach; but what I'm most sorry about is for anyone not to have a personal relationship with Christ."

Jayden didn't know how to answer that. Edna at least stood by what she believed. Jayden admired that in a person; it's just that faith didn't have an effect on her one way or another.

"I love the room," Jayden said to get off the subject of religion.

Edna smiled. "Good. Now that's settled, dinner is at six. Like the ad says, 'Meals included.'"

"Thank you, Ms. Sullivan…I mean, Edna. I know I'll love it here."

Edna looked down, then up, as if puzzled. "You only have one suitcase and a box."

"This is it," Jayden said, feeling slightly embarrassed. "I weeded out the things I didn't need and brought with me the things I couldn't live without," she added, hoping Edna wouldn't question her further.

"Smart girl," Edna said in approval. "Unpack and then come on down for a bite to eat. I make a mean cheeseburger."

Jayden waited until she heard Edna rummaging in the kitchen, then closed the bedroom door. It was the first time she felt she had a chance for a new start. Tossing her suitcase on the bed, she popped open the lid. After she put away her clothes in the bureau drawer, she removed the unwrapped gift and card Jonathan had given her. She felt guilty for not opening his gift yet.

Jayden flung herself on the bed. *I think I'm finally home.*

Five

The aroma of caffeine percolating early the next morning brought Edna to her feet. Following the scent, she found Jayden busy in the kitchen.

"Good morning," Jayden said cheerfully. "Hope you're a coffee drinker?"

"My goodness, I can't remember the last time I had someone make coffee for me."

"Here, let me pour it for you," Jayden said.

"Thank you, hon. So, tell me, what's on your agenda today, if you don't mind me asking?"

"Job hunting."

"Mercy me, you sure don't let grass grow under your feet. But that's admirable. So often people don't appreciate how hard it is to earn a dollar. I suppose you'll be looking for work across town at the new strip mall that opened up. Seems like that's where all the jobs are moving to."

"Actually, yesterday when I was on the bus coming through town I saw a *Help Wanted* sign in the window of a drugstore not too far from here."

Edna stroked her chin, trying to visualize the location Jayden was talking about. "Oh, that'd be Jerome's; it's on Locust Street."

"I don't really know the name of the streets. I do know it's walking distance from here."

"It's the only drugstore left downtown. He and his family are of the Jewish faith. Wonderful people. When Willum—that's my dearly departed husband—and I moved here in the late 1950s, Mr. Weiskopf and his wife, Ruth, were so kind, showing us around town and all. We spent many a Friday night with them playing bridge. Ruth had the most delightful stories. Always had a moral to each one. No one could tell a story like her. It was like stepping back in time, reliving a part of history."

"What do you mean?"

"Well, for example, many members of his family were murdered under the orders of Henrick Hemler and Adolf Eichmann in those despicable concentration camps. He was a young boy at the time, but he still carries those awful numbers they branded on his arm. Such courage and strength they had. God's chosen people. You know the old saying, 'What doesn't kill us makes us stronger.' We've all had sorrows in our life, honey, but it's how we handle and grow from these tragedies that's important."

Jayden thought of her own personal losses. She raised her mug of coffee in a toast. "Here's hoping he still needs help."

The coffee mugs clanked together.

"Here, here," Edna said.

∽╟∾

Jayden walked the two blocks to the pharmacy. The row of buildings looked vacant except for Mr. Weiskopf's, and he only had a few loyal customers left. Most retailers had left the downtown area for the more prosperous suburbs. It wouldn't be long before Mr. Weiskopf's would end up like the rest of the other stores. He couldn't compete, not with the new chains offering door prizes, coupon days, and promotions. All Mr. Weiskopf could offer was a good cup of tea and great conversation.

Jayden paced back and forth in front of the store, rehearsing her speech: "Good morning, sir. I saw your sign in the window, and I would like to put in an application." Or, "Good Morning, my name is Jayden Arman, and I'm your new employee."

Just be natural. Calm down. Don't make it seem as though you're desperate.... Who are you fooling? You are desperate! Ready or not, Jayden moved inside the store and waited for someone to greet her.

Finally, a short, squatty man practically ran out from behind the counter. "I said, 'May I help you?' And what are you doing with my sign in your hand? You shouldn't touch things that aren't yours."

"I'm sorry. I didn't hear you. This sign, well, I'd like to apply for the position you are advertising for."

He shook his head. "You are not what I need. I'm not looking for a girl for this job. I need a boy who can lift, clean the store, stock shelves. This job isn't for you. So—" he pointed his pudgy finger at his display window—"please put the sign back."

"Excuse me, Mr. Weiskopf. I don't mean to appear pushy or rude, but your sign didn't distinguish if you were looking for a male or female. If that's what you wanted, maybe your ad should have been more specific. But I'm here now, and I can do any job you need."

Mr. Weiskopf, glasses perched on the bridge of his nose, glared at her. "I think you're being smart with me, young lady. I'm very busy, and I will ask you again to put my sign back in the window."

"Sir, I can do the job, please," she insisted. "I'm stronger than I look. I'll make a deal with you. Hire me on a trial basis for two weeks, and if I'm not what you want, I'll leave. But please, give me a chance. I need a job."

"This job would not be suitable for a girl. You'll get dirty. I need someone to watch the store when I'm not around, and there are a lot of hooligans—troublemakers—in these parts."

She held firm. "Two weeks—that's all I'm asking. If I don't work out for you, I won't ask any questions. I'll just leave."

The elderly man shook his head as he walked towards the back of the store. "You should try one of those swanky stores across town. I'm sure they could use some young girl."

"I can't."

"Well, you can't work here either. Now you must leave unless you're going to buy something."

"I can't look for work across town because I don't have a way to get there."

Mr. Weiskopf stopped in his tracks. "That's why you want to work here? just because it's close to where you live?"

"To be truthful with you, yes."

"At least you're honest. People aren't honest anymore. So, where do you live anyway? There are no apartments left on this side of town."

"Edna Sullivan's."

"Where?"

"Edna Sullivan's boarding house—or, at least it used to be a boarding house."

"Oh yes, Edna and Willum's red brick two-story."

"Yes, sir."

Mr. Weiskopf stared off in the distance as if remembering them fondly. "The Sullivans were customers of mine…well, they were more than that. Willum and Edna were friends to me and my Ruth many years ago. When Willum passed away, we didn't see much of Edna. I think the last time I saw her was at my Ruth's funeral. Is Edna in good health?"

"Yes, sir. I just met her yesterday, but she seems to be in good health."

"Well, young woman," he said, changing the subject, "got to hand it to you, you're very persistent. Against my better judgment, you got yourself a job."

"Really! Thank you so much. I promise you won't be sorry."

"There's one stipulation: I'm taking your advice and hiring you on a trial basis. If I don't like your work, or if I don't like you for that matter, no ifs, ands, or buts, you have to leave."

"It's a deal," she said shaking his hand.

"I must be out of my mind," he scoffed at her.

<hr>

Over the next several weeks Jayden and Mr. Weiskopf developed a mutual respect for one another. Each morning he served hot tea and bagels, and she was his captive audience, listening to his stories of the war. But it was her pleasure and privilege to be taught life's lessons from him. He was such an inspiration.

He shared with her the story of his family. She learned that when Mr. Weiskopf was a child they had lived in Poland. His father owned a shoe repair shop, and his mother and aunts were always busy taking in garments for repair.

"To this day, I remember the look in my father's eye the day he came home and said something was terribly wrong. He said we had to prepare to leave immediately. My father didn't frighten easily, so when we saw his urgency...I can't put our fear into words. So many families were being ripped apart. The weak were of no use to the Germans, and the strong went to work in harsh weather with little food from sunup to sundown.

"Men are supposed to be the strong ones. You know, like it's a sign of weakness to cry. No more do I feel that way. It's not exclusively a woman's emotion. I still have visions of the hundreds of people crammed into box cars without food or water. They were on their way to different concentration camps. When the people died from starvation or illness, the soldiers cast the bodies in ditches as though they were removing rubbish. I was horrified when I saw one of my mother's sisters thrown into the heap. When I cried out, I was struck in the back of the head by the butt of a rifle. No one was allowed to help me. When I came to, I noticed what looked like snow falling from the sky. As I touched my face I realized it was soot. I must have looked shocked, because one of the other men bent down and told me that it was from the ovens.

"Every night I prayed with my elders so God would hear the cries of his people and set us free. The atrocities of war...how can a human being created by God treat another with such disregard for life? It is God's promise each and every one of us will stand before him in judgment one day."

She only hoped that Mr. Weiskopf was right. Then all the people who had falsely accused her father of a crime he didn't do would pay the price.

Six

Jayden noticed Mr. Weiskopf slipping on his overcoat and hat. "You going somewhere?"

"Yes, I think I may go home and rest for a spell. Will you be okay here alone? It looks like it might rain, but if you need me, call."

"Of course. Don't worry about anything here. I'll do just fine," Jayden said, elated that he placed so much trust in her. She would make certain not to disappoint him.

The overcast sky turned quickly to a threatening deep charcoal. The smell of ozone was in the air. Any minute, the rain would pour down. Relatively sure she wouldn't have any customers in the store, Jayden reached into the refrigerator and pulled out her sack lunch. She sat on a stool and decided to write Jonathan a letter. She hadn't even told him about her job.

August 31, 1977
Dear Jonathan:

    It seems like a long time since I left Odessa, and in other ways it feels like just yesterday. A lot has happened and, I'm pleased to say, they are all good things. First, I found a place to live in a boarding home. Well, it's not exactly a boarding home any longer. It's the home of a wonderful lady named Edna Sullivan.

    Has anyone taken my place on the bench in front of the church? Just kidding. I do miss our talks and have every intention the next time I come to town to see Emma, and to call you.

    Within a day of being here, I found a job at a small pharmacy in town. The owner is Mr. Weiskopf. It's so interesting to hear him talk about his past.

    How are you doing? My boss has left me in charge of the store while he is out. I know it seems like such a small thing, but you have no idea what a big thing that actually is. Just to know he believes I can handle it makes me feel good about myself.

Since we're having quite the rainstorm right now. I need to go and close up everything. I'll write more next time. Please let me know how you're doing.

Sincerely,
Your friend, Jayden

Seven

The storm moved through town with a fury. The rumbling drumroll of thunder was followed by bright flashes of electrical current charging through the atmosphere. The inside lights flickered off and on while shadows bounced in the aisles. It unnerved Jayden, but she'd never admit that to Mr. Weiskopf or he'd never leave her alone again. The tumultuous downpour was quickly turning the parking lot into a water reservoir.

Jayden rushed around checking all the windows. The forceful winds caught the screen door and blew it open, practically ripping it from the hinges. She struggled to close the front door when she thought she saw the image of someone running towards her. It was a man. His long strides hurdled across water-filled potholes. He was heading right for her. The driving rain stung her skin as she waited for him to cross over the parking lot.

"Come in, hurry." It took both of them to close the door.

"Boy, you're a welcome sight." The man slid on the wet linoleum the moment he stepped inside. Rainwater streamed from his clothing, forming puddles where he stood. His drenched T-shirt clung to his broad chest, revealing a well-toned body. *An athlete, probably a football player.*

Jayden watched as his strong masculine hands, the kind that aren't afraid of hard work, wiped the water off his tanned face. He ran his fingers through his hair, slicking it back as he squeezed the water out. Their eyes locked. He had glacier blue eyes, unlike any color of blue she had seen.

"No problem; it wouldn't have been quite humane to leave anyone standing out in this storm."

"This was pretty unexpected, wasn't it?" he asked.

"No, not really. I heard the forecast on the radio earlier predicting the storm would hit, but I thought it would be later this evening."

"I haven't listened to the radio at all today. Usually I do, but today I've been working outside laying brick."

Pegged that right. Definitely a man used to a little physical labor.

"Laying bricks? What type of work do you do?"

"I'm a landscaper during the summer for my father. We're putting in a fountain for a business across town. I was on my way back when the truck broke down at the light a couple of streets over. Well, the rest is history."

"Uh huh," Jayden said, not taking her eyes off of him. *That's all you can think to say to him? "Uh huh"?*

"I'm sorry. I didn't even introduce myself. My name is Daniel Taylor." His handshake was firm yet gentle.

"Nice to meet you. I'm Jayden Arman." Her tender flesh felt the rough calluses on his palms.

"Sorry about the water mess," he said.

"No problem, I'll get it later; besides, the floor needs a good cleaning. But you're drenched and probably cold. All I can offer you are some paper towels to dry with."

"I am a little chilly, but I do have some dry clothes…back in the truck." They laughed at the same time.

What a natural beauty, Daniel couldn't help but think. *A real celebration for the eye.* He was captivated. Jayden was different, not like so many of the young girls hiding behind layers of makeup. San Antonio was a fairly good-sized town, but he had been part of the crew to revitalize the downtown area and been inside Mr. Weiskopf's pharmacy many times. He couldn't recall seeing her. She had the kind of face he could never forget.

Daniel slapped his forehead. "I almost forgot why I was running over here. I need to borrow a phone. I saw the light on in the store, and then I saw you, so I headed right over. My truck is still in the middle of the road."

"Maybe you should have stayed in your truck until the rain let up," she suggested.

"It was just a light drizzle when I started out and then a couple of thunder claps and swoosh—it was like the dam broke."

Jayden handed him the telephone, then moved away from the counter, as if to offer him privacy.

"Hi, Marsha, is Bill around?" Daniel kept Jayden in his field of vision. "Bill, hey, it's me, Daniel. Oh, come on, I call you more than when I'm in trouble. But I am in a bit of a predicament. Yep, it's the truck again." Daniel smiled at Jayden. "The alternator? I was going to get to it but, well, you know." Daniel laughed out loud. "Address, uh, wait a minute. I'm sorry, Ms. Arman, but what is the address here?" he called.

"223 Locust Street."

Daniel repeated the address to the person on the phone. "Yes, downtown past the old First Bank. Thanks, Bill, I'll watch for you."

"The rescue team should be here soon," he told Jayden, watching the sky as the storm passed over. "Looks like the rain is slowing down."

The sun made a valiant attempt to break through granite-colored clouds. There was comfortable silence between them. Daniel wasn't ready to leave, but he couldn't think of a good enough reason to linger.

"Guess I've taken enough of your time. I'll wait outside."

"Oh, I really wasn't that busy." She hesitated. "I mean, I'm always busy, but the threat of the storm probably is keeping people at home. It's been slow here."

"Good—if I'm going to be a nuisance, at least it was on a slow day for you."

Daniel had the most incredible smile, Jayden thought. Straight, ivory white teeth made even whiter by a deep, bronze tan. He was so different from the other boys she knew from school with their crude ways of getting a girl's attention.

"You can wait inside if you'd like," Jayden offered. "I was going to get a soda; would you like one?"

Daniel perked up. "Thank you; I'll buy." He began to fish around in his pockets, as if looking for some loose change.

"It's on the house." Jayden opened a couple of cold bottles. She handed one to him.

"Is Mr. Weiskopf gone for the day?"

"You know Mr. Weiskopf?"

"Of course. Most of the community does. He's a legend around these parts, which brings me to another question."

Jayden was a little nervous about what he was going to ask.

"Have you been working here long? I'm only asking because I don't remember ever seeing you, and I come in quite often."

"No, actually I've been working here for a couple of months. I moved here from Odessa, Texas, and decided to do something new and adventurous when I graduated."

"So you picked up and moved to San Antonio alone?...Or maybe that was a little forward of me. I don't mean to get personal." Daniel winked at her and she blushed.

"No, it's all right. I did move out here alone. Guess I wanted to be independent."

"I know what that's like. It's always nice to get away from the same old routine and venture out on your own."

"Precisely."

Daniel couldn't get over how remarkable she was. *Wow! Who would have guessed today you'd meet the woman of your dreams?*

The two of them were engrossed in conversation when another man walked in. "Hope I didn't interrupt," he said. "I wasn't sure if you heard me honk, so thought I'd better come inside."

"Sorry, Bill, you're right. I didn't hear you honking." Daniel introduced Bill to Jayden.

"It's a pleasure." Bill extended his hand to her. "I'll get this troublemaker out of your hair." Bill looked several years older than Daniel, but it was plain to see that they were good friends.

"He wasn't too much of a handful," she teased Daniel.

"Well," Daniel stammered, "Guess I'd better run along."

Bill raised an eyebrow at his friend's awkwardness. "I'll pull around to the front door."

Daniel waited inside the doorway with his hands in his pockets. Then, just before he ducked out the door, he called back, "It's been a pleasure, Ms. Arman."

"It certainly has, Daniel Taylor, it certainly has," she replied.

Daniel looked back one more time before he got in the car.

"I hope you at least asked for her number?" Bill teased.

Daniel wasn't good at this sort of thing.

"You didn't, did you?" Bill looked over at him.

"No, I didn't, but I'm sure I'll run into her sooner or later."

"Last chance."

"Drive, drive," Daniel said.

Jayden tried to make it a habit to write inside her journal each night before she retired, but it didn't seem to work out that way lately. So she pulled it out and began.

> *August 1977*
> I couldn't wait to write tonight. I don't know where to begin. There was a terrible storm today, more lightning and rain than I'd seen since moving here. Well, in walked the most gorgeous man. We spent some time together talking. I couldn't get the butterflies to settle down in my stomach. I hope I see him again, but I'm probably reading more into this than I should. Whatever would a man like that see in someone like me?

Daniel Taylor was a rare breed among young men. After graduating from college, he had decided to take some time off to discover what he really wanted out of life. It was a great source of contention between him and his father. "You just spent a fortune on a college education," his father had reasoned. "What's to find out? A man needs to find an honest job and bring home a steady paycheck." At times, his father had a tendency to hound Daniel about money and work matters.

Daniel respected his parents and valued their opinion on most things, but he also wanted to experience life for himself. So, with a lot of protest from his parents and some solid persuasion from Daniel, along with a lot of prayer, he had boarded the plane headed for the African continent to spend a month serving the people there.

When he'd returned home, he'd worked with his father for the summer. But he couldn't shake the thought that God was calling him to Africa. He'd fallen in love with the country…and the people. He longed to go back.

But now, for the first time since he'd stepped onto African soil, something was holding his heart back from returning there…and it had everything to do with the hazel-eyed woman he'd just met in Mr. Weiskopf's pharmacy.

Eight

Most evenings, Edna and Jayden could be found sitting on the front porch sipping iced tea and enjoying the night air. Though Edna looked forward to those times with Jayden, she also worried how much the young woman kept to herself, isolated from others. Every time Edna tried to learn about Jayden's family, she ran into a dead end. The young Jayden was closed-mouthed. It was the same when the topic of religion was brought up; Jayden always changed the subject.

What happened to make her have such a lack of faith in God? And in humankind, for that matter?

Edna knew she had to tread lightly. The last thing she wanted to do was have that wall Jayden had built around herself go up any higher.

❧❧

The first couple of months after leaving Odessa, Jayden was consistent about calling Tilly to check on Emma. In the beginning, Tilly was cordial, giving glowing reports on the child but never allowing Jayden to speak with her. For the last several weeks, however, Jayden's calls had gone unanswered.

It was a blessing in disguise when Mr. Weiskopf announced he was giving Jayden a three-day weekend for all her hard work. Immediately, Jayden picked up the phone calling Tilly to ask for permission to visit. To her surprise, the number was disconnected. Tilly had a new number, an unlisted number. There was no choice left in the matter. She would catch the bus and head to Odessa unannounced. Jayden packed a few articles of clothing in a small bag and was having a cup of coffee when Edna joined her.

"My, my! You going so early?"

"Oh, good morning! I hope I didn't wake you."

"Not really. I needed to get up and start moving. If I lay around for too long, I feel worse. My old bones need some exercise." Edna poured herself some coffee and sat at the kitchen table.

"Mr. Weiskopf not only gave me a weekend off but a three-day weekend. I decided to take full advantage of that and go visit someone I haven't seen in a long time."

"Around here?" Edna asked.

"No, I'll be going back to Odessa."

"Odessa? That sounds like fun. I've been so worried about you being all alone at your age and just working, then coming back here hanging out with an old fogy."

"For your information," Jayden said, "I can't think of anyone I'd rather be with."

There was something different about Edna, Jayden thought. Her eyes seemed dull. She looked completely drained of color, her breath coming in short spurts.

"Are you feeling okay, Edna? You look a little pasty."

Edna waved her off. "Don't worry about me. I'm fine. But don't you try to get off the subject at hand."

"Which would be?" Jayden asked.

"Don't be coy with me. You know very well what I'm talking about. I really appreciate the fact you enjoy spending time with an old woman, but it ain't right. You need to be with people your own age. Tell me now. Do these friends happen to be of the male persuasion?" Edna asked with a sparkle in her eye.

"No, nothing like that." Jayden didn't want to admit that at her age she'd never dated a boy.

"Honey, a pretty young thing like yourself? The boys should be falling at your feet...but you got to get out there and meet some."

"I will, in time."

Edna leaned closer. "I know you may not want to hear this, but I'm just feeding you a little information. You can do with it what you want. I hear that the youth group at my church has an exceptional program. I think they meet at different times during the week to make it convenient for everyone."

"I've never been one to join a group," Jayden said.

"I can understand it's uncomfortable for some people. But I wanted to throw it out there and then you make the decision. If you decide to try it, I know someone who would be pleased to escort you. In fact, he's the grandson of one of my best friends."

Jayden smiled. "A blind date? No thanks."

"I know what you're thinking. *The boy must be unattractive or a complete nerd.* But I can guarantee he's anything but that. There are lots of girls who think he's dreamy."

"Dreamy?" Jayden smirked.

"All right. Whatever you kids nowadays call it. In my day we would have called him a real catch," Edna said.

"I'll let you know when I'm ready, but I wouldn't hold my breath. I can't remember the last time I set foot in a church…except maybe on one or two occasions."

"Just give it some thought."

"We'll see. I better run. The bus leaves around ten, and I plan on coming back home sometime on Monday, so don't worry about me."

"Would you set an old woman's mind at ease?"

"Of course—anything."

"Call me when you get to Odessa. I want to know you got there safely."

"I promise. I'll give you a call once I've reached my friend's house."

"Thanks, Hon."

Jayden started out the door, then stopped to look back at Edna. "You sure you're fine?"

"Yes. Now go on and stop making a fuss."

Edna waited until she knew Jayden wouldn't walk back in. She opened the cabinet where she kept some of her medication, reaching for her nitroglycerine pills. With trembling hands she brought the glass of water to her lips. "Lord, I'm not ready just yet. Please give me more time to be with her."

The eight-hour trip to Odessa felt like it would never end. No sooner had the bus come to a stop than Jayden leaped to her feet, waiting for the folding doors to open. Her pace was quick until Tilly's house came into view, then she broke into a full run.

It didn't appear that anyone was home at Tilly's. The window blinds were drawn. There was no car in the driveway...but then, that didn't mean anything. Tilly usually kept her car in the garage.

Jayden felt a strange sense of foreboding. Emma's toys were usually strewn about the yard. Now there were no signs that a child lived there.

Jayden knocked on the door and waited. When there was no answer, she ran her hand over the lip of the window ledge feeling for the spare key, usually left there for emergencies. It was still there. She slipped the key into the lock and cautiously opened it, calling out for Tilly the entire time. There was no sign of life inside.

"Tilly? Emma?" Jayden called out, but there was no response.

The familiar backfiring of the old station wagon brought Jayden to the edge of the porch. Tilly pulled in the driveway. Any second now, Emma would look out of the car window and see Jayden standing there. She couldn't wait to hold her in her arms again. Her heart pounded with anticipation. Tilly opened the door to the back seat and grabbed a bag of groceries.

Strange. There was no sign of Emma. Jayden moved from the shadows into the light to get a better view.

Tilly looked up at Jayden. She squinted against the sun as she lowered her sunglasses. "Jayden? What in blazes are you doing here?"

"Hi, Tilly. I tried calling, but you have an unlisted number."

"That's right. So, what are you doing here?" Tilly didn't look Jayden in the eyes. "I had to change my number. Too many prank callers."

"Why didn't you call me and tell me?"

"I thought I did. You took it upon yourself to come anyway?"

Jayden had lived with the woman for ten years, yet the tone in Tilly's voice was one she'd use with a stranger.

"I've been out of town visiting my cousin Frieda. I got back into town yesterday," Tilly said.

"Where is she—Emma, I mean?" Jayden's stomach knotted.

"I don't want to discuss it out here where everyone can hear. Come inside." Tilly brushed past her. The screen door slammed.

Jayden stopped just inside the entryway.

"Let me put these groceries away. Can I get you something to drink?" Tilly offered.

"No, thank you, I'd just like to see Emma."

"Well, I want something to drink." Tilly looked nervous.

"I thought I could take Emma to the zoo today if it was okay with you, and then, if you don't mind, could I stay here tonight and catch a bus back to San Antonio on Monday?" Jayden asked.

Tilly came out of the kitchen with a soda in her hand. "She's gone." Tilly tilted the pop bottle against her lips and took a big gulp.

"What do you mean, gone?"

"What part of that didn't you understand? I mean she's gone. If you must know, I placed her with another foster family."

Jayden stared at Tilly. Did she hear right? "I don't get it."

"She no longer lives here. Okay?"

Jayden broke out into a cold sweat. Her knees started to buckle. Feeling lightheaded, she leaned against the wall for support.

"It makes sense this way, Jayden," Tilly spat. "I've been doing foster care for years, and now I need to do something for me. I've spent the better part of my life always taking care of kids or a husband. Besides, after you left, I couldn't ever cheer that child up. It's only right she be with others her age."

"What are you saying, Tilly? You've always thought of yourself first!"

Tilly backed away from Jayden. "Well, for your information, Ms. Smarty Pants, I have every right to do with my life what I want. What are you complaining about? Didn't you stay on here while you finished school?"

"Yes, and the day I turned eighteen, you shoved the apartment ads in my hand. Of course, all in the name of love. Right, Tilly?"

"That's not fair. I thought we understood one another."

"You're a piece of work." Jayden brought herself to a standing position.

"I did what I had to do. That child was more than I could deal with. Whining about this and that. She drove me nuts. You only have yourself to blame."

"That child has a name." Jayden gritted her teeth. "And me to blame? What are you talking about?"

"I couldn't control her moods any longer."

"What do you mean 'her moods'? She's a little girl, and she felt abandoned by me when I left. You never called me, not once, to let me know you were thinking about doing this. Why?" she screamed in Tilly's face. "Why?"

"You have no right to talk to me that way, understand?" Tilly scolded her.

Jayden pushed Tilly aside, running down the hallway until she reached the room the girls had shared for five years. Emma's favorite stuffed animal was still on the bed. Jayden walked over and sat down. She picked up the stuffed puppy and stared at Tilly, who now stood in the doorway. "What have you done?" Jayden fought back the nausea.

"I didn't know if you were coming back."

"If I would come back? You knew I would come back. I called you every week. You never let on anything was wrong or that you were thinking about doing this."

"I don't owe you any explanation. I did what I felt was right."

"Where can I find her?" Jayden pleaded.

"I can't tell you because I don't even know that information. All I know is that she has a new foster family. You shouldn't worry so much about her. I bet she's adjusting just fine."

"Emma forgot this," Jayden said, holding the toy dog.

"No, she didn't forget it. The day Emma left it was so sweet." Tilly smiled as though what she was about to say would make everything all right now. "She ran into her room and asked me to give the stuffed dog to you when I saw you again so you would never be alone."

The events had unfolded so quickly, Jayden felt as though she was on one of those spinning rides at a carnival and couldn't get off. "What do I do now?" Her eyes pleaded for an answer from Tilly. "Tell me, please. What do I do? I gave her my word."

Tilly stood in silence.

Jayden clutched the toy animal tightly against her chest and rocked back and forth on the bed. *What will I do without you?*

Tilly stood, wide-eyed, against the bookcase now. "Stop it. I'm not the bad guy here. You were in no position to take Emma, were you? You don't even have your own place or the financial resources to support a child. Besides, you act like you two were related or something."

"Because we aren't blood related? I know how important that is to you. After all, how many times did you remind me I wasn't your real daughter or that it was your house and not mine?"

"Well, you both had mothers. It's not my fault your mother died or Emma's mother didn't want her. Do I have to make up for both of your misfortunes?" Tilly argued. "And don't use that same old excuse that I was paid for caring for you two because there wasn't much money." Tilly looked down at her fingernails as though she was going to file them.

Jayden didn't know how to respond to that. Tilly was right about Jayden's financial resources, but she knew how to bite down to the bone with her sharp tongue.

Jayden's hopes and dreams of reuniting with Emma had just been dashed at the whim of one person. A relationship built on trust and love had been carelessly tossed to the side as though it had no worth. The vision of a frightened Emma sickened Jayden.

"I will never forgive you for this, Tilly. Never." Jayden leaped to her feet, stopped to glare into Tilly's eyes for a moment, then left the house.

Once outside, the fresh air helped with the nausea. Jayden fell to her knees, digging her fingers into the cool earth as though trying to hold onto her sanity. A primal, guttural grief rose up from the very core of her being. She didn't care who heard her.

What am I going to do, Emma? How can I help you now? I don't even know if you're safe. The helplessness was overwhelming.

"It's not my fault!" Tilly yelled one last time from the front porch.

Jayden's world was spinning out of control.

"Miss," a next-door neighbor called out, "You okay over there?"

Jayden didn't look up. Instead she brushed the grass and dirt from her pants. "No one can help me now," she mumbled. "No one."

Nine

Jayden had no idea how she got back to the bus station, but found herself sitting on a bench there, staring out the window. Desperate to hear a friendly voice, she remembered Jonathan. Fishing in her bag, she found his business card and headed for the payphone.

"Hello, Baxter residence," the woman on the other end of the line said. It had to be Jonathan's sister, since he lived with her.

"May I please speak to Jonathan?" Jayden tried to steady her voice so the woman wouldn't detect her emotional state.

"I'm sorry, but Jonathan isn't home right now; may I take a message?"

"That's all right. I'll try later."

"If he gets home soon, would you like me to tell him who called?"

"Yes, I mean no, I'm not at a place where he can call me back. Will you please tell him that Jayden Arman called? I'm at the Greyhound bus terminal. Do you expect him home soon?" Jayden didn't want to seem too frantic, even though she was.

"The Greyhound bus station." Jonathan's sister repeated the location slowly, as if she was writing it down. "Actually I haven't heard from him all day, but the closer it gets to dinner the faster I expect I'll hear from him." She laughed.

"Thank you. I'll be here awhile longer. The last bus for San Antonio leaves by 8:00 p.m. tonight."

"8:00 p.m. Got it. The moment I hear from him, I'll give him the message."

"Thanks."

Jayden hung up the phone and tried to compose herself. She found a corner in the station where she could be alone and collect her thoughts. An employee busied himself stringing Christmas lights from window to window, adding a little Christmas cheer. A small aluminum tree, the support base missing, was propped up by several magazines.

It's probably seen better days. Bored, she picked up an old *Field and Stream* magazine, when the janitor brushed her foot with his push broom.

"If you don't plan on spending the night here, I'd go up to the counter and get my ticket if I was you," the man said.

Jayden looked at her watch. *7:45 p.m. He's not coming. Well, maybe another time, Jonathan.*

"One ticket to San Antonio," she said, handing the cashier a twenty.

"She won't need the ticket." Jayden turned around to see Jonathan standing there. Suddenly her fear was replaced with comfort. "Jonathan, you have no idea how glad I am to see you."

"I'm sorry I wasn't here sooner. I didn't know you were coming to town," he said. Concern creased his brow.

"It's not your fault. It was a spur-of-the-moment thing. My boss gave me time off."

"I'm glad you're here. What's going on?" Jonathan said.

Without warning, Jayden broke down.

Jonathan led her to a bench. "I'll get you something to drink."

"No, I'm okay. I can't believe I fell apart like that in front of you." Jayden wiped her eyes with a tissue.

"I want to help. No matter what it is; I'm here for you."

She could tell from his eyes that he meant every word. But she said, "There's nothing you can do. Besides, I don't have time to talk about it now. My bus will be leaving soon."

"Forget the bus. If you have to leave tonight, I'll take you myself."

"I don't want to impose on you."

"You're not imposing on me at all. We're friends, aren't we?"

"Of course we are."

"Then as far as I'm concerned, friends are there for one another. Come on—let's get out of here. I know a quiet place where we can talk. All I need to do is make a quick call."

You shouldn't have involved him in your problems, a little voice inside her whispered. But she had to talk to someone, and burdening Edna wasn't an option. With such a questionable past, Edna might ask her to leave, and who could blame her? No, it was safer to talk to Jonathan.

"Let's go to the church and use one of the offices," he said, helping her to her feet.

When they arrived, the church parking lot was completely empty. The main chapel was pitch-black inside. The silence was eerie with only the occasional click from the heat thermostat echoing throughout the building. Jonathan unlocked one of the office doors and flipped on the light. He motioned for her to take the overstuffed high back chair for comfort. Then he sat next to her.

"I don't even know where to begin." She curled up in the leather seat.

"Take your time; I have all night."

"It's Emma."

A worried look came over Jonathan.

"I didn't mean to frighten you. Emma's not sick or anything like that, or at least I don't think so," she explained.

"I'm not following you."

"That's all I can tell you. I don't know anything for sure because she's gone." Fresh tears rolled down her face.

"Gone? Gone where?"

"I need to be honest with you. I told you Emma was my sister."

"That's true, isn't it?"

"That depends on who you ask. To me, she's my sister. To the legal system we're nothing more than foster sisters related by an unfortunate turn of events."

"Foster sisters?"

"She couldn't have been any more of a sister to me if we had been blood relatives. Do you understand what I mean?"

"Yes I do."

"I couldn't bring myself to tell you I was a ward of the state. It's nothing I'm really proud of."

Jonathan reached over and grasped her hand. "You have nothing to be ashamed of. It does answer a question I've had all along, though."

"What's that?"

"I often wondered why you would never let me pick you and

Emma up at your house. Is that the reason? You were afraid I'd find out?"

"It was a bad situation."

"This may seem a bit forward, but why were you in foster care?"

She debated her answer. If she considered Jonathan a true friend, she couldn't hide her past from him. "This is hard for me to tell anyone."

"You can trust me," Jonathan said.

"My mother is deceased."

"I'm very sorry to hear that."

"She was murdered."

Jonathan tried not to look surprised, but he was afraid she could read the shock by his expression.

She smiled wryly. "Not quite what you were expecting to hear, am I right?"

"Well no, it's not."

"Oh, it gets better. My father...well, he is"—Jayden laughed nervously—"the one who supposedly did it." She started to tremble.

"Jayden, I don't know what to say. Where is your father?"

"Serving time in prison. But I don't believe he did it."

Jonathan's heart went out to her. He knew it was hard for Jayden to share something so private and painful. His hand tightened around hers. "That must have been a horrible time in your life. I don't know how you came through it as well as you have."

"I'm not sure I have come through it. For years, all I wanted was to be a normal kid with a mother and father. I wanted my childhood back. After my mother's funeral, I was sent to live with a foster family that, by all practical purposes, should never have been licensed to care for children."

"That's where you met Emma?"

"She was a newborn when she came to live in the foster home. I took care of her as though she were mine."

"No one can deny your love for her. I saw it in your eyes every time she was around, and I see it now when you talk about her."

Jayden walked to the window and looked out into the night.

"There's more. I never knew my grandparents on either side. A couple of years back, I went through my mother's belongings."

"What did you find?"

"It seems my mother had twin sons."

"So she was married before?"

"Her sons, my half brothers, were born out of wedlock. For some reason, there must have been an agreement that her mother, my grandmother, would raise one of her sons, and the other son was put up for adoption."

"Why would anyone do that? It seems pretty cold to me." He was amazed at the burdens Jayden had carried all her young life.

"Believe me, I've witnessed firsthand how unfeeling people can be."

"Have you tried finding out where your grandmother is living? She may hold the key to where your brothers are."

"Actually, yes. It's a long story, but I did find a letter that my grandmother wrote to my mother right after I was born. Needless to say, when I wrote to that address explaining who I was, the letter was returned to sender and there wasn't a forwarding address."

"Did you try calling the telephone operator to see if there's a number for them?"

"I've tried everything without success. Yet I think I may have seen my grandmother and maybe one of my brothers."

"What do you mean?"

"I know this is starting to sound stranger by the minute, isn't it?"

"It's fine—go ahead." He was delighted she was opening up and talking to him.

"As I look back, I think I met them unknowingly at my mother's funeral."

"That had to be very troubling. To possibly be standing face to face with members of your family and not even know them. I can't imagine going through that. You're very brave."

Jayden shrugged. "I don't know about that, but something has always troubled me. If that was my grandmother and she knew I was her granddaughter, why didn't she say something to me?"

"There's no way to know what goes through someone's head or

why they act the way they do. Maybe after all this time she was ashamed." Jonathan tried to comfort her.

"Who knows? That's ancient history. Finding Emma is more pressing." She sighed.

"May I ask you something?" he said gently. "And if you feel it isn't any of my business, just tell me. Okay?"

"Okay."

"Why did you leave Emma behind? I mean, couldn't you have taken her with you?"

"Where would I have taken her? I had no home, no job, no money, not to mention, I have no legal rights to her. No one is going to allow someone like me to have guardianship of a child."

"Could you have stayed in town to be closer to Emma?"

"Yes. I thought about that, but there were too many memories here. I needed a fresh start. But the plan all along was to visit Emma every chance I got."

"You weren't real fond of your foster family, I take it?"

Jayden didn't turn to face him. "That's water under the bridge. I don't ever want to discuss them."

Jonathan knew he'd hit a sore spot, so he moved on. "People don't just up and disappear, Jayden. Someone knows where Emma is."

"The agency isn't about to tell me what foster home she's been placed in. There are all types of legalities. All I know is what Tilly says. Emma was voluntarily removed from her care to another home, a home where there are other children her age. I can't say that was a bad move for Emma's sake. It's just that I would have liked to know this was going to happen so maybe I could have been there for her…you know, to ease the transition for her. I would like to believe Tilly did it for Emma, but I know Tilly. She's concerned about no one but herself."

Jonathan stepped closer to Jayden. He wanted to hold her and let her cry on his shoulder, but he didn't want her to misinterpret his motives. So instead, he simply asked, "What's plan B?"

"Plan B?"

"You're not going to just roll over and let them get the best of you, are you?" he asked, trying to spark a little fight in her.

"You don't understand."

"You're right, I may not know exactly how you feel. But I do know if there was someone in my life who meant as much to me as Emma means to you, I wouldn't rest until I found that person."

"There's nothing I can do." Her tone sounded defeated.

"I never figured you for a girl who would give up if a few obstacles were in your way." Jonathan watched her closely and was rewarded by the glint of anger in her expression.

"Who said I'm giving up?" Jayden's eyes narrowed. "I would never give up on Emma."

He smiled. "That's what I was looking for—that fire in your eyes. We can't give up."

Startled, she looked at him. "We?"

Then, a second later, as he held his breath, she blurted out, "Edna! I promised her I'd call when I got here."

"Use this phone. It'll be fine."

"I'll call when I get to a motel for the night."

"There's no need to go to a motel. You can stay with me and my sister; she won't mind at all. In fact, you can take my room. I'll take the couch. Then, after I teach my class at church tomorrow, I'll drive you home."

She paused. "I don't know. I feel like I've been one royal pain. Here I am unloading all of this on you, and now I'm kicking you out of your room."

"Are you kidding? I prefer the couch," Jonathan teased. "That way, I'm in total control of the television programming."

"If you're sure, I'll take you up on your offer. You do realize that it's a long drive back to San Antonio?"

"Good. I haven't taken a road trip in quite some time. It'll be a nice diversion."

"If you'd known you were befriending someone from the wrong side of the tracks, I'll bet you'd have run the other way." She laughed.

"Wrong side of the tracks? I don't appreciate you talking about my friend like that."

"I come with a lot of baggage, trust me." Jayden was starting to relax a little.

"The Lord doesn't give us more than we can handle."

Oh, Jayden, Jonathan thought, *how glad I am to see you. And how much I want you to know Him.* It was hard to mask his feelings for her, even though he knew he needed to. Now was not the time.

"Hmm, then since you have an 'in' with him, maybe you could ask Him to help us find Emma," she said…and smiled.

❦

When Jayden reached Jonathan's house, she wrote her thoughts and feelings in her journal.

December 1977
Today my world has fallen apart. Everything good in my life is taken from me. Emma and I have been separated by someone so heartless. As I lie here alone in Jonathan's room I'm trying to piece together why. There are no answers; there's only hatred. But I find it is my hatred towards the one that has ripped Emma from me. If it wasn't for Edna and Jonathan pulling me out of the depths of depression, I'm certain I wouldn't be here at this moment.

Ten

"Where did you meet her again? Church?" Jonathan's sister asked as they sat together in the kitchen.

"It's a long story, but yes, you could say I met her at church."

"What's so long about that story, little Brother?"

Ten years older, Cynthia mothered Jonathan sometimes against his protests, but he treasured his relationship with her, especially after the death of his parents and the loss of Gina, his treasure.

He knew it wasn't the right time to share his personal tragedy with Jayden; he didn't want to minimize what she was feeling. And he also wasn't going to break Jayden's confidence, even if it was with his sister. At the same time, he didn't want to sound mysterious, or her sisterly red flags would go up.

"How long have you known her?"

"For a few months, but I really only see her once a week or so…"

"So you don't know that much about her?"

Cynthia was reverting to the mother role and Jonathan knew it. "I know enough for now." He reached over and patted her hand.

"Well, you're a good judge of character, and I trust you."

"It's part of my job to connect with people and to help them but…"

"But this is a little different? You can't fool me, Jonathan Michael Baxter. I've seen that look on your face before, and I am thrilled."

It had been a long time since his heart had felt this way. Soon the three-year anniversary of the death of his beloved Gina was approaching….

Gina had been full of spirit—brightening up a room the moment she walked in. When Jonathan announced the two of them were getting married, Cynthia couldn't have been more pleased. Gina had already become the sister she never had.

Two months after the wedding, Jonathan and Gina announced they were expecting their first child. Immediately Jonathan started drafting plans to build a cradle with his own two hands. All the while, Cynthia and Gina spent hours looking at swatches of material and wallpaper designs for the nursery. At first the pregnancy wasn't anything out of the ordinary, even though Gina complained of unusual fatigue and bruising.

"Nothing to be alarmed about. First-time mothers are always 'nervous Nellies,'" her obstetrician said, passing off her symptoms.

Jonathan, not liking the cavalier response, decided they needed a second opinion. After reviewing the lab results, Gina and Jonathan were asked to come in so the physician could talk to them face to face. Frightened for her husband, Gina asked Cynthia to come along to support him.

"My dear...," the doctor started.

"Anytime a doctor starts out by saying, 'My dear,' it can't be good news." Gina laughed nervously.

"In all the years I've been practicing medicine, I've never found it easy to tell people bad news."

Gina started to cry.

"You have a blood cancer," the doctor said gently. "Leukemia, to be precise."

Jonathan turned pale. "Leukemia. Okay, but there's a cure for that, right? I think I read that somewhere."

"There has been some success with experimental drugs, but Gina, I don't want to give you false hope. I believe you are in the advanced stages of leukemia. To be sure, we'll need to biopsy the bone marrow."

"I think I'm going to throw up." Gina held her stomach and ran out of the room, Cynthia right behind her.

Jonathan was stoic. "Okay, then tell me what we can do to help her and the baby."

The physician walked around to the front of his desk and closer to Jonathan. "We can treat the symptoms to keep her comfortable."

"Treat the symptoms. Don't act as though you're trying to spare my feelings." Jonathan snapped out of his chair, gripping the back of it so tightly his knuckles turned white. "Treat the symptoms? Is that doctor lingo for 'there's nothing we can do'? Spit it out! Stop treating us as though we can't handle whatever it is. Or are you afraid to say my wife doesn't have much time?"

The physician averted his eyes to the floor.

"Oh, dear Jesus, don't let this happen to her," Jonathan cried out as he leaned against the wall for support. "She's pregnant. What do we do?"

"There is no treatment I can safely recommend. It would be of no benefit for her. As far as the baby, at this stage, it would never survive. If Gina lives until her due date, maybe we could do a caesarean section."

"What are you saying—*if* she survives to her due date? That's only five months away!"

"I know. This is hard for me to tell you this."

"Hard for you? This is *my* wife and baby. They're my life." Jonathan crumbled into a chair. "How long does she have?"

"Two months." The doctor cleared his throat. "Three months at best."

The women walked back into the room just as Jonathan was grabbing his jacket to leave. "Come on," he said, "let's get out of here."

The rest of the day was a blur. No one spoke, as though not speaking about it made it less real.

Six weeks from the date of her diagnosis, Jonathan was sleeping by Gina's bed when she reached over and touched the top of his head.

"Gina?"

"I'm going home now," she said, and took her last breath....

The memories were still fresh, even now, but Jonathan knew he must go on and live.

"No, my dear matchmaking sister," Jonathan said. "Jayden and I are friends, and that's it. It's not that I wouldn't like it to be more, but it can't be anything else."

"I'm not following you," Cynthia asked.

"Tonight was the first time Jayden trusted in me enough to share a very private part of her life. I can't destroy everything I've worked for to gain that trust. My witness for Christ could be damaged if she thought I might have taken advantage of her vulnerability."

"You know her better than I do. I'm sure you have your reasons."

Just then Jayden stepped into the kitchen.

"Good morning!" Jonathan greeted her, just happy she was there.

"Good morning." She walked to the table and pulled out a chair.

"Coffee?" Jonathan offered.

"Yes, please." She turned to Jonathan's sister. "You must be Cynthia. I'm Jayden Arman. Jonathan has told me so much about you."

"Well, none of it's true." Cynthia laughed. "Don't believe a word of it. It's a pleasure to meet you, Jayden. Jonathan speaks very highly of you."

Jayden looked over at Jonathan who was now standing by the stove. They smiled at one another.

"Did you sleep okay?" Jonathan asked her.

"I don't think I woke up once in the night."

"Good. I was hoping you couldn't hear Jonathan's snoring from the living room," Cynthia teased her brother.

"Okay, don't gang up on the only man in the room. Besides, I don't snore."

"Can I get you something to eat?" Cynthia asked. "We have cereal, or you can have bacon and eggs."

"I don't usually eat breakfast. I survive on a couple of cups of coffee until lunch."

"So that's the secret to staying so slim. Would you look at the time?" Cynthia pushed her chair in. "I'd love to visit more with you, but I'd better not be late for church again. Guess I'll see you there, and we can talk after."

Jayden looked to Jonathan for a rescue.

"Jayden's going to rest up here while I teach my class, then I'm driving her home…to San Antonio," Jonathan said.

Cynthia's mouth hung open. "As in home of the Alamo?"

"That would be the one." Jonathan left it at that and hoped Cynthia would, too.

"Hopefully I'll see you again soon," Cynthia said.

"I'd like that. Thank you for allowing me to stay in your home."

"You're welcome anytime. When do you think you'll be home, Jonathan?"

"I'll probably get a room when I get there and head back in the morning."

"I'd prefer you do that. I don't want to worry about you being overtired and driving on the road."

"Yes, ma'am," he said, saluting his sister.

"Watch it, mister. Nice meeting you, Jayden." Cynthia waved as she hurried out the door.

"She's something else." Jonathan shook his head.

"I like her."

"Yeah, she's okay. Guess I'd better run along too. I should be back from church by 10:30 or so."

"Thank you for offering to drive me home."

"Don't thank me yet. You may be bored to tears by the time I get you there."

"You? Boring? Not a chance."

"I'll ask you that question again after the trip. See you in an hour or so."

When Jonathan got to the car, he started it but just sat there. He was happy to see Jayden but also knew he'd have to go through the pain of seeing her leave again. This time he didn't know if his heart could take it.

Eleven

"Sorry it took all day to get here, stopping for lunch and dinner," Jayden said.

Jonathan turned off the car engine and removed the keys. "No problem. It was a lot of fun."

"It didn't even seem like it took that long. You, Jonathan Baxter, are a very enjoyable person to be around. I was such a wreck last night, but I couldn't think of anyone I'd rather talk to than you."

"That's really nice to hear. I hope you feel as though you can always talk to me. Why don't you let me walk you to the door?"

"Ordinarily I'd say yes, but I think I'll just sneak in and hopefully won't wake Edna. Tomorrow I'll share with her some of what I shared with you yesterday. Poor Edna has tried so many times to ask about my family, and I've always avoided the topic. It's not fair to her. Do you have any idea where you'll stay for the night?" Jayden asked.

"I saw a vacancy sign at the motel right outside of town."

"The Wagon Wheel. I had the great fortune to see why it's such a great rate."

"Ahh, so you know firsthand?"

"My first night in town."

"That doesn't sound good, but all I need is a place to rest my head."

Jonathan waited until Jayden went inside the house.

⊰⊱

The kitchen light was on. Jayden tiptoed in, easing the door closed, and latched the door bolt and chain behind her.

"Jayden, honey."

Startled, Jayden whirled and saw Edna sitting at the base of the stairs.

"I didn't mean to scare you," Edna said. "I've been worried."

"Why were you worried? I told you I'd be home on Monday, and it's only Sunday." Jayden didn't want to put any extra burden on this sweet woman.

Edna put one hand on the banister, easing herself up. Jayden winced at the popping and creaking of the older woman's joints and reached out her hand. "Here, let me help you."

"Thank you, sweetheart."

"I'm going to take a shower and go to bed," Jayden said, turning to make her way up the stairs.

She was already up three steps before she heard Edna. "Jayden, dear, can we talk?"

"I'm really beat. Can we do this tomorrow?"

"Someone called earlier today for you. She said her name was Tilly Jenson."

Jayden was already at the top of the staircase when she stopped. "Did she say what she wanted?"

Edna lifted an eyebrow. "I'm not about to have this conversation while you stand up there and I'm down here. You need to come down here."

"Okay, but I don't have a lot to talk about." Jayden slowly stepped down the staircase until she stood in front of Edna, fighting back tears. "I'm not sure what you want me to say."

Edna put her arms around Jayden, holding her tight.

"Please just let me go upstairs and rest," Jayden begged. "We'll talk about it tomorrow. I promise." Jayden tried to catch her breath between sobs.

"Go ahead and cry. Edna has got you now."

"I don't...," Jayden stammered between her cries, "I don't want anyone to care about me. I'm worthless." But as she spoke those words, her arms wrapped tightly around Edna, deeply afraid to let go.

"Oh, my sweet girl, please don't ever say that again. You have so much worth in this world. I love you as my own daughter."

Jayden drew back, surprised, and studied Edna. Love radiated from the older woman's eyes. Her comforting touch was that of a mother.

But for Jayden, this was unfamiliar territory...with feelings that were long dead and buried.

"It hurts so much." She sobbed uncontrollably.

"Let's go into the living room." Edna motioned Jayden down on the couch and propped her feet up on the ottoman.

"I'll be right back. I'm going to make us both some hot cocoa."

Jayden's muscles were tense, causing her head to throb. Guilt gripped at her insides. *A promise to an innocent child. You can't even do that right. Why didn't you just let me say good-bye to her, Tilly, why?*

Edna's Bible was on the edge of the end table. Jayden picked it up, opening the front cover.

> To my beautiful, loving wife and mother of our daughter. I thank God every day for blessing me with you in my life.
> Your faithful husband,
> Willum
> *July 12, 1951*

What kind of power do You claim to have to be able to give believers hope? I need you to perform a miracle for me! Jayden thought, angrily. The Bible slipped from her hand, making a resounding thud as it hit the floor.

A minute later Edna entered with a tray of hot chocolate. "Mind if I sit next to you?"

Jayden didn't answer; she merely scooted over. Tears streamed down her face. She leaned her head against the back of the couch, closing her swollen eyes.

"Edna, what did Tilly say to you?"

"Nothing, really. She just said you came to visit her. She was worried, that's all, honey. She wanted to make sure you got home all right. What happened to make her worry?" Edna reached over to hold Jayden's hand.

Carefully contemplating her response, Jayden said, "No matter what she may have told you, take everything with a grain of salt. Tilly Jenson and I don't have the best relationship."

Was she making matters worse by sounding so mysterious? Jayden wondered. Edna deserved some kind of explanation—even if the consequences were that she was asked to leave.

"I didn't want you to know anything about me," Jayden said.

"Why? What are you afraid of?" Edna asked.

"Not so much afraid as embarrassed of who I am and where I came from."

"You have nothing to be embarrassed about; everyone has a story to tell."

Jayden stood up and walked over to the fireplace mantel, trying to decide where to begin. Then she began to share her story. "I'll tell you who Tilly Jenson is. She is…*was* my foster mother." Jayden didn't turn around to see Edna's face. "You always asked about my family, and it wasn't like I didn't want to tell you; it's just I don't have one. For ten years, I lived in foster care…since losing my parents."

"I'm so sorry, hon," Edna said. "Were they in some kind of an accident?"

Jayden spent the next hour going over every grisly detail.

"And you have never met your brothers?"

"No."

Edna's expression was full of love and compassion—no judgment. She hugged Jayden again. "Oh, my poor girl. And when was the last time you saw your father?"

"At my mother's funeral. But I wasn't allowed to even talk to him. I hope one day new evidence will be presented to set him free, and we can be together once again."

Jayden felt a strange freedom. She had carried the burden of these secrets herself for years, and now two people knew her past: Jonathan and Edna. She had faith in them both.

Jayden took another sip of hot cocoa before continuing on. "I was placed in foster care because there were no family members."

"God sent his guardian angels to help you through this," Edna said quietly.

Jayden stiffened. "Please don't take this the wrong way, but if there is a God, why does He allow horrible things to happen to His people? I mean, how can you trust in a relationship like that?"

"I know you're hurting, Jayden, but you can't blame God when things go wrong. We've all suffered a loss of one kind or another. And faith? I choose to hold onto it. It's what helps me get through the day. I can't imagine going through life without it."

"There's something else." Jayden started wringing her hands.

"Go ahead, hon."

"I haven't told you about Emma."

"Emma?"

"Yes, Emma. The legal terminology for our relationship was *foster sisters*. But we were far more than that. I was with Emma most of her life, except for the last few months. I'm all she has and…now, that has been taken from us."

"You've had to grow up before your time, sweetheart. A baby taking care of a baby."

"That never mattered to me; I was committed to Emma. Tilly made a promise to care for her while I was gone…and she didn't follow through. Not only that, she didn't tell me until after the fact. She tossed Emma aside like an old shoe! And Edna, I don't know where she is." Jayden was now sobbing hysterically.

Again, Edna gathered Jayden into her arms, rocking her gently.

Finally, when she was able to talk, Jayden continued. "I wanted to visit Emma, but she was gone." She told the rest of the story.

When she was done, Edna patted her hand. "You did the best you could, and from the sound of it, Emma was a very lucky little girl. She'll never forget you and what you did for her. God has certainly tested your strength."

"I don't mean to be rude, but unless you've had the kind of losses I've had in life, I don't think you can understand," Jayden said.

Edna opened the heavy leaded-glass door to the cabinet. She quietly handed Jayden a white, satin-covered photo album.

"What's this?" Jayden asked.

"Go ahead, start at the very beginning."

The first section of photos was of a young Edna, beautiful and full of life, her body limber and free from the destructive forces of rheumatoid arthritis. This was followed by family pictures at picnics, leaping over frothy waves at an unknown seaside park, and friends of the family who seemed to be enjoying themselves for the camera.

Jayden looked at the Edna on the page, then back to the older Edna by her side. Deep chestnut hair was now replaced with snow white tufts, and a once unlined flawless complexion showed years of wisdom and life experience.

Guess it's inevitable that time slips away and you can't get back what you've lost, Jayden thought. *But why is it, then, that moving forward can be so paralyzing?*

A picture slid out from the back of the book, falling to the floor. "I hope it didn't come loose because of me," Jayden apologized.

"It didn't come loose," Edna said. "I meant to dispose of it long ago, but there must be a reason why I hung on to it."

It was a picture of her father, she explained. He stood alongside a black sedan. His balled-up fist hung to his side. He wasn't a pleasant looking man.

"Papa," she said, her tone emotionally detached, "was the meanest man alive. He disguised himself as a man of God—a Baptist minister—but I think he was more of a dictator interpreting Bible passages for whatever was convenient to him. For example, the passage 'spare the rod and spoil the child.' Many a time, he'd head out back to the old weeping willow tree and break off a switch or two, the perfect tool for tanning our backside. I'd have welts on my legs that would last for weeks. He was such an unforgiving man.

"Right then and there, I promised myself when I left home it would be a cold day in—well, you know what I mean—before I would set foot in my heavenly Father's home or my earthly father's home, for that matter. I didn't trust any man…that is, until I met my Willum. Tender and loving as they come, and yet, still a God-fearing man. Willum helped me understand that all men aren't like my daddy. I just can't thank the Lord enough for not turning His back on me.

"Years later, I saw my father one last time before he passed. Never once did that old man say he was sorry or even acknowledge his wrongdoing, not once. And I was okay with that. My heart had long been healed. Look here, this is Willum," she said, pointing to his picture, "my rock."

"If you don't mind me asking, when did your husband pass away?"

"Let me see…going on twenty years now. Never did remarry; just couldn't bring myself to be with another man after him."

Jayden started to close the album, but Edna placed her hand between the pages. "There's more."

Jayden turned the next page. The remainder of the album was dedicated to a child—Edna's child. There were pictures of an infant, lying on a blanket, dressed in a satin dress and an oversized bonnet that swallowed her small head. Then a picture of her in the arms of her adoring father as he gazed lovingly down at her. Jayden tried to imagine what her own father must have felt like the first time he held her in his arms.

Page after page contained milestones of the tow-headed child: crawling, walking, her first tooth.

"She's adorable."

Edna said with pride, "She's my Mary Beth." Although the images on the pages were old, Edna delighted in sharing every detail, as though they had happened yesterday.

The last picture was of Mary Beth in a tire swing, suspended by a rope dangling from the tree branch. Her head bent backward, and long blonde strands of hair swept the ground while her feet pointed to the heavens. The resemblance between her and Emma was uncanny. Below the picture was a tribute:

> To our Mary Beth, one of God's angels who blessed our lives for five wonderful years; our lives are richer because of you.
> Love Mom and Dad

"Are there more pictures of her?"

"No, this is the last picture of my baby." Edna's tone was wistful.

Dread swept over Jayden. What had happened to Mary Beth? "I'm sorry, Edna. I don't mean to pry."

"Don't be sorry, hon. I appreciate the opportunity to talk about her."

Jayden sat quietly, listening to Edna tell the story of Mary Beth.

"She was a precocious child, always into something. We lived in Greensboro, North Carolina, when she was born. We had a Cape Cod-style two-bedroom house by the river. In the spring, some of the loveliest flowers with the most radiant colors filled the river's bank. It was so picturesque. Mary Beth loved flowers, especially the ones by the water's edge. I told her over and over again, 'Never go down to the river alone.' Why was I expecting a child to listen to me? The temptation was too great for her. You want to talk about guilt? I was her mother. I should have done everything in my power to make sure she would never go down to the river without supervision."

Edna's expression turned solemn as she replayed the tragic story on that fatal day. "I'd completely forgotten about this picture. Seems like we had no use for picture taking after she was gone. I suppose I put the camera at the top of the closet, and there it sat, until we sold the house. I just threw the film into a cardboard box and forgot about it. I got curious one day, I suppose, and took the film in for developing. This was the only picture on the roll.

"Willum's mother was visiting from Tennessee. She offered to baby-sit for the afternoon so Willum and I could go into town and do a little shopping and maybe take in a picture show. Mary Beth had been sick with a cold, so we told Grandma Sullivan to keep her in the house. It was starting to get dark; I guess we lost track of the time."

Jayden felt sick, knowing the story was about to take a drastic turn for the worst.

"I was the first one to see the flashing lights of the police car. 'Something happened to Grandma,' I told Willum. Never in my wildest dreams did I think it was my child.

"Willum swerved the car to the left and then to the right, gravel spitting like little BBs from underneath the tires. Never saw that man panic before that night. When I got out of the car, a crowd of people were standing around. People I'd never seen before. Everyone just turned to look at me and then back at the small lifeless body lying on the ground.

"I thought I heard someone scream. I looked over, thinking it was Grandma, but she was sitting on the porch with her head down. My husband was crumbled in a heap, pounding his fist on the ground. Turned out I was the one who was screaming.

"I walked over to the little body. Everyone moved aside. Her blonde curls were matted with river debris. Lying next to her was a handful of flowers. She'd gone all by herself and picked them.

"I can't tell you how long I sat there, holding my baby and

humming her favorite song. I just wanted her to wake up and sing with me. Finally, someone took her from me and wrapped her body in a blanket.

"Angry at God? You bet I was. I couldn't find comfort in His Word or in His house any longer. My marriage, my life was falling apart. I didn't want to live. Everywhere I looked life was going on, and all I wanted to do was shout from the rooftop, 'What is wrong with you people? Don't you know my little Mary Beth is dead?' I wanted everyone around me to suffer as much as I was suffering.

"Willum was desperate to hold onto what we had left. He begged me to get help or talk to the pastor of our church. For what? What could anyone say to bring my child back? Willum never gave up on me or us, for that matter. He prayed for God to show him the way to help comfort me. So I grudgingly went to church one Sunday with him. Strange, but it was as though the sermon was written just for me and Willum. 'If we believe in Jesus, we will reap our reward in Heaven.' I was reminded that one day I would see Mary Beth again in her perfect form. Well, that's all I needed. You see, one day I will see Willum and my baby again. That was God's promise."

"I'm so sorry. I feel so selfish," Jayden offered.

"Life is difficult. At one time or another we all have heavy burdens to carry. But now we have to put our heads together and find your Emma. You see, where there is a will, there is a way. I happen to have a friend from my Sunday school class, and if I remember correctly, her granddaughter works with adoptions or something like that. I can give her a call and see if there's any way we can get information on Emma's whereabouts."

"I appreciate it." Jayden hesitated. "But this is my problem, not yours. I'd rather deal with it in my own way."

Edna's eyes turned sad, and she looked at the clock mantel. "I'm pretty beat, honey. What do you say? Let's head to bed and clear our minds. Tomorrow is another day, and we can come up with some plans. Then if you still decide to do it alone, that will be your choice." Edna was slow in easing herself out of her cozy spot on the couch. "The way I see it, Jayden, you have a big job ahead of you."

"What do you mean?"

"Seems to me, you need to start from square one and get some questions answered—one step at a time. My first priority would be to write to my father and request a visit."

"He always refuses a visit with me."

"I see. Well, maybe it's time to be a tad more assertive. You have every right to at least hear your father's side of the story. It's hard to move on when you have so much lingering doubt."

"I've tried."

"Then try again. When you're ready, I'll help you write the letter. Maybe you need to let him know that you need this from him in order to put the past behind you and move on with your life."

"If he says no…"

"Then he says no, but I think you owe it to yourself. You're an adult now, so maybe he'll be more willing to talk. You need to get that settled once and for all. Then there's the issue of Emma and your brothers. It won't be easy, and it could take some time and money, but if need be, we'll hire us one of those fancy detectives."

"Time I have; money is another issue."

"Not really. I've got a little stashed away for a rainy day. It ain't much, but for whatever it's worth, I can't think of anything I'd rather use it for."

"I couldn't let you do that."

"I can't take it with me; besides, it's for a good cause."

Jayden was moved. No one had ever made such a generous offer to help before. "I may not share your belief in a higher power, but I know luck must be on my side. I found you."

"Rationalize it anyway you want. You didn't get here by chance or luck. Believe me when I tell you there's a Higher Power and His name is the Lord! We have to put our trust and faith in him. Man will let you down, but not our heavenly Father. And I can tell you another thing."

"What's that?" Jayden asked.

"You do have a family. You and I are family." Edna reached for her hand, and Jayden pulled her to her feet.

"Thank you, Edna. I can't tell you how much I appreciate you listening to me go on and on. I love you."

Jayden surprised herself in saying it, and Edna seemed surprised to hear it.

"Thank you, sweetheart," the older woman said, her voice choked with emotion. "That's the nicest thing I've heard in a long time. I love you too. Now let's get a little shut-eye and things will look so much clearer in the morning. Besides all that, you're probably exhausted after the bus ride home."

"Actually, I didn't ride the bus home; a friend of mine drove me."

"That must be some friend to drive you all the way from Odessa, then back in the same day. One hard drive," Edna said.

"Jonathan Baxter, that's his name. I believe he's staying at the Wagon Wheel and plans on leaving in the morning."

"Why don't you call the motel first thing tomorrow and invite him over for breakfast? Or, better yet, we'll all eat out. I just love those buttermilk pancakes with hot maple syrup over at the Waffle Tree."

"Thank you, Edna, for being so understanding. You've always made me feel that this is my home."

"Jayden, you've made this house a home."

Jayden waited for Edna's light to go off before she went into her room. She slipped an oversized T-shirt over her head and folded the comforter down to the end of the bed. She reached over to turn out the light when she noticed the Bible Jonathan had given her lying in the drawer of her nightstand.

"It's time to open you," she said.

It was a beautiful, wine-colored Bible with her name engraved in gold lettering. Inside, Jonathan had tucked a letter inside.

Dear Jayden:
    I've really enjoyed being your friend. I pray that you will have a happy life and a bright future. In the Bible, you will find the key to that future: "Delight yourself in the Lord and he will give you the desires of your heart." Psalm 37:4.
    Your friend,
    Jonathan

Jayden sat quietly for a few minutes. She had never heard such talk. If only it could be true. Maybe one day she'd try to figure out what all the hype was over a book written so long ago.

Deciding to write to her father before she lost her nerve, she pulled out a tablet of paper. After settling into a comfortable position, Jayden gave some thought as to how to start. Several crumpled pages later she started to put down what was on her mind.

Dec. 1, 1977
Dear Jeffrey, Dad,
    How can writing a letter to your father be so hard? But it is. I started the letter over probably ten times before I decided to just go with what is on my heart. It's sad not to know what to say to you. At first I thought if it was an informal letter, then I might come off sounding cold and heartless. If I write and tell you how very much I miss you, would you disregard me? There is so much I want to tell you about my life and the person I've become. Surely there is some part of you that wants to know who your little girl is now that she has grown into a woman?
    But then, maybe that's all speculation on my part. If the truth be known, I don't know who you are any more than you know who I am. Would we recognize one another if we passed on the street?
    If you noticed the postmark on the letter you are aware that I live in San Antonio now, just in case you do decide to write back. Please know that I do not blame you for anything. That is one of the reasons I need to see you. I want to hear from your own mouth what happened the day my mother died. Allow me this opportunity to put it to rest and move forward in my life. Nothing you could tell me would be worse than not knowing at all.
    Sincerely,
    Your daughter,
    Jayden

Jayden turned out the light. "We'll see if you answer me, Dad. We'll see."

Her sleep was sound that night. In a dream she saw a man dressed in white in the distance standing on a grassy hillside. The man held out his arms, beckoning to her. "Come to me, all you who are weary and burdened, and I will give you rest."

She had no fear. There was something so peaceful and serene about him. Instinctively, she knew she was looking into the face of God. Falling to her knees, Jayden asked His forgiveness for not believing in

Him. His hand cradled her face.

"He who believes has everlasting life."

"You don't know who I am or about my past," Jayden protested.

"My child, I knew you in your mother's womb." He smiled and stroked her hair. "I will never leave you."

Twelve

The knock on the bedroom door startled Jayden. She knew it was time to get up, but she didn't want to leave the comfort of her bed. She decided if she ignored the knocking, it would stop.

"You still sleeping in there?" Edna hollered from the other side of the door. "I know you don't have to work today, but let's get cracking. I've got a full day planned for us."

Jayden stretched and yawned. "I'll be there in a minute."

"Come on now, time's a-wastin'."

Edna was talking sweetly, but it was still annoying to someone who wanted to remain in bed. Jayden snuggled deeper under her covers where it was warm and toasty. Suddenly, she remembered her dream…or was it a dream?

Edna repeated the instruction this time with a light tap on the door. "Hello…rise and shine."

"I'm up now." Throwing her legs over the side of the bed, Jayden sat up, her feet touching the cold floor planks. She moaned and retreated under the blankets.

"I don't hear you moving around in there."

"I'll be down in a minute. I promise."

When she heard Edna downstairs, rummaging around in the kitchen, Jayden threw on her robe and walked out of her room. She leaned over the banister to say something and stopped…cold. She couldn't believe her eyes.

The entryway was decorated with papers and Christmas boxes.

"What's going on here?" Jayden asked as she came down the stairs.

Edna was standing in the middle of the living room. "Land's sake, would you look at some of these old decorations?" As she held up an ornament by its string, the glass ball rotated, casting shades of varying colors about the room.

"It looks like a cyclone hit the place. Where did all this come from?" Jayden inched her way over to Edna, careful where she put her foot.

"All this stuff? From Christmases long ago. Goodness, sounds like an advertisement for a Hallmark movie, doesn't it?" Edna laughed. "Believe it or not, I used to deck out this old house every Christmas. I lost my desire for it, though, when Willum passed on. Couldn't rationalize going to all that trouble just for me. Now that you're here, that's all changed."

"Please don't go to all this trouble on my account. I appreciate it, but Christmas is just another day to me."

"I hope to change that attitude," Edna said. "To be perfectly honest, I'm doing it for me too."

"Good—as long as this isn't all for me, then I'll help." Jayden tried not to let on how excited she was to be a part of Christmas in a home full of love.

"Did you try calling your friend to see if he'd like to have breakfast with us?"

"I'll call right now."

Edna started to unpack the boxes filled with memories.

"Operator, can you please give me the number for the Wagon Wheel motel?" Jayden asked. "Thank you."

After several rings, a disinterested, nasal voice spoke between yawns. "Wagon Wheel."

"Jonathan Baxter's room, please."

"Mr. Baxter checked out this morning."

"I see…thank you."

"Guess he's on his way back home," Jayden told Edna.

"That's a shame. I would have loved to meet one of your friends."

"I'm sure there'll be another time. Now, what's in all these boxes?"

"A lot of it's just junk. I'll hang onto the ones that mean the most to me. Will you look at this?" Holding a brilliant glass star by its cord, Edna laid it carefully on the couch. "Doesn't look like one piece is broken, and I can't imagine why. It wasn't packed well at all."

Jayden reached inside one of the open boxes and pulled out ornaments that were tangled together by their hooks. One immediately stuck out. It was a glass snow globe with a picture of Edna's Mary Beth. "We need to put this one near the top of the tree where the star is," Jayden said.

Edna's eyebrows knit together. "Let me see that." Her eyes filled with tears when Jayden handed the globe to her. "My baby. Funny, I can remember when this picture was taken—after Mary Beth lost her first tooth. This will definitely go right to the top. You know, one day, when you marry and have children, I'll cover this tree with their pictures."

"I like that idea." Jayden gave Edna a hug.

Just then, there was a knock at the door.

Edna dried her eyes. "These allergies make me all teary-eyed. Who in the Sam Hill could be at the door?" Cinching her robe tightly, Edna peered through the Venetian blinds. "Some young man, probably selling magazine subscriptions or something."

Edna was about to open the door when Jayden stopped her. "No, wait." Jayden peered out of the window first.

"What's wrong?"

In a way, Jayden half-expected Jonathan to stop by before leaving town. When she saw it wasn't him, she was disappointed. "Nothing, I guess I thought…"

"Let me get the door before someone thinks a bunch of nuts are looking out the window and whispering behind closed doors."

When Edna opened the door, she gasped. "Oh my, oh my! Will you look at this?"

"Delivery for Jayden Arman," the kid said, handing Edna a large vase with a dozen lilies.

Jayden took a step closer.

"Will you look at this," Edna said. "The delivery boy said they're for you."

"There must be some mistake; why would anyone send me flowers?" Jayden looked puzzled.

Edna parted the flowers, searching for a card. "Here's something," she said, handing it to Jayden.

"Go ahead. You can open it," Jayden said.

To Jayden:
Thank you for allowing me to be a part of your life. I am truly blessed. Will call when I get home.
Your friend and confidante,
Jonathan

Edna took a deep breath of the fragrance. "Beautiful, absolutely beautiful. I just love lilies."

Jayden couldn't help but smile. "I can't imagine why he would have sent these to me. They're really nice, though, aren't they? I'll put them on the kitchen table for us both to enjoy."

"*Nice?* Honey, that word doesn't do them justice. Besides, do you think Jonathan sent these flowers for me to partake in their fragrant petals? Maybe you should put them in your room."

"I'll bet Jonathan would be happy if I allowed both of us to enjoy them."

"Friend, huh?" Edna winked.

"Yes, friend." Jayden wanted there to be no question about her relationship with him. "If you really want to know, Jonathan is a youth pastor. So, even if I was interested, his only interest is leading me down the path of the straight and narrow."

"If you say so." But Edna didn't look convinced that was all to the relationship.

"Okay, enough talk about Jonathan," Jayden said. "What are the plans for the day?"

"First, let's go through these boxes and determine what else we need for the tree. Then we'll get dressed and go tree shopping."

"With all the boxes lying around, are you sure you don't have a tree stashed in one of them?" Jayden laughed.

"You just go get dressed, missy. We're burning daylight."

◈◈

It was only two weeks to Christmas, so, despite the record-breaking cold, the holiday shoppers were out in full force. Christmas carolers strolled up and down the streets, inviting everyone to join in. The town square was decorated with every kind of twinkling lights imaginable.

The clip-clop of horse hooves on the street pulling a carriage added to the old-world charm. The air smelled clean and fresh with just a touch of pine.

The ladies' auxiliary booth sold cinnamon donuts and hot chocolate. In the center of the town square was the main attraction, which made parents leave the coziness of their homes to brave the frigid weather: Santa Claus in his red velvet suit.

There were two lines of anxious children and tired parents all waiting for their chance to read from their endless wish list. The entire scene reminded her of an oil painting of a country Christmas.

"Well, would you look right over there?" Edna pointed across the street at a tree vendor. "That's the same vendor Willum and I used to buy our trees from."

"Evening, Ms. Edna. Good to see you again."

After a pleasant conversation with her old friend, Edna and Jayden decided on a beautiful pine tree that was just the right size. With Edna on one end and Jayden on the other, the women managed to get the tree back to the car.

"On the count of three...one...two...three." With one big heave, Edna and Jayden swung the tree so high it cleared the roof of the car, landing on the other side.

"Guess we didn't know our own strength," Edna said, belting out one of her familiar laughs.

"Let's give this another try, shall we?" Edna started to count again when a man's voice called out to them from across the street.

"Having trouble?"

Jayden couldn't see who it was, but his voice sounded familiar. When he walked out of the shadows and stood under the street light, her heart jumped. It was Daniel Taylor. Would he remember her?

"Daniel," she muttered under her breath.

Edna made a beeline right for him like she knew who he was. "Honey, you're a sight for sore eyes."

She called him "honey." Why in the world would she call someone "honey" that she didn't even know?

"I saw you trying to get the tree on top of the car and yelled out to you, but guess you didn't hear me," Daniel said, giving Edna a big hug.

81

"Come on over here. There's someone I want you to meet." Edna turned around and stood Daniel in front of her. "Jayden, this is Daniel. You know, he's the one I told you was my best friend's grandson. The one I wanted you to meet?"

Jayden stuck out her hand to shake his. She waited for a sign of recognition in his eyes; something to tell her he remembered meeting her before. If he did remember, he sure didn't show it. *Someone like him probably forgot you the moment he walked out the door.*

"It's nice to meet you." she said.

"Thank you. It's nice meeting you. Looks like you ladies could use a hand. Ya'll go ahead and get inside the car and turn the heater on. This will only take me a minute to strap down."

Jayden watched as Daniel picked up the tree without the slightest effort. "There you go, Ms. Sullivan. It's tied down good enough to get you home."

"Thank you, dear, but now I have another problem," Edna said. "We couldn't get this tree up on top of the car. I wonder what luck we'll have getting it down and into the house?"

"Would you like me to follow you home and take it inside?"

"If it's not too big of an imposition, that would be wonderful."

"It would be my pleasure," Daniel said.

⋘⋙

Jayden and Edna went inside the house while Daniel cut the strap that secured the tree. They watched out of the living room window as Daniel lifted the tree up on his shoulder with ease and propped it in the corner of the room.

"Thank you so much, Daniel. What would we have done without his help, Jayden?"

Jayden couldn't believe it. Edna was playing matchmaker.

"Yes, thank you."

"Oh heavens!" Edna had her hands up to her cheeks.

This will be interesting to hear what she wants Daniel to do now.

"I had every intention of buying a new string of lights before I came home. Daniel, unless you need to run along, would you be a sweetheart and put this tree up in the stand by the window while I run up to Kresge's and buy a set?"

By now Jayden was completely embarrassed.

Daniel glanced over at her. "That would be..."

Edna didn't give him a chance to answer. She never even took off her coat. Before they knew it, she grabbed her car keys and made a mad dash out of the house.

"I'm sorry," Jayden said.

"For what?" he asked.

"I suppose for not giving you a choice to leave."

"I always have a choice, and I want to stay right here. I was hoping to have time alone with you." he said.

"You were?"

"Yes, there's something I want to tell you."

"What's that?"

"How happy I am to see you again."

"You are? I mean you didn't' act like you..."

"Remembered you? I haven't been able to get you off my mind since we met."

Jayden was pleased—stunned—she'd made a lasting impresssion.

"Well?" he asked.

"Well, what?"

"This is where you come in and say you've been thinking of me too."

"I was trying to place where I've seen you before." She laughed as Daniel frowned at her. "Just kidding. Ever get your truck fixed?"

"Sure did. Have you rescued any more stragglers from a storm?"

"Hmm, let me think," she said, smiling. "Can't say that I have, but then again I don't think we've had a storm like that since."

Daniel made one final turn of the screw into the pine's bark. He stood back and examined the trunk to see if the tree leaned. "Good. It looks straight up and down. A little sugar water and the needles will stay fresh."

"Sugar water?" she repeated verbatim as though taking notes.

"Guess it feeds the tree and keeps the pine needles fresh. In any event, it's something my family always does, and it seems to work."

"Would you like some hot tea?"

"That would be great."

Within minutes they sat at the kitchen table sipping hot tea. He winced.

"Sorry, it's a little too hot, I'm afraid," Jayden said, blowing the steam off of her cup.

"It'll cool." Daniel gestured toward the snow collecting in varying patterns on the windowpane. "I love the Christmas season, don't you?"

"Can't say that I love it. It seems way too commercialized."

"You're not a Scrooge now, are you?" he teased.

"No, I just never really understood what the big deal is."

"So you're not a people watcher? I get a kick out of the ones who have presents piled high in their arms, and they do this juggling act trying to get from the store to the car."

Jayden rolled her eyes in a playful manner.

"Okay, if people-watching isn't your thing, then do you enjoy looking at Christmas lights? Or how about time around the table with family and friends?"

"I was never one to enjoy crowds."

Everything Daniel talked about sounded wonderful, but they were his experiences. She couldn't relate, but she envied him.

"In any event, that's not what Christmas is all about," he said. "I guess people do commercialize it. But if it wasn't for the birth of our Lord, none of us would have any hope."

She certainly wasn't going to get into a debate over the birth of Christ with him.

"So, tell me about yourself," Daniel asked.

"There's nothing to tell really." This was another topic she didn't feel comfortable discussing. "Why don't you tell me about yourself?"

"Okay, what do you want to know?"

"Start with your family."

"I have a mother, a father, a sister, a grandmother, a dog, a parrot, and a salt water aquarium," he teased.

"Okay, now can you elaborate some?" Jayden laughed.

"You'll be sorry, but here goes."

When he spoke of his family, she couldn't help but feel a sense of jealousy. He was so proud of them even if they had a difference of opinion in what he should do with his future. Daniel shared with Jayden a little about them and how they lived as a family. His mother was the stereotype stay-at-home mom. Daniel said it was comforting to come home and share his day with her.

"It may sound like the *Leave it to Beaver* sitcom," he said, "but when my sister and I came home, there would be a plate of cookies or apple wedges and a drink. Going out to eat was left for special occasions like birthdays because Mom believed in preparing a wholesome meal for the family. She took pride in caring for us."

Jayden had never known anyone with such a fairy tale childhood. Tilly Jenson didn't work outside the home either. The difference was that, most times, Tilly didn't know if Jayden was coming or going. Life appears blurry when you're looking through the bottom of a whiskey glass.

"I hope whenever I marry and start a family, I'll be able to offer my wife the same opportunity," Daniel said.

Jayden frowned. "Don't tell me you're one of those male chauvinists who think a woman's place is in the home? Isn't that kind of old-fashioned? Don't most women want a career, a family, and the whole nine yards?"

"In my opinion, raising an emotionally healthy child is the most important job a person can do."

"I hope you're not saying that raising a child is strictly a woman's responsibility."

"No way! It's a partnership. I guess I believe that if my wife has the opportunity to be with our child instead of leaving him all day with a babysitter, well, it just seems like the ideal situation," he reasoned.

Worried she had come on too strong, she murmured, "I didn't mean to sound so defensive."

"No, not at all. You were just stating your opinion." He smiled. "You're entitled. And now, it's your turn. Who is Jayden Arman?" Daniel asked with genuine interest.

Great, here it comes: the ten-million-dollar question. Should I tell him how it really is and run him off now? Jayden opted for telling enough to satisfy his curiosity but not enough to let him know her story. "There's not much to tell. I'm like everyone else. As soon as I graduated from high school, I left town to start a life for myself." At the moment, those words sounded so much better than telling him the grim details.

"Where are you from?"

"Odessa, Texas."

"Oil country?"

"Yes." Jayden hoped if she kept her answers short and to the point, he'd bore of it all and move on to another topic.

"Most of your friends are still back there then?"

"Friends…well, I'm not one to have a lot of friends. But I do have one very dear friend. His name is Jonathan Baxter."

"A guy?"

"Is there anything wrong with that?"

"No, not at all. Guess I was just expecting you to say a girl's name, but a guy, no, nothing is wrong with that."

"I've never had a friend quite like Jonathan."

"You never dated him?" Daniel asked.

"Dated? No, of course not. Besides, Jonathan is a minister."

"What does that have to do with anything?" he asked.

"It has a lot to do with the fact I wouldn't…I couldn't date a minister."

"Why? Is there a law against it?"

"No…but anyway, I think you'd like Jonathan."

"I'm sure I would. He sounds like a nice person."

"He is. You know, I just thought of something. Jonathan called me last week and said he'd be coming to San Antonio sometime in the next couple of months."

"That's nice of him to come for a visit," Daniel said.

"Actually, I think it's more for business. He's looking into possibly applying for a position at that new church across town."

"Maybe the three of us can go to dinner when he comes into town," Daniel said.

"I'd really like that. In fact, I think that's a great idea."

"Good—just let me know when and where."

Jayden quickly turned the questioning back to him. "Where did you go to college?"

"New Mexico State."

"And after college?"

"I went to Africa, and one day I hope to go back."

"Africa?" She couldn't hide her surprise. "I'm sorry, it's just I've never known anyone who has left the North American continent. I only know what I've either learned in school or gathered from reading *National Geographic.* How fascinating."

"Fascinating. That's putting it mildly. It was the most incredible experience of my life."

"How in the world did you ever end up there?"

"It's a long story."

"I've got plenty of time; that is, until Edna gets home and wants help stringing lights."

"I'll give you the shortened version. During my senior year at New Mexico State, I had the opportunity to receive extra credit if I attended a one-hour Q & A seminar on preventable childhood diseases. One of the guest speakers was a new pediatric physician who spoke about the clinic he was building in the village of Mukumbra. It's a remote primitive area along the Zambezi River. I originally thought about signing in to get the credit and then cutting out a little early. Boy, am I glad I didn't. It turned out to be the most mentally stimulating and thought provoking lecture I'd ever heard.

"After class, I introduced myself to the guest speaker. He introduced himself as *Zareb:* that's what the people in the village called him. It means 'protector.' Everyone calls him Doc. I wanted to know more about the villagers he dealt with and the specific problematic areas. More importantly, what could I do? His wife, Rachel, taught school along with a group of volunteers."

"What do the villagers call Rachel?" Jayden asked.

"*Safiya.* It means 'pure one.'"

"Sorry to interrupt. Please go on."

"At dusk," Daniel continued, "Rachel and Doc talked to the villagers about our Savior. He said if I was interested in joining their work, they were in great need of help. It seems some of the elders of the village prefer men to teach the male children."

87

"To make a long story short, Doc became my mentor and friend. He invited me out for the summer. I can't even begin to tell you how much that changed my life. Oh, you know, I think I have a picture of Doc and Rachel." Daniel reached into his back pocket and pulled out his wallet. Inside was a picture of his family and, on the reverse side, a picture of Doc and Rachel.

"It's not the best picture of Doc," Daniel said. "I remember when this was taken; he was determined not to shave to see what he would look like with a full beard. The last I heard he never made two months of not shaving. Rachel won that battle." He laughed.

"This is Rachel?" Jayden pointed to a blonde woman with a kerchief tied around her head. "She's very pretty."

Both Doc and Rachel wore bright yellow and blue wraps—some type of beautiful ceremonial garment, perhaps.

"Yeah. She's pretty neat. She has a wonderful sense of humor and the patience of Job. I guess she needs it to put up with Doc." Daniel laughed again. "I've never had friends like the two of them. They're truly an inspiration."

"You're a lucky man to have such wonderful friends and such fond memories."

"I agree with you there. So, I know what you mean when you speak of your relationship with Jonathan," Daniel said, putting the picture back into his wallet.

"Tell me something about your time in Africa." Jayden said, genuinely interested.

So Daniel spoke about Africa, bringing the continent to life with romantic, descriptive words.

"You know what I miss the most about Africa?" he said at last.

"What's that?"

"The sunset. Until you've seen the sun set in Africa, you don't know what you're missing. Words can't describe it."

"I've seen pictures."

"Seeing pictures and actually being there…there's no comparison."

"Try to describe what the sunset looked like just as though you were there right now," Jayden said.

Daniel had to think quickly. How could he respond? Was this a way to set up a date with her? "Next time I see you," he said, "I'll bring some incredible pictures that I took."

"I'd love to see the pictures, but maybe some other time. For now, I'd love for you to tell me in your own words what you saw."

"All right, I'll give it my best shot. Sit back and close your eyes. I'll try to describe it so the images will come alive in your mind."

Daniel couldn't take his eyes off Jayden. *You're more beautiful than the African sunset*—that's what he wanted to say. *Good grief,* he told himself, *say that out loud and she's sure to run the other way. Better stick to describing the sunset.* His mother had always told him that one day he would know when the right one came along, and she was right. The "right one" was sitting across the table from him.

"Imagine this," he began, "an artist holding a palette of vibrant colors in one hand and a brush in the other. Starting at the top, he makes deliberate wide brush strokes, gliding one brilliant deep shade of amethyst followed by another with each shade getting lighter and lighter than the one before it. This continues on until the earth meets the sky.

"Then, when you thought it couldn't get any better, an enormous fireball displays an array of fireworks shooting burnt coral against the purple sky. Finally, the sun slips behind the desert's backdrop. And it doesn't end there!" he said with enthusiasm. "Once the night takes reign in the sky, the desert comes to life with all the nocturnal creatures. The earth is so miraculous. Our heavenly Father created everything for us to enjoy."

Her face was alight with pleasure. "Go on, don't stop there. I want to hear more."

"Guess I could tell you about the village of Mukumbra."

Jayden nodded.

"There are no modern conveniences. No air conditioning, refrigeration, toilets that flush, or running water—things most people here take for granted. If I wanted water, I'd go down to the river and bring it back in a wooden bucket."

"What about wild animals?" she said.

"Well, we have the Doc fairly well-trained by now," he teased.

"Seriously, did you see all kinds of different wildlife?"

"Of course, I lived in their territory."

"Any dangerous ones?"

"Only if you mess with them. For the most part, if you leave them alone, they'll leave you alone."

"What are the people like?"

"Poor, but proud. The time I lived among them I followed their customs. You know the old saying, 'When in Rome…' It was important to learn from them as much as I hoped they would learn from me. I wanted them to know about acceptance and mutual trust. I stayed in a mud hut with a straw-thatched roof. There were no paved roads, and the mode of transportation was either on foot or by donkey. All in all, I missed three months of my favorite television shows like *All in the Family*, if you want to call it missing something. You can't measure what I gained.

"My primary reason for going to Africa was to help Doc and Rachel. I thought I was going over there to change how the natives live; you know, help them change their backwards ways. It was I who came away from there a changed person. It might sound corny, but you can get so focused on just yourself that you miss what's really important in this life. These people see the beauty in all creatures."

"But they're so primitive," Jayden said.

"Are they? I question that. I could go into my newfound philosophy about living off the land, getting back to basics, and on and on, but that would put you to sleep for sure."

"No, it wouldn't. I'd like to hear it."

"Maybe some other time. But I will tell you this: I fell in love with the children there."

Jayden waited for him to elaborate.

"The kids are so eager to learn. Their minds are like little sponges soaking up everything you teach them. In the evening, when the sun goes down, it's a time to rest and sit with the adults of the tribe. We talked to them about our Lord and the wonderful plans He has for each one of us if we believe in Him. Now keep in mind, these people pray to false gods and idols. It's not easy to tell the people there that their centuries-old traditions are wrong.

"I was a little worried we might upset them. Instead, they listened and occasionally would look to the heavens when they asked questions about God. An invisible God who sees and knows all is a hard concept for people right here in our own country, who also have trouble understanding something so abstract."

Jayden knew that feeling all too well.

"The people in the village became my second family," he said softly, "and I miss them."

"That must have been an amazing experience," Jayden said.

It's now or never, Daniel decided. He paused, then blurted, "Are you seeing anyone?"

Jayden abruptly set down her tea cup, as if his change of subject had taken her completely off guard. "No, I'm not seeing anyone."

"I've been told I can be good company; of course, that was said by my family." He chuckled.

"There's no doubt in my mind about that," Jayden said.

"So then, I can see you again?"

"My goodness, you're forward. I wouldn't object to it, I suppose; that is, if I get to know you a little better."

"That's the whole idea behind going out on a date, isn't it? To try and get to know someone?"

"Daniel, I have to be up front with you."

"I'm listening."

"We're different."

"Good. I like different. I'm assuming your friend Jonathan is different from you as well?" Daniel said.

She was no match for his wit. "You're right there. Jonathan and I are nothing alike."

"See, that's a good thing. I'm not looking for someone just like me either. How boring would that be? That way everyone brings something different to the table."

She appeared nervous. "As long as they have something interesting to contribute."

"I think you're pretty interesting just like you are," Daniel said.

"Well, we do have some significant differences that may not blend real well."

"Like different beliefs?"

"I don't believe in God," she stated bluntly. "That could be a point of contention between us."

He wasn't completely surprised she didn't believe in the Lord or have a belief system. Edna had shared with his grandmother a few personal details about Jayden, especially the big secret, her indifference to the Lord. Of course, Molly felt compelled to forewarn her grandson.

"Grandmother, it isn't Christian to be gossiping," he lovingly scolded her.

"Land's sake, honey, I wouldn't ever gossip. It's just that Edna wanted you to meet this young woman, and I thought in all fairness to you that I should tell you a little bit about her," Molly offered as an excuse.

"Call it whatever you want, but the bottom line is Edna shared information with you she shouldn't have and now you're sharing it with me; sounds a lot like gossip," he said, giving her a loving hug. Daniel's grandmother played an active role in his life. Respect for her was an understatement. She was the voice of wisdom in their home, so he trod lightly when it came to correcting her.

"I don't mean to continue using Jonathan as an example, but if he is a minister I think I can safely say he has a belief in God, and yet, you are friends with him."

"True," she said.

Something about Daniel made Jayden feel comfortable, like she'd known him forever. But a man like him? He was way out of his league. He deserved a woman who didn't have a past like hers. She came with a lot of baggage.

"Yoo-hoo...you here, Jayden?" Edna called out from the living room.

"In here," Jayden said.

Edna swung open the café doors leading to the kitchen. She was thrilled to see Jayden and Daniel enjoying each other.

"Did you get the lights for the tree?" Jayden asked.

"I surely did, but I think I'll just put them on tomorrow. Oh, by the way, thank you for all your help tonight, Daniel. I don't know what I would do without you. Turn out the lights before you go to bed, hon. I think I'll just go upstairs and leave you two young people alone to visit."

"You can stay, Ms. Sullivan. I probably should be running along anyway."

"Don't go on my account, Daniel."

"No, that's fine. I really need to go. I promised the family I'd spend a little time with them tonight." There was an awkward pause, then Daniel said good night to both of them and closed the front door behind him.

"You could have at least walked him to the door," Edna said, nudging Jayden toward the door.

By the time Jayden opened the front door, Daniel was almost to his car. "Daniel," she called out to him, "drive carefully."

"Go back inside before you freeze," he said, unlocking his car door.

"We didn't set a time to meet again; you know, to get to know one another," she stammered.

"Not a date? Right?" He smiled.

"Definitely not a date."

"How about tomorrow then?"

"Tomorrow?"

"Unless you have something else to do?"

Daniel had the most incredible smile.

"Call me tomorrow. We'll see." She watched as he drove off. Her instincts told her she shouldn't let this one get away, but how fair was it to him to get involved with someone with a past like hers? She watched until she could no longer see his car. "Good-bye, Daniel." She had barely stepped back inside when the phone rang.

"I'll get it," she called out to Edna.

"Hello?"

"Hello, yourself."

"Jonathan, what a surprise!"

"I hope it's not too late to call."

"No, no, it's fine," Jayden said.

"I'm sorry I didn't call when I got home, but there was a little situation that needed my immediate attention."

"I hope everything is all right."

"Just one of the kids in my group. But, yes, everything is good."

"I was just talking about you," Jayden said.

Jonathan's ears perked up. He needed a little ego boost. "You were? Who to?"

"Daniel. Someone I met back in the beginning of summer. I don't really know him well, but it turns out his grandmother is a friend of Edna's. Next time you come to town, we should all have dinner."

"Daniel. Hmm…dinner; that sounds great." That wasn't exactly what Jonathan had in mind when he came to town. In fact he was hoping to come back to San Antonio on Valentine's Day to surprise her. It stuck in his mind the time she told him about a movie she had seen where the couple ate by candlelight while romantic music played in the background and off to the side was a small dance floor where they danced into the early morning hours. It was what she wanted to do with the man she fell in love with one day. He wanted to do something special for her, something she had only dreamed of. But now that wasn't about to happen if Daniel came along.

"Oh my gosh, I almost forgot…the flowers you sent. Why did you do that? They're gorgeous, but you shouldn't have."

"You're welcome. I wanted to express my appreciation to you."

"For what?"

"For trusting in me enough to share your personal story."

"I do trust you, Jonathan. What I want to know is if you're still coming down around Christmas?"

"No, that's really a busy time for churches. I plan to come around the middle of February." Jonathan hoped the tone in his voice didn't sound deflated.

After they hung up the phone, he stared at the picture he'd taken the day she graduated, the one he kept framed sitting on his desk. *Why can't I just accept that we will be nothing more than friends?*

Thirteen

Dec. 18, 1977

This is an exciting time. This will be my first real Christmas. Edna has decked out the house with lights, and we have a magnificent tree with every kind of ornament you can think of. I personally think she went all out on my behalf, but I have to admit I'm enjoying it. Almost three weeks ago now, Daniel Taylor and I met for the second time when I was in town. We've been seeing one another almost daily but as friends. It has been a wonderful time. Turns out we do have something in common, our love for photography. At every opportunity he teaches me about the different lenses and how to use them. I can't get over how smart and well-traveled he is. Daniel says he has told Doc and Rachel about me. I do hope one day I'll meet them.

Daniel has been practicing the solo he will sing in the church choir for the Christmas program. I told him I'd go, but only to listen to him so he shouldn't get any ideas that this will become a habit. As always, he is very understanding. Haven't heard from Jonathan in awhile but again this is his busy season.

A day before Christmas, and there was still so much to do. Jayden never imagined how much preparation went into Christmas dinner. Edna always had the kitchen countertops dusty with flour as she made one pie crust after another. The aroma of baked goods filled the house. Fruit of every kind sat in bags waiting to become part of a fruit salad or a pie.

"Are you feeding an army?" Jayden teased.

"Some of this will go to the less fortunate and some to friends," Edna explained.

Jayden was always amazed at Edna and her enthusiasm for life. She made every day worth celebrating. It just took some adjusting to. Holidays back at Tilly's weren't too much different from any other day. For Christmas and Thanksgiving Tilly would have a turkey with a bowl of cranberries and store-bought pies. She'd put it on the table and say, "Every man for himself."

The tree was always the scrawniest on the lot mainly because it was the cheapest. If the check for the girls came in on time, there might be a couple of presents under the tree for them. Otherwise Tilly would say, "It's better to wait for the after Christmas sales, anywho."

Edna handed Jayden the keys to her car. "Would you run and get a couple of cans of evaporated milk for me, hon?"

"Sure, no problem. Just let me get dressed and I'll go right away."

When she opened the bureau drawer to pull out her sweatshirt, she saw the letter she had tucked away for safekeeping. She'd received it two days earlier from her father. It was unopened. Jayden didn't want anything to ruin her Christmas, and if he didn't want to see her or correspond with her it would accomplish nothing more than upsetting her. *What I don't know right now won't hurt me. After tomorrow, when Christmas is over, then I'll read it.*

The remainder of the day was full of finishing projects.

⁂

At 6:00 p.m. Daniel came to the door to pick Jayden and Edna up for the Christmas program.

Once at the church, Daniel separated from them while Jayden and Edna joined Daniel's parents, the Taylors, who were already saving a seat for them in the front row. Good thing—there wasn't an empty seat anywhere.

Edna leaned over and whispered, "He's really good."

Edna was right. Jayden was surprised how much of a treat it was to hear Daniel sing. He definitely was a man of many talents.

The lights dimmed, and a soft blue light lit the way for Daniel and six backup vocalists to walk to the front. He picked up his guitar and the microphone. The piano started, followed by Daniel strumming a chord. Daniel's deep baritone carried throughout the church with such quality and strength that Jayden was mesmerized. He sang of the birth of the Lord with such passion, it sent chills down her. Edna and Mrs. Taylor were moved to tears.

By the end of the program, Daniel had joined the choir, and they had the entire congregation join hands to sing along. Daniel walked down from the platform and held out his hand for his mother, Edna, and Jayden to join him on the stage.

"I can't," she whispered to him.

"You'll do fine," he whispered back.

Jayden didn't want to make a scene, so she relented and went up front, standing next to him.

The verses to the song were easy enough. The same line, "Praise him! Praise him!" was repeated over and over. Many of the people raised their hands in the air to give praise. At the end, Daniel still had Jayden's hand in his as he shook hands with everyone around him, introducing her as his very dear friend. Finally, he faced Jayden. She was surrounded in the blue light—like an angel sent from heaven.

Daniel had never expected to fall in love with Jayden, especially since she didn't share in his love of the Lord. However, for all her talk about not being a Christ follower, Daniel couldn't bring himself to believe she truly meant it. There was a side of Jayden he'd witnessed that was innocent. He was confident in the power of prayer and believed that one day Jayden would accept Jesus as her Savior.

"Merry Christmas," he said, embracing her.

"Merry Christmas, Daniel." She couldn't explain it, but something felt different. Maybe she was just caught up in the moment of all the excitement. *It'll pass,* she thought.

Fourteen

The sun had barely peeked through when Jayden heard Edna shout from downstairs, "Get on down here. Come see what Santa left!"

Jayden rolled over and squinted at the alarm: *7:00 a.m., December 25, 1977.*

After dressing, she headed downstairs for breakfast. But when she reached the bottom of the stairs, she couldn't believe her eyes. Edna was in her green plaid flannel pajamas, sitting in front of the Christmas tree draped in gold garland.

"Where did all of this come from?" Jayden asked.

"Santa." Edna laughed.

"Very funny. We agreed to exchange one gift each, am I right?"

"Yes and no. We agreed to think about the exchange gift idea, but we never revisited that suggestion, if you remember."

"Now you're getting nitpicky, don't you think? You know very well what we promised, or at least I thought we made an agreement," Jayden said.

"Oh well, punish me. I wanted you to have a very special Christmas," Edna said smugly.

Jayden put her arms around Edna and squeezed. "Merry Christmas and I love you," she whispered.

Edna held Jayden, tears filling her eyes. "Dearie, you've brought laughter and joy back to these walls…and to this old life. So go on, open these gifts. I want to make sure everything fits." Edna made a loud noise as she blew her nose into a hanky.

For the next hour, Jayden modeled one outfit after another, making a fuss, to Edna's delight, over each article of clothing.

"You'll never know how much fun I had buying for you. I love buying girl things. And the styles. Well, they are kind of different but I had a great time." Edna beamed.

"Oh my goodness! I've been ripping through the gifts, and you haven't opened my gift to you." Jayden placed a red foil-wrapped box with curling ribbon tied around it on the coffee table in front of Edna.

"My, what could this be?" Edna asked, carefully inspecting it. The look on her face said it all when she examined the contents inside the small box.

"It's a locket," Jayden quickly explained.

"I see that. I don't know the last time anyone bought me such a fine piece of jewelry."

"Open it," Jayden pleaded. Edna made several attempts at the clasp, but her arthritic fingers wouldn't cooperate. Jayden took it from her and, with a quick flip, opened it. Inside was a picture of Willum holding Mary Beth and on the other side was Jayden.

Edna held the locket close to her heart and smiled. "I don't know quite what to say."

"Say you like it.'"

"Oh, it's more than that. I *love* it."

"I hope you don't mind, I took a picture out of your photo album and had a small picture made. I trimmed it down enough so it would fit inside it. The original picture is back in the album, so don't worry."

"I'm not worried," Edna said. "I will keep it close to my heart and never take it off. The three most precious people in my life."

"Let me help you," Jayden said, fastening the gold clasp.

"Now, looks to me like there are a couple more gifts under the tree. I took the liberty and looked at the tags. One is from your friend Jonathan Baxter and, of course, the other is from Daniel."

"Jonathan?" Jayden stood immobile. "I wish he hadn't done anything. I didn't send him a gift. I wonder what it is."

"It won't open itself up," Edna said.

"Okay, okay." Jayden held the square box in her hand. "*Fragile* is stamped a couple of times across the box."

"Here, use this to cut through the tape." Edna handed her a pair of scissors. Shredded newspaper was packed in around the contents, and a note lay on top.

"It's more protected than Fort Knox. What does the note say?"

Edna laughed.

"It says, *Jayden, I thought of you and Emma when I saw this; hope you enjoy. I'm sure you'll know why as soon as you open it and hear the music.*"

"Oh my, will you look at that!" Edna reached for her glasses to get a better look.

"It's a music box." Jayden held it up for Edna to see. When she opened the box, a ballerina danced around on a spindle to the music.

"Wait," Edna said, her eyes closed and a finger pressed against her temple. "I know that song. It's 'Close to You,' isn't it? Bet you didn't think I knew that."

"Here's a note," Jayden said.

> Now that you've opened the music box and wound the key to hear the song, let me explain. Remember the time we took Emma to the park and all she wanted to do was put on a solo performance for us?
> Whenever you open up your music box you'll see your little blue-eyed ballerina dance again.
> Merry Christmas,
> Jonathan

"This isn't one of those dime-store music boxes. It's real wood. Looks like some kind of mahogany. It cost some money."

"Now I'm embarrassed I didn't send him anything. I'll give him a call later today."

"That would be nice…. Now, what else do we have here?" Edna asked mischievously.

"I don't know." Jayden's curiosity was piqued.

Edna pulled the package out, with different colors of curling ribbons dangling from it.

Edna read the tag aloud: "*To Jayden, From Daniel.*" Then she sat on the edge of the couch, antsy with anticipation.

"I can always open it later," Jayden said teasingly, knowing all too well that Edna wouldn't be able to wait.

"Oh no, you don't! I'm dying to know what it is." Jayden took her time opening the package.

"If you don't hurry it up, I'll do it for you."

"Okay, okay."

Jayden removed an 11x14 picture, elegantly matted and enclosed in a gold leaf frame. It was of an African sunset taken by Daniel. He'd had it blown up for her. The colors were breathtaking. The setting sun was so vibrant and vivid she felt as though she could feel its warmth.

"Let's see it," Edna asked.

Jayden held it up for Edna to see.

"Oh my! Oh, would you look at that. What a lovely picture. Where in the world did he buy that, I wonder?"

"He didn't buy it. I'm sure Daniel took this photograph when he was in the African desert."

"How on earth would you know that?"

"Daniel described the sunset perfectly to me. The picture is exactly how I imagined." Jayden couldn't take her eyes off of the picture. To her it was a most precious gift, a gift from Daniel's heart. Finally, she turned to Edna. "Guess I'll start picking up this mess."

There was a twinkle in Edna's eyes. "Not so fast. I have a very special request for you."

"Oh."

"Will you accompany me to church? Now before you say no…"

"I wasn't going to say no."

"Did I hear you right, or are my ears deceiving me?"

"Yes, you heard right."

"That's the best present you could have given me."

Over the last several weeks, Edna had noticed how God had been working on Jayden's heart. It was such a blessing. And now the young woman had two men—both of whom seemed worthy—in her life. When Jayden had opened the sunset picture, the expression on her face had said it all. Edna was convinced. Jayden was a woman in love.

Fifteen

Once they reached the church, Edna walked slightly ahead of Jayden.

"I have to get ready for choir," Edna said, "so sit wherever you want, hon. I'll meet you right after the service."

Jayden chose the back pew, where she could be inconspicuous. As the congregation started filing in and greeting one another, she became more acutely aware that she was out of her element. Picking up a hymnal, she flipped through the pages, trying to appear as though she was well aware of church proceedings, when a group of kids sitting a couple of rows in front of her started horsing around. Jayden held the hymnal up in front of her face. It was awkward not knowing anyone. She felt very out of place.

The pastor took the pulpit. After a couple of songs he asked everyone to turn and greet the person next to them. *Great, another uncomfortable moment.*

Then a deep voice said, "It's good to see you." Daniel leaned forward. He sat in the row directly behind her.

"Oh—it's good to see you too. I didn't know you were back there."

"If I'd known you were going to come to the Christmas service, I could have picked you and Edna up." Daniel moved up next to her.

"I didn't know I was coming until this morning."

"Do you mind if I sit with you?" Daniel said.

"Not at all. In fact, thank you for joining me. Besides, it gives me the opportunity to tell you how much I loved my gift. It's unbelievable."

"You're very welcome. Thank you for the new camera case. It'll work very nicely. Guess you could tell how worn out my old one was."

Jayden grinned. "Oh, was that a camera bag you had?" She laughed.

Daniel smiled. "Point taken."

"Before we all pray," the pastor said, "I'd like to ask each and every one of you to join hands with the person beside you. Let us take a moment to honor family and friends either close to home or on the other side of the country. Relationships are such an important part of our lives and without them, we suffer greatly. God didn't intend for us to be alone."

After the service, Daniel turned to Jayden. "Pretty good sermon, don't you think?"

"It was."

"What are your plans for the rest of the day?"

"Dinner with Edna, and after that, I don't really know."

"I'll be going over to my grandmother's right after church. We went by this morning to pick her up, but she wasn't feeling well."

"I'm sorry to hear that," Jayden said.

About that time, Edna walked up to the two of them. "You ready to head home and check on that turkey?"

"Whenever you are," Jayden said.

"Oh, I almost forgot. Grandmother wanted me to give this to you." Daniel handed Edna a loaf wrapped in foil.

"Molly, Molly. That woman knows how much I love her pumpkin bread. Is she doing any better, Daniel? With her health the way it's been lately I don't know when she found time—or the energy—to do this. I'll give her a call."

"I'll talk to you later, Daniel." Jayden loved being in church with him, or anywhere for that matter.

On the ride home, Edna talked and talked, but Jayden was thinking about the church service and the story of the birth of Christ. She had so many questions. For instance, the virgin birth? It was almost too incredible to believe. *But I suppose that's the premise behind faith.*

Jayden pulled Edna's car into the driveway. "You go ahead and go inside. I'll put the car away in the garage."

She watched until Edna had stepped into the house, then leaned her head back. "God, I'm not sure if you exist and if you do, you've probably given up on me by now. But I wanted to thank you for my life now, and the people in it."

103

After a fabulous Christmas dinner, Jayden pushed away from the table. "Edna, you're some cook."

"Thank you, hon. Until you came to live with me, I didn't really cook big meals any longer. I thought I'd lost the touch. So don't disappoint me and give up eating so soon."

"If I don't stop now, I won't be able to make it up the stairs." Jayden laughed. "One thing's for certain: you haven't lost your touch for cooking. It was wonderful."

"After we clean up this mess, I think I'll pack up a little food and head over to Molly's house. Would you like to go with me?"

"I have an idea. Why don't I clean up everything, and you run along to Molly's? She may not be up to visitors anyway."

Edna was already starting to cover some of the dishes to take to Molly's. "That's probably a good idea since Molly could have that flu bug that's going around. No reason to expose both you and me if she does. I'll stay a couple of minutes and leave."

Right after Edna left, Jayden picked up the phone to wish Jonathan a Merry Christmas and to thank him for the wonderful gift, but no one answered the telephone.

He must be busy.

Just as Jayden finished putting the last covered dish in the refrigerator, she heard the sound of a car.

She expected to see Edna come through the side door, so she went into the living room to pick up the clutter. Then she heard a knock.

"Edna, did you forget your keys again?" she callout.

It wasn't unlike the older woman to forget her house keys. For some reason, she didn't like keeping her house keys and car keys on the same ring. "Makes for too many keys to sort through," she reasoned.

Jayden opened the door and saw Daniel standing there. "What are you doing here?" she blurted.

His face fell. "I can see by your expression that coming over unannounced wasn't a good idea."

"Oh, no, it's all right. I was just surprised. I thought it was Edna."

"I left my grandmother's a few minutes ago, and she's over there."

"I know," Jayden said.

"Edna said you offered to stay home and clean up the dishes. She thought she left her house keys on the kitchen ledge and asked if I could get them and bring them to her so she wouldn't bother you to let her in if you were busy."

They both walked to the kitchen ledge and looked. "There are no keys here," Jayden said. Then a thought struck her. "Wait a minute, Daniel. Call your grandmother's house, will you?"

"Sure but…"

"Just call over there and let me speak to Edna."

Edna answered Molly's phone on the first ring.

"Your keys aren't on the ledge. Any idea where else they could be?" Jayden asked Edna. She had a gut feeling this was a set up so she and Daniel could be alone on Christmas Day.

"Oh, you found them the minute Daniel walked out of the house…in your purse the whole time?" Jayden winked at Daniel. "How's Molly doing? Send her my best."

After hanging up the phone, Jayden turned to Daniel. "Looks like this may have been a plan to get you over here to see me."

A slow smile spread across his face. "I can't say I'm angry about that. Besides, Edna was kind enough to bring over some food for my grandmother. It's the least I can do to come over here and help with the dishes."

"I'm glad you're here, but I don't need help, really."

"The truth of the matter is, I was hoping to see you," Daniel said.

"You just saw me at church today."

"That was *hours* ago." He laughed.

"I enjoy your company, too. And if you haven't noticed, I also enjoy your stories."

Daniel gestured toward the sunset picture propped up against a wall. "I'm glad you took the picture off of my hands. Otherwise I'd have thrown it out." He winked at her.

"Are you nuts? This is a gorgeous picture. I will treasure it always."

Their eyes locked for what seemed an eternity. Daniel moved his face close to Jayden's, took her face in his hands, and kissed her cheek ever so gently.

"Jayden, I'm not expecting anything," he said softly. "Just being with you like this is enough."

"I'm glad you understand. I want to take it real slow."

"I won't apologize for what I'm about to say, though. I'm falling in love with you."

"Love." She exhaled. "That's a mighty strong emotion. Do you honestly think you know me well enough to say what you feel for me is love?"

"Why is it that as soon as I start to feel close to you, this invisible barrier comes up between us? I get this strange feeling sometimes you want me to walk away. Well, it won't be that easy. I don't fall in love every day. It's not something I toss about lightly. I *am* falling in love with you, and all you need to do is accept the fact that you're worth loving. I will wait for you." Daniel put his arms around her and held her close.

"It would be wonderful if it could always be like this," she murmured.

"But it can be…if that's what you want," Daniel countered.

Jayden didn't answer. For now, being in Daniel's arms, feeling the beat of his heart, was perfect. *There's no other place I would rather be.*

⁂

Later that night, with Edna in bed, Jayden enjoyed some time alone while the house was quiet. It was a time to reflect back on the events of the day. It was the first time she had ever enjoyed Christmas. While she sat next to the twinkling tree lights, she stared at the letter that lay in her lap, the letter from her father. Jayden was glad she'd made the decision to wait until the end of the day before she opened it. Nothing could spoil her day now.

The moment she opened the sealed envelope, a strip of five pictures fell out. It was one of those instant pictures where you put in a dollar and sit inside a booth. It was Jayden and her father making faces at the camera. In the last pose, Jayden leaned against her father as he looked down at her.

Dear Jayden,

I received your letter, but it was difficult to answer right away. It sounds as though you are doing very well for yourself. Congratulations on your graduation. I'm sure you did great. So you are living in San Antonio in a boarding home and have a job in a pharmacy? Do you plan on college at all? I hope you give it some consideration. It opens so many doors for you.

Anyway, health-wise I'm doing fine. My emotional state is another issue, but that's not your concern.

I'm not ready for you to come for a visit. I know that may disappoint you, and I am sorry for that. This is not a good place for anyone to be. Let me give it some thought, and maybe down the road we can discuss it. However, with that said, I would like to receive your letters from time to time to tell me how you're doing.

Love, Jeffrey (Dad)

It wasn't exactly what she hoped he'd write, but on the other hand he didn't say he didn't ever want to see her, so there was hope.

Sixteen

Feb. 14, 1978

 I don't have a lot of time to write. Jonathan is on his way to town. He phoned not more than 30 minutes ago to let me know he should be here by 2 p.m. I can't wait to see him. We haven't talked as much as we used to when I first moved down here, so there's much to catch up on. Daniel and Edna will be coming to dinner with us. I think it's only right to introduce Jonathan to the man I love.

 At first Daniel seemed a little bothered by the fact we were going out as a group on Valentine's Day, but those plans were made long ago. I'm sure Jonathan didn't give thought to what day it was when he planned on coming down.

 Well, better find something to wear. Until later.

"Are you excited?" Edna asked after commenting on the many different outfits scattered across the bed.

"Yes! It seems like such a long time since I've seen Jonathan, but when I think about it, it's only a couple of months."

"I'm anxious to meet him. What does he know about Daniel?"

"Daniel?" Jayden shrugged. "He knows I've been seeing him and that I care a great deal about him. I think he's very happy for me."

"That's good. Now"—Edna cocked her head toward the clothes on the bed—"you'd better settle on an outfit quickly. Daniel just arrived, and you don't want to keep your friend waiting for us at the restaurant, do you?"

"I'll be right down."

❧❦

The parking lot at the restaurant was so packed Daniel decided to let the women out first and then park.

"We'll wait for you inside," Jayden said.

"Table for 2?" the maitre d' asked.

"No, four. We're meeting someone here," Jayden replied. Suddenly she saw Jonathan, already seated at a nearby table, waving her over. "There he is now."

"Jonathan, I'm so glad to see you!" Jayden embraced him.

"Me, too, and you look great," he said.

"Thank you. I'm happy. Let me introduce you to Edna. Daniel is parking the car."

Jonathan gave Edna a hug and handed her a white rose. "I've heard so much about you, Ms. Sullivan."

"Now, don't you go making me feel old. Call me Edna."

"Edna, it is," he said.

Just as they were about to sit down, Jayden noticed Daniel standing at the front entrance looking for her. "Over here," she called. Then, when he reached the table, she said, "Daniel, I want to introduce you to Jonathan."

The two men shook hands.

"Jayden has told me a great deal about you and your ministry. It's a pleasure to get to meet you finally," Daniel said.

"Likewise. I've heard such wonderful things about you, as well. Jayden tells me you're involved with a mission in Africa?"

"Yes, in a small village by the Zambezi River."

Over dinner the four of them exchanged stories as though they'd always been friends. There was never that uncomfortable lag in conversation. Daniel and Jonathan talked theology, while Edna and Jayden sat and listened. Edna, who was also well versed on the Bible, made an occasional comment for clarification.

Jonathan was fascinated to hear about Daniel's experiences in Africa. "I can't imagine the satisfaction you must have had living among the villagers and teaching them, and I'm sure they taught you a lesson or two."

"More than a lesson or two. Here I was this green kid from Texas. When I look back on it, I must have stepped off that plane with a huge ego. I planned to teach these people how to think modern; you know, do things the civilized way. Wow! How arrogant on my part! Turns out

I was the pupil, and the village was my teacher."

Edna waited for a pause in the conversation. "I don't want to rush you boys, but we've been sitting here for a spell. Let me make a suggestion. Why don't we all go back to the house for some coffee and pound cake?"

"It depends," Daniel said. "Did you make the pound cake?"

"Of course. Store-bought doesn't taste fresh."

"That sounds great, Edna," Jonathan said, "but I should probably head back to the motel."

Daniel spoke up. "If I were you, I wouldn't pass up the opportunity to have a piece of Edna's cake."

"Really, Jonathan, come back to the house with us," Jayden said.

"It does sound tempting." He wavered. "Okay, on second thought, I'd love to have a piece of cake."

Daniel reached for the check to pay when Jonathan objected. "It has been such a pleasure to be here with Jayden and to meet both of you. Dinner is on me."

Seventeen

The women finished drying the last saucer, then Jayden joined Daniel and Jonathan on the front porch. Jonathan leaned against a wooden porch beam. He smiled as soon as he saw Jayden. Daniel could see in Jonathan's eyes how much he cared for Jayden, but there was no jealousy. Jonathan was a man of character and would respect his relationship with Jayden.

Daniel stood up and took Jayden's hand. "Will you thank Edna for me? I'd better run along. Tomorrow I'm helping my father move some cement blocks to a new job site. Jonathan, it was a pleasure to meet you. I hope the next time you're in town we can get together."

"Do you have to go right now?" Jayden asked.

"I really should." He leaned over and kissed her cheek.

"I'll walk you to your car."

"No, you stay and visit. I'll call you tomorrow."

He looked back briefly as she waved good-bye.

"He seems like a real nice guy," Jonathan told Jayden.

"I'm so glad the two of you hit it off. I think he's pretty special too."

"Sounds serious." Jonathan watched Daniel drive off.

"I feel so alive when I'm with Daniel. He's everything I've ever wanted in a man. This may be premature, but I think I'm in love with him. But…"

Jonathan remained silent. It was hard to hear her say she loved another man.

Jayden moved to the edge of the porch and looked out into the night.

"So why the long face?" he asked. This was a difficult conversation to have with her. On the one hand, he was pleased Jayden was allowing herself to seek out a healthy relationship, and on the other hand, he wished she was seeking it with him.

"I don't feel special enough for Daniel," she said.

He was stunned. "Why on earth do you feel that way?"

"It's nothing I want to go into right now."

"Jayden, I thought we got past all of the secrets. You should know by now you can trust me."

"It's not that I don't trust you; it's just something very personal. Something I don't share with anyone. Please just accept that and don't be offended," she pleaded.

"All right. But if you want to talk…"

"I know I can always count on you."

It was quiet for a moment as Jayden struggled inwardly. She didn't want anyone to know that Douglas Jenson had stolen from her what she had hoped would be a special gift to her husband on their wedding night: her purity. She felt like used goods, and Daniel deserved better.

Jonathan interrupted her thoughts. "May I ask you a question?"

"Uh, sure."

"Do you think Daniel might have marriage on his mind?"

"I'm sure of it. Why do people always assume a couple should get married?" Jayden said.

"It's generally the natural progression of things. Man meets woman. They fall in love and want to spend a life together," Jonathan reasoned.

"I'm happy with things the way things are," she said. But she didn't know who she was trying to convince—Jonathan or herself. To marry Daniel would be her dream.

Jonathan settled his back further against the porch beam. "May I make a suggestion? You need to resolve your past, Jayden, so you can move on with the future; otherwise, you'll never reap the full benefits of the love God intended between a man and a woman."

"I know. I'm trying."

"Glad to hear that. I didn't come up here to harp on that subject and put you on the spot. The last time I was here you said you were going to write to your father. Did you?"

"Yes, and he wrote back."

"That's fantastic. Was it…"

"A good letter? I suppose. He hasn't agreed to see me again, not just yet, if that's what you're wondering, but he did ask some questions about me."

"That's an improvement," Jonathan said. "And there's something else. A few weeks ago, I had dinner with Cynthia and her boyfriend, Trey. He just happens to be a social worker in Midland. A couple of weekends ago, he invited me to go with him for a little target practice, and afterwards we sat around the shooting range and just chatted. We got on the subject of his work and I mentioned to him about Emma's situation. I hope you don't mind."

"No, but what did you tell him?"

"Basically, that Emma was in foster care, her approximate age, and just some generalities. I found out a little information, but I thought it better to tell you in person instead of in a letter or over the phone."

"Tell me. What?"

"Trey inquired with some of his colleagues in Odessa. He asked about her. Come to find out, one of his friends that he went to graduate school with handled her case."

"Oh my gosh. He knows where she is."

"Trey was hesitant to tell me because his neck's on the line. Come to find out, Emma isn't in foster care at all."

"What are you saying?"

"I'm saying she was adopted."

"Adopted! That's impossible. She was in foster care for five years because there wasn't a family who wanted to take a chance on her."

"She's with a family all right. The good news is there may be a way to find out where Emma is."

"How? If she's been adopted, then she has a new last name."

"That's true, but Trey found out something interesting. After the adoption was granted, the adoptive parents requested the records not be sealed."

"What does that mean?"

"When most adoptions are granted, the records are closed to prevent people from coming in and out of the new family's life and disrupting it. Evidently, the people who adopted Emma have requested to leave the adoption open."

"Open, sealed, I'm confused."

"Open adoption means it may be possible to contact her new parents through the courts. You see, Trey said the people that adopted her must want relatives or people who have Emma's best interest at heart to remain in contact with her."

"Do you think it's a possible I'll be able to see Emma again?"

"I can't say for sure, but everything Trey told me leads me to believe there's a strong chance. Trey knows the ins and outs of the court system. He has offered to speak to one of the judges he knows personally to see how to contact Emma's family. It will all need to be done legally."

"Oh, Jonathan, I might get an opportunity to see her again?"

"Keep in mind there's always a slim possibility they may feel it's not in her best interest to see you."

"I don't believe they'd do that," Jayden said. "Not if Emma has told them anything about me. I just need to have faith." Jayden looked off into the night. She closed her eyes and pictured the blonde child in her mind, happy at last to have a home to call her own.

Jonathan sat back in the chair. *Faith.* He heard her correctly. God was working miracles right before his very eyes. Jonathan knew only the Lord could make such a transformation happen. God heard Jayden's heart. Through all her trials, it was the Lord who carried her, the one who gave her the endurance she needed to stand strong.

Jayden sat next to Jonathan. "I love you, dear friend," she said to him. "What would I do without you?"

"I love you, too." He loved her as his sister in Christ and for who she was. She was everything he wanted in a lifetime partner, but it wasn't his choice. God had other plans for his life.

Eighteen

"**E**veryone gone?" Edna asked.

"Daniel left a little while ago, and Jonathan just left to head back to the motel."

"Well, my dear, I know one thing for sure. I'd hate to be in your shoes."

"Why?"

"For starters, you have two handsome, intelligent men who are obviously crazy about you."

"That's ridiculous. I do believe Daniel loves me, but Jonathan? It's Jonathan's job to care for and love everyone."

"Go ahead, keep those blinders on. I know I'd have a hard time choosing between the two. Both are God-fearing men; you couldn't go wrong with either of them."

"I think your imagination is running wild." Jayden laughed, then sobered. "However, Jonathan asked me something odd."

"What's that?"

"He asked if Daniel might be thinking marriage."

"That's not odd, if you ask me. When people are in love and they're together as much as you and Daniel are, that's usually the next step."

"Not for me. Marriage isn't always the answer to happiness. Just look at the divorce rate."

Edna threw up her hands. "Marriage has gotten a bad name…I'll agree there. People jump in and out of relationships without a thought. I'm sure the Lord's heart is broken over what He intended to be a holy bond between a man and a woman. Everyone looks for the easy way out. But the grass isn't greener on the other side."

"Edna, you and Willum's marriage was the last of its kind."

"You think so? Things aren't always as they seem. Willum and I had our fair share of problems."

"Well, if I ever marry, I hope I can have close to what the two of you had." Jayden smiled. "Oh, by the way, Jonathan told me something incredible tonight. I may be able to find Emma." Jayden relayed everything Jonathan had shared with her.

"Honey, that's wonderful. What's the next step?"

"Jonathan's going back first thing in the morning. When he sees Trey, he'll ask him to pursue this."

"I told you God has a plan. It's all in His time, not ours. Go into this with little expectation and a lot of prayer."

"I've been praying there would be a way to find her," Jayden said.

Edna did a visible double take at the word *praying*.

Jayden rolled her eyes. "Don't get your hopes up. It's not that I particularly believe in prayer, but at this point, I'll try anything."

"I've seen some miraculous things happen when people turn their problems over to God."

Nineteen

Jayden opened her bedroom window and watched from above, her heart full, as Edna puttered in her garden. The red and violet tulip bulbs Edna replanted in the spring had broken through the earth's winter crust. Edna looked adorable in her oversized straw hat and dirt-stained dungaree with a smudge of freshly tilled soil smeared across her cheek. Dandelions and crabgrass didn't stand a chance once Edna was on weed patrol. It may have been a small flower bed in the back of the house, but to Edna it was as grand as the Butchart Gardens.

Edna looked up and saw Jayden in the window. "When will Daniel be here?"

"Any minute now."

"Ruidoso…" Edna looked away, as though remembering the place fondly. "Did I ever tell you Willum and I went there on several occasions?"

"You never did."

"It's a lovely place. Least it wasn't overrun with shopping malls and such."

"I'm looking forward to it," Jayden said. "Daniel's parents and sister are already up there."

"Molly said they usually rent a nice log cabin for a couple of weeks in the summer."

"According to Daniel, it has two bedrooms and a fully stocked kitchen. I'll share a room with his sister."

"What a romantic getaway," Edna commented. "The two of you walking hand in hand up in the mountains, the fresh scent of pine; sitting by a campfire gazing into one another's eyes…"

"Why aren't you a romance writer?" Jayden teased.

"I smell love in the air." Edna placed her hand over her heart.

"You're impossible," Jayden said.

But Jayden knew Edna was right. She was deeply in love with Daniel. "I'd better get a move on. Daniel will be here any minute. I'll see you in a few days, Edna. Now, don't you stay out in the sun too long."

Jayden closed her bedroom window and took a final look in the mirror. She wore just a hint of makeup and her hair was loose around her shoulders—the way Daniel liked it.

A rap on the door sounded at that instant.

"Coming!" Jayden raced down the stairs and opened the door.

"Need some help?" Daniel laughed, gesturing toward her feet. She only had one shoe on.

"Would you believe I just bought these sneakers? One of them fits, and the other seems too snug."

"Here, let me help before you fall." Daniel knelt down and placed her foot on his bent knee, then eased the shoe on.

"Like Cinderella and the glass slipper," she joked with him.

"You are like a princess." And she could tell by his expression that he wasn't joking.

He stood and took her hand in his. "Oh, I almost forgot. Do you like magnolia trees?"

"Magnolias, well yeah, I guess so."

"My father ordered a couple extras and can't use them for the job he's doing. It's not worth sending them back for credit so he thought maybe you and Edna might like one for your yard."

"I'd love it, and I'm sure Edna will too. Let me go tell her. She's in the garden."

"If you tell me where you want it, I'll plant it for you."

"That's up to Edna to decide."

"Decide what?" Edna was walking around the front of the house.

"Daniel's father gave us one of his magnolia trees."

"How marvelous! Magnolias in bloom are such a sight. If you'll take it out back, I'll keep it watered until you can get it planted for me. In the meantime, I'll find the perfect spot for it."

"While you're doing that, Daniel, I'll throw my overnight bag in the car." Jayden kissed Edna good-bye.

"You have a safe trip, hon, and give his parents my best."

Daniel and Jayden jumped in the car and honked the horn as the Volkswagen Bug sputtered.

Edna was about to go inside when she noticed the mail carrier coming down the street. He'd been delivering mail in the neighborhood for over twenty years.
"I can set my watch by you, Richard."
"How you doing today, Ms. Sullivan?"
"Good—and you?"
"Can't complain."
"Was that the kids I saw driving off?" he said.
"Sure was; they're off to the Ruidoso mountains."
"It's pretty cool up there in the night; hope they packed some warm sleeping bags."
"They're staying with Daniel's parents in a cabin."
"Not roughing it then?"
Edna sorted through the stack of mail Richard handed her. "What's that?" She came across a letter for Jayden. It was postmarked Maine. The return address was from a Henry Kirkpatrick, Attorney at Law.
"I'm sorry, what did you say, Richard?"
"I just said the kids aren't roughing it if they are staying in a cabin."
Edna was distracted by the letter. "No, guess not."
"Better run along, Ms. Sullivan. You try and stay cool now, ya hear?"
"Thanks, you do the same." Edna went inside and laid the letter on the hall tree so Jayden couldn't miss it when she came home.
But she couldn't help but worry. *What on earth would a lawyer want with you?*

Twenty

"I hope the family won't be too much of a handful for you this weekend," Daniel said wryly.

"I've been looking forward to this."

"Just remember you said that!" He chuckled.

Daniel couldn't have been happier that Jayden had agreed to come. She was now incorporated into a Taylor tradition. Yet he had ulterior motives for this weekend, something he'd planned for the last several weeks down to the speech he'd written. After all, it wasn't every day he proposed marriage. It was all planned by Daniel that he and Jayden would stay on an extra day after his family left. In the evening around a romantic fire, he'd ask her to be his wife.

He'd discussed his intentions with his parents, and they were ecstatic for him. "Just like a woman," his father had said when Daniel's mother started to cry.

"You won't find a sweeter girl," his mother said between sniffles. "Guess I should look at it like I'm not losing a son but gaining a daughter."

"Jayden is one of a kind." His father patted him on the back. "It's time me and you start talking partnership in the landscaping business. You need to start earning some money to support a family."

"Let's not jump the gun, Dad. She hasn't said yes yet."

"There's not a doubt in my mind she'll say yes," Daniel's mother said. "Who couldn't love you?"

"Spoken like a true mother." Daniel gave her a kiss.

Maneuvering up the winding mountain roads now was exhilarating. Daniel handed his camera to Jayden so she could capture some of the scenery.

"Daniel, wouldn't you love to live up here where it's secluded, only going into town for the necessities?"

He smiled and nodded. He loved the way Jayden marveled over simple things. Looking through her eyes, Daniel felt as though he was experiencing everything for the first time.

"A couple of more turns around the mountain and we're almost there." Daniel was anxious for Jayden to see the place.

When she began to tug on her ear because the climbing altitude caused her ears to pop, he offered her a stick of gum. "Try chewing on this. It helps." He tugged on his own ear. "There it is! Welcome to the Taylor mountain escape." He pulled into an alcove.

"Daniel, you said it was a small place. But this is the size of a regular house. It's incredible." She got out of the car and stretched her legs.

"Ya'll come on inside," his mother called, waving at them from the open window.

"The air even smells different."

Daniel wrinkled his nose. "You're used to smelling pollutants."

"Hey! What took you guys so long to get here?" Daniel's younger sister Rebecca, otherwise known as Becca, ran towards them. She grabbed Jayden around the waist and gave her a bear hug. "Come on. I want to show you my secret hideout."

Daniel groaned. "A place where no boys are allowed." His sister rolled her eyes at her brother.

"Should I put my bag up first?" Jayden asked.

"Nope, let lover boy take it in for you. If we hurry, you might be in time to see my deer."

"*Your* deer?" Daniel said.

"All right, it's not my deer but every time we come up to the cabin, it just so happens she comes to see me."

"Because you feed it."

"So what?"

"Don't you girls be gone too long," Daniel's mother called after them. "Becca, I could use a hand with dinner."

"All right, Mama," she said. Then, in a side voice to Jayden, "I get so tired of having to always help with dinner."

"Becca, you're lucky to have such a nice family. Not everyone is so fortunate."

"I know, I know, but just because I'm the only girl I'm expected to do the housework while Daniel and Dad get to work outside in the sun and dirt."

"Come on, show me this special place of yours," Jayden said. Jayden was convinced Becca took her further out of the way than she needed to but Jayden played along. The trees were full and the sunlight couldn't shine through. When the girls came to a stream, Jayden said, "We don't have to cross that, do we?"

"No, just sit here and watch." Becca patted a spot on the ground beside her.

Jayden couldn't put her finger on the animal sound Daniel's sister was trying to imitate. It was kind of funny. "Look over there," Becca squealed.

"Well I'll be. It is a deer." Jayden was impressed.

"See, that's my deer."

The deer cautiously put one foot in the water, then another. The animal looked around and then practically leaped across the rocks until it was on the other side.

"Wow, he's magnificent," Jayden said.

"Watch this." Becca inched her way close to the deer.

"Be careful." Jayden stood ready to grab her.

Becca pulled a branch from a bush. The deer took a couple of steps forward and one back before starting to nibble on the berries. Then the snap of breaking branches frightened the animal off. The two girls looked to see who was coming. It was Daniel.

"Daniel," Becca said, exasperated, "you scared him off."

Jayden walked over and put her arms around him. "She was right. The deer came right up to her."

"Well, it is her deer." He rubbed the top of his sister's head. "Mom sent me to get you two. Dinner is on; besides, it's getting dark."

Sitting around the dinner table without the interruption of the television set was nice. Jayden learned so much in one evening about Daniel's family. Mr. Taylor told stories of his ancestors and his childhood. He had everyone in stitches.

While the girls did the dishes, Daniel and his father picked up their guitars and started to play. Jayden and Mrs. Taylor stood inside the doorway listening.

"I didn't know Mr. Taylor played guitar."

"Oh yes! In fact, that's how Daniel learned to play." Becca bolted out of the kitchen and went over to her father.

"Why don't we have a sing along?" Mr. Taylor suggested.

"That's our cue." Mrs. Taylor coaxed Jayden to join them.

"I'm not a singer."

"Neither are we." Daniel laughed.

It was one of the best times she'd had. Daniel's family was like him. Lighthearted and fun to be around.

"We need a picture of this," Daniel said.

"You left your camera in the car. I'll go get it," Jayden said.

"Be careful. When it's dark up here, it's *really* dark," Mr. Taylor said.

Dark wasn't the word, Jayden decided. Pitch black was a more accurate description of the night. The only light came from the cabin.

Jayden searched the back seat of the car. "Here it is." She shut the door and was heading back to the cabin when she paused. Overhead were thousands and thousands of silver specks in the sky.

Daniel joined her. "You okay out here?"

"Look at that." She pointed up.

"The constellations are pretty incredible, aren't they?"

"I've never seen anything like it."

"I arranged it all for you," he teased.

"Daniel, I'm happier right now at this very moment than I've been in a long time."

"Me, too."

Twenty-one

"We are leaving with more than we brought up," Mr. Taylor teased his wife. "Okay, the car's all packed. Guess you two will head back in the morning?"

"Probably before 8:00 a.m."

"Daniel, make sure you put the fire out and that everything's locked up before you leave," his father said.

"Yes, sir, will do."

His mother leaned over and gave her son a kiss. "Good luck." She winked at him.

Daniel's sister, a very typical twelve-year-old, leaned out of the car window. "Go take your pictures, lover boy."

"Becca," Daniel said sternly to his sister.

"Rebecca, get your head back inside the car." Daniel's mother's tone was amused.

"Bye, now." His little sister made a face.

"Kids." Daniel rolled his eyes.

"She's great—very spirited."

"Thanks for being polite."

"I mean it. I love your family. And what did your mother mean, 'good luck'?"

"Nothing. Just being Mom. Let me grab the camera, and we'll go for a walk."

Jayden walked slightly ahead exploring a new path. It was all he could do to keep up. She never ceased to amaze him. There was a childlike quality to her, finding wonder in every living thing, yet there were times when it seemed she was a million miles away.

"Don't you love the way nature has an internal clock? Depending on the species of plant, they come to life right on cue. It's that way with wildlife. If you think about it, all the animals run on a clock. For example, bears hibernate…and look at that squirrel over there."

"I'm looking." Daniel acted interested in the biology class for her benefit. But he was completely entranced by her.

"The squirrel is picking up nuts to store, I assume. They all have a job to do to survive."

"Like I've always said, 'Life's a miracle.'…I have an idea. Come stand under this pine." He positioned her the way he wanted her and then focused the camera lens.

"Didn't you say we were going to take pictures of nature and not me?" she said.

"Why on earth would I want to take a picture of you?" Daniel teased. "It's the tree I want a shot of. I thought if you stood next to it everyone will be able to see how large the tree is in comparison to, say…a person." Sounded like a good excuse to him.

"Sure."

"Perfect—now, don't move." He walked around the tree, snapping one picture after another as though he was doing a professional photo layout for some high-class magazine.

"Now, for one good close-up." Jayden crossed her eyes and stuck out her tongue, trying her best to make the goofiest face she could think of.

"Very funny," Daniel said, "very funny."

"Oh, come on, you don't want a picture of me. I'd break the camera lens."

"Yeah, you're right." He laughed.

"Hey! Thanks a lot."

Jayden sat down by a brook and pulled out her journal.

July 17, 1978

This has been one of the most enjoyable times of my life. For the past week I've spent the days and nights at a little piece of heaven in the mountains. For the first time, I've tried my hand at fishing. Surprisingly, I was the one who caught a trout. Beginner's luck. The days are spent walking and taking pictures with Daniel when I'm not in town with his mother. That woman can find a bargain anywhere. It's been wonderful here with Daniel and his family. It's given me such a nice perspective on family life as I watch the interaction with Daniel's parents and sister.

Today Daniel and I are alone as everyone has gone back home. At this very moment, I'm sitting on a blanket watching Daniel focus his camera lens on a robin. As I watch him, I take note of his every movement. The way he loads the film in the camera and the way he scopes out his target. There is nothing about this man I don't find fascinating.

"Got it!" Daniel said, looking over his shoulder at Jayden. "What are you doing?"

"Writing in my little black book." She moved the book so he couldn't see it.

"Ah, you brought that with you in the event this didn't work out?"

"A girl's gotta be prepared."

Daniel lay next to her on the soft grass, his hands tucked behind his head. He squinted against the light as it sifted through the thicket of trees.

"Do you ever feel restless?" Daniel asked.

Jayden set her journal down on the ground beside her and leaned back on her elbows, looking into his eyes.

"Describe restless," she asked.

"My definition is when I bore of the mediocre and need something to give meaning to my existence."

"Wow! That's some definition. I usually don't get bored, but when I do, I guess I find something to fill my time."

"See, filling time to me is such a waste. I believe each one of us has been placed here for a reason."

"Is this going to get philosophical?" Jayden asked.

"No, I just don't think we're here by accident; I believe God has a plan for us."

"Do you know what your mission in life is?" she asked.

"I know one thing for sure: it's not to be a landscaper." Daniel frowned.

"It's an honest job."

"No offense, but that's something my father would say."

"I didn't mean to…"

"I know you didn't. It's just I don't want to spend my life putting in brick gardens or cement fountains. There has to be more."

There was a slight hesitation, then Jayden asked, "Did you prefer living in Africa?"

Daniel sat up and looked at her. "You think I'm a dreamer, don't you?"

"Not at all. I just think maybe you should be realistic." The instant the word slipped from her tongue, she winced. "I'm sorry. I shouldn't have said that."

"No offense taken. At least over there I felt like I was doing what I was meant to do." Daniel reached for her hand. "I knew you would understand if anybody did."

Jayden did share his love for adventure. He cupped her face in his hands, stroking her soft porcelain skin with his fingers, and then gently kissed her.

"I'm getting hungry, are you?" she asked abruptly.

"We just had breakfast."

"Must be this fresh air." Jayden started to head back to the cabin.

❧❦

Jayden was torn. Torn between leveling with Daniel and telling him her dark secret, then letting him decide for himself if he wanted to continue a relationship with her. Daniel only knew what she presented to him and eventually that could come back to haunt her.

At the same time, though, she wasn't ready to give him up if he chose to walk away.

Am I being selfish by not telling him? she wondered.

Twenty-two

"Here, let me help you," she said as Daniel carried in kindling for a fire.

"You can help by putting the album on the player."

"I heated up some leftover chili. Hope that's all right with you," Jayden said.

"Whatever you made is fine with me. Come on over here. Let's eat in front of the fire."

Jayden carried the bowls of hot chili on a tray. "Down here on the floor?"

"Sure—it'll be our indoor picnic." Daniel spread a blanket out in front of the stone fireplace.

After they ate, he stretched out on his side, facing her.

"Aren't the fire embers pretty the way they dance around the logs?" she asked.

"Yes, very pretty," he murmured.

"You're not even looking at them." Jayden poked him in the arm.

"Caught me. But I'm looking at you, and you're so beautiful." Daniel kissed her.

Jayden let out a laugh.

His eyebrows rose. "What's so funny? Hope it wasn't my kiss."

"No, of course not. It's just something Edna said before I left."

"What did she say?"

"That sitting around a campfire gazing into one another's eyes was so romantic."

"Do you agree with her?" Daniel asked.

"Absolutely."

"I'm glad you think it's nice." He sat up.

"What's wrong?" she said.

"Come with me. There's something I want you to do for me."

Daniel sat Jayden in the chair, then got down on one knee.

"Daniel, please…" Her stomach tensed.

"Jayden, you know I love you."

"Yes, and you know that I love you, too." Before she could say another word, he slipped a one-carat diamond engagement ring with a plain white gold band on her finger.

Her mouth dropped open. She took in a deep breath and held it.

"You really do need to breathe," he said, smiling.

"A ring?"

"Do you like it?"

"It's incredible."

"It belongs to my grandmother. When I told her how I felt about you and that I was going to ask you to marry me, she gave this to me to give to you."

"My goodness. This is priceless." Jayden started to cry.

"This last year with you has opened my eyes and heart. I want to share my life with you. How could it get any more perfect than marrying your best friend? There's nothing we don't know about one another," Daniel said with confidence.

Jayden looked away.

"This may sound old-fashioned, but I am your biggest fan. I want to be your everything. Your supporter and your encourager. When you need a helping hand, I want my hand to be the one you reach for. When you carry a burden, I want to carry it for you. We will have our ups and downs, and life may not always be as perfect as it is at this very instant, but my promise to you is that I will be there as your companion, your confidante, and your husband through the laughter and the tears, through the hard times and good times." He paused and took a deep breath. "Jayden, will you be my wife?"

"Oh, Daniel, I don't know what to say. This is so unexpected."

"Say yes."

"I love you, I do, but…"

"In love, there are no buts," Daniel said.

"There is no other man in this world I'd rather marry than you, but I can't, not now. Do you understand?"

Daniel stood up. "No, I don't understand. I must have missed something. You say you love me. You say you would want to marry me."

"But there are things about me that you don't know. Things I haven't shared with you."

"Then let's talk. I want to know everything about you."

"We need to pack up and leave," Jayden said.

"You want to run away."

"Don't spoil the weekend."

He studied her. "I'm sorry if you think I've spoiled the weekend. I just asked you to marry me and now you're telling me there are things I don't know about you, yet you're not willing to talk about it with me?"

"Please Daniel, don't do this."

"Each time I think we're progressing and moving forward, bang! Just like that, you sabotage it. What is it, Jayden? How can I help you? How can I help us? I've prayed a lot about this."

"The truth of the matter is, Daniel, we come from very different walks of life. You have an incredible family. I have Edna, and that's fine, but she's all I have. Don't you find it odd I don't talk about my family? Because I sure find it strange that you don't ask a lot of questions…"

"Jayden, I have asked, and you always find ways to avoid the topic. So now, tell me, please. I can handle whatever it is." He held her by the shoulder.

"You want to know?" Jayden brushed off his hands and looked him in the eyes. "My mother is dead. To top that off, my father was accused of her murder. He is serving twenty years to life in the state pen."

Daniel looked aghast.

"Oh wait, Daniel, you wanted to know everything? It gets better than that. I grew up in a terrible foster home where my foster father was…" Jayden thought better of going forward with the specific details of Douglas Jenson's abuse.

Daniel's eyes grew wide. "I'm so sorry, honey. I didn't know." He started to put his arms around her again, but Jayden stood and walked away from him.

"There's more. In foster care, there was a little girl named Emma that I took care of for five years. Recently, I discovered she's been adopted by a family and I may never see her again."

She heard Daniel sink into the chair, and she went on. "Until recently I thought I was an only child, but it turns out my mother had two sons before she met and married my father, and I have never met them, nor do I know even where they are."

Jayden turned, and her eyes met Daniel's disbelieving ones. She hadn't meant to sound harsh to him. The words had just come out that way. "I'm sorry. None of this has anything to do with you."

Daniel reached her with several swift steps. "But, Jayden, it does. I can't tell you how sorry I am that you've endured so much heartache in your life." He gathered her in his arms. "But I don't love you less or feel differently about you. I want to be there with you in your journey to find Emma and your brothers. And about your father, Jayden, if you…"

She stepped back and put her fingers to his lips. "Thank you for understanding, but this is something I want to resolve before I plan a life with anyone."

She didn't look into his eyes again as she walked away. She knew what she'd find in them. *Hurt.* She didn't want to hurt him, but she had to take care of some things first.

Daniel watched her as she walked out of the house and stood, gazing at the heavens, a few feet away. If she didn't want to move forward with him, then after today, he would put distance between them. He knew just how to do that.

⊰∂⊱

It was shortly after midnight when they arrived back at Edna's. Neither Daniel nor Jayden made a move to get out of the car.

"I'm sorry if I seemed angry back at the cabin." Daniel knew he owed her an apology, but he couldn't bring himself to look into her eyes.

"You have nothing to be sorry for. Let's just get past this. I love and care for you…"

"But not enough, right?" Daniel stared ahead, his hands gripping the steering wheel.

"I'm not settled in my life right now. Maybe in time…"

"I don't want to put undue pressure on you," he said. "It won't be an issue any longer." Daniel didn't want to sound petty but somehow it was coming out that way.

"That's not what I meant," she said quietly.

He reached over the back seat and grabbed her overnight bag.

She leaned in to give him a kiss good-bye, but he couldn't respond. He felt frozen.

"Call me tomorrow?" she said.

"I don't know. Let's just see how it goes."

At that moment, Jayden knew her worst fear was coming true. Daniel would walk away.

"Is that what you want?" Jayden said.

"Right now it's what I need. It's painful for me to stand by and watch you go through something you won't allow me to be a part of."

The porch light went on. "I better go in," Jayden said, her heart aching.

Daniel stayed in his car while she ran inside. The light went on in her room. How could he have misread their relationship? Tomorrow he would write Doc and accept his offer to return to Africa.

Twenty-three

Edna pressed the off button on her alarm. She eased herself into a sitting position and then sat on the edge of the bed. A searing pain shot right through her hips, radiating down to her knees. She opened the nightstand drawer and took two painkillers.

"Lord, give me the strength to make it through another day with these worn-out joints." Edna slid her feet into her slippers.

On the way downstairs, she opened Jayden's bedroom door to see if she had made it home all right. Jayden was still asleep with the covers pulled up over her head.

Edna walked outside, picked up the paper, and started the coffee. She was sitting at the table reading the comics when she heard Jayden moving around.

"I'll put on an egg for you," Edna said the moment Jayden came downstairs.

"I don't feel like eating."

"Something wrong?" Edna was worried that Jayden had seen the letter from the attorney and was upset.

"Yeah, something is very wrong. Daniel asked me to marry him yesterday."

"Be still my heart. Excuse me if I don't quite see why that's a problem."

"It's a problem because it's poor timing."

"Poor timing. You have a man who would go to the ends of the earth for you, and you call that poor timing? Honey, don't you recognize love when you see it?"

"It's not that easy; if it were, I would have said yes."

"So the problem is…?"

"Edna, I'm not going to drag Daniel or his family down my path until I have a good idea who I am. I can't do this to them. What a stain on the Taylor name, and I'd be to blame."

"Oh, I get it. You haven't been honest with him or even given him a chance to decide if he could handle it or not. You're making that decision for him, right?"

"Yes, I have! And it's not that I haven't been honest. I did tell him some things yesterday...he was supportive, but I'm not ready."

Edna leaned closer to Jayden. "Mark my words, if you let him go because of stubbornness that you have to go on this journey alone, you may not get a second chance."

"Can we not talk about it anymore?" Jayden fought tears.

"That's fine, but please think about what I said. Did you see the letter lying on the hall tree when you came in last night?"

"What letter?"

Edna shuffled down the hallway, then came back to hand a letter to Jayden. "This is from an attorney in Maine. It's had my curiosity up since it came."

Jayden opened the letter and, upon Edna's prompting, read it aloud.

> Dear Jayden:
> My name is Henry Kirkpatrick. The courts forwarded your letter to me. My wife and I have adopted Emma. I understand you're very close to Emma, living five years with her in foster care.
> From the first day we brought her to live with us, she spoke of you daily. You have requested contact with her and, after careful consideration, I believe it would be in the best interest of Emma for you to have visitation with her.
> At the end of this letter I'm sending a number where I can be reached any time of the day. Please call us collect and we can prepare to make arrangements for you to visit Emma. All expenses will be paid by me. You just need to find the time to be able to come.
> I know this may be awkward for you, staying with people you don't know; therefore, I hope you'll be able to bring someone along with you. All expenses for you and a companion will be paid by me.
> Sincerely,
> Henry Kirkpatrick

"Edna, I'm going to see Emma!"

"That's wonderful, hon."

"Will you go with me?" Jayden asked.

"I've always wanted to see Maine; let me think about it."

"Please, just come with me."

Edna smiled. "Okay, you've twisted my arm."

"You know what I'm going to do?" Jayden said.

"What's that?"

"I'm going to call the Kirkpatricks and then, after that, I'll give Daniel a call. It was awful how we left it last night."

"It's going to be a glorious day," Edna said.

Jayden was halfway up the staircase when she stopped. Then, before Edna knew what was happening, Jayden was in her arms.

"My...my...what's this all about?" She patted Jayden on the back as they hugged tightly.

"I want you to know how very lucky I am that you're in my life."

"It's all God's plan for us."

"I'm starting to believe there may be something to all this prayer stuff." Jayden went upstairs to make her call.

Edna couldn't believe her ears. "Thank You, dear Jesus, for giving me wisdom and the patience not to give up on her."

Uncoiling the garden hose, Edna was about to turn the water on and set the sprinkler when Jayden came out in the backyard, grinning from ear to ear.

"Well?" Edna asked.

"If Mr. Weiskopf will give me a week off it looks like we're going to Bangor, Maine, in a couple of weeks. They're anxious to meet you, as well."

"What kind of people did they sound like?"

"Very nice."

"Did you speak to Emma?"

"Yes. She sounds so grown up. Do you know that they have her in a private school for special education? She's even learning to play the piano, and she swims now."

"Sounds like Emma lives with a good family. We need to think about what to pack for Maine. Not sure what the weather is like. Haven't been on a trip in...oh, I don't know when. My old joints aren't going to enjoy the cramped quarters of the airplane, but I wouldn't miss out on this opportunity for anything."

"Did you call Daniel?"

"I did. We talked briefly. He said he was helping his dad with something. But he's going to pick me up later. Funny—he said he had to talk to me about something, too."

Twenty-four

Jayden was anxiously waiting for Daniel in front of the house when he pulled up. She didn't even give him an opportunity to get out of the car before she hopped in.

She leaned over and kissed his cheek. "You're not going to believe this!"

"Sounds like good news. Tell me what's going on." He turned off the car's engine.

"I told you about Emma, right?"

"The child in foster care?"

"Yes. To make a long story short I received a letter from Emma's adoptive parents."

"But how did you…"

"Let me finish. I called and spoke with them today and with Emma. Edna and I are flying out to Maine to visit with them."

Daniel was visibly taken aback. "You're going to fly out to Maine and stay with people you don't know?"

"Crazy, isn't it?" Jayden could barely contain her excitement.

"How did you find out where Emma was so you could write to these people, or is that another long story?"

"Well, Jonathan has helped me resolve some of this, and I'm certain…"

Daniel looked shocked. "Jonathan has helped you? I've asked for how long for you to let me in, to let me help you with whatever I can, and now you're telling me that Jonathan helped?" He paused. "I think this all boils down to the fact that you don't completely trust me."

"I do trust you, but I also wanted to protect you."

"Protect me? From what? I didn't think it possible to feel any more humiliation and hurt, but you have proven me wrong. Then whatever it is that you're protecting me from, I do hope you and Jonathan can solve it."

"Daniel, Jonathan only knows because there was a time, before you and I were together, that I needed a friend, so I confided in him."

"And we've been together for over a year and you didn't feel the need to share any part of this with me?"

"You're right. I was wrong not to include you." Jayden felt badly that she'd upset Daniel…again.

"No, I was wrong. I thought we had an open, honest relationship. I'm sorry for whatever it is that you're going through, and I do hope it works out. But I thought when you wanted to talk to me tonight that it was to tell me you've had a change of heart."

"I do love you, Daniel."

"Well, I have some news of my own." Jayden didn't like the tone in his voice. "After yesterday, I decided I wouldn't be able to stay around here and continue dating you only as a friend. I love you…enough to ask you to be my wife. About a month ago, Doc asked if I could come back to Africa. They're in dire need of help since a couple of the school teachers went stateside."

Jayden's heart started to race. *Please don't tell me you're going back over there.*

"I can't go on the way we have been, especially since it seems I was the only one who wanted more out of this relationship."

"That's not true," she said.

"This morning, I left a message with the Red Cross to tell Doc and Rachel I would be back within the next month. My passport's still good, and I'm using my savings to get a plane ticket. The organization they're with will reimburse me once I've worked over there for…"

"For how long?"

"A year."

"You're thinking of staying over there a whole year?"

"Not just thinking about it. I *will* be staying over there for a year. It will be for the best."

Jayden was stunned. *How did all of this go from such a beautiful weekend to this?* "Are you sure this is what you want?"

"Yes and no. What I really want, I can't have."

"I know I don't have the right to say this," Jayden said, "but I don't want you to go. I'll miss you so much." She couldn't believe it had come to this.

Daniel looked at Jayden. "You'll be missed, too."

Jayden watched, a minute later, as Daniel pulled away from the house. *I kept my secret from you so I could keep you close. I feared if you knew, you'd leave. Now you're further from me than I ever dreamed possible.*

Twenty-five

Jayden barreled down the stairs fully dressed.

"Are you actually going into work today?" Edna said.

"Of course, why wouldn't I? I need to work as much as I can right now since Mr. Weiskopf is letting me off for the entire week when we go to Maine."

"I promised I wouldn't meddle, but I can't sit by and watch you and Daniel part ways like this," Edna said, reaching for a dishcloth.

"It will be fine."

"Why don't you be honest with yourself? I heard you up most of the night, and it's because Daniel is leaving today."

"Edna, please don't." Jayden was trying not to break down in front of her.

"You can't fool me." Edna tossed the dishcloth on the counter.

"Daniel and I will move on," Jayden said in a tearful voice.

"Oh, is that right?"

Jayden walked to the sink and rinsed out her coffee mug. "I'd better get going."

"You're exhausted, sweetheart. Why don't you give Mr. Weiskopf a call and tell him you're not coming in today? He'll understand, I'm sure."

"I need to keep busy."

"What you need to do is to stop letting pride get in the way. Just give Daniel a call so you don't waste any time with regret."

Jayden didn't answer. She knew Edna had her best in mind, but didn't know how to respond.

Edna sighed. "I'm so sorry. I just feel so helpless."

"I'm not upset with you, but it was Daniel who said it has to be this way."

"Daniel said that?"

"Okay, maybe not in those words, but this is the way it has to be. I'll see you tonight."

Edna waited for Jayden to leave the house, then phoned Molly immediately. "Good morning, Mol. How's the weather over in your neck of the woods?"

Edna knew Molly would know exactly what she meant...and she did.

"It's pretty gloomy here. How about over there?"

"I'd say about the same. What are we going to do about these two?" Edna asked.

"Well, they're too old for us to send them to their rooms. We can't make them kiss and make up." Molly laughed.

"I'll tell you something right now. I don't know about Danie,l but Jayden didn't sleep at all last night. If she wasn't walking the floor, she was in the kitchen getting something to drink. I'll be—what in the world makes young people so stubborn? The girl might have gotten a couple hours of sleep...if that."

"Then that was two hours more sleep than Daniel got. I did everything except put the phone in his hand," Molly said.

"Tell me Daniel's itinerary again. I think I have a little plan that could work." Edna wasn't one for scheming, but this time was all in the name of love.

"What's that?" Molly asked with a childlike curiosity.

"Mr. Weiskopf. I know he'll help us out with my plan of action. He loves both of those kids."

"Edna Sullivan, what on earth is up your sleeve?"

"I don't have time to go into it now. I need to give him a call before Jayden gets to work. Talk to you later, Mol. Keep your fingers crossed."

"Will do."

141

Molly enjoyed the intrigue of it all, but in her heart she hoped it would eventually work out between the two kids.

"Who's on the phone?" Daniel asked as he walked into the room munching on a piece of toast.

"Uh, it was a wrong number." Molly couldn't think fast enough to give Daniel another answer. *God forgive me,* she thought.

He quirked an eyebrow. "For a wrong number, you sure talked quite awhile."

She frowned. "You just never mind. Now, are you gonna let me fix you something decent to eat besides an ol' dry piece of toast? No telling how long it'll be before you get a good meal. What do those folks eat over there anyway?"

"Nuts, fig leaves, and ground rock." Daniel gave his grandmother a hug.

"You know, young man, you're not too big for me to get a switch after."

"I'll do fine over there. I made it last time, didn't I? I still have a couple of hours before I need to get to the airport. Is there anything I can do for you before I leave?"

"Can't think of a solitary thing and if I think of something that needs fixin' when you're gone, your daddy will do it." Then Molly decided to push from her end a little. "Are you packed and ready to go?"

"Ready as I'll ever be."

"Any last-minute calls you need to make?"

"Can't think of any."

Daniel knew where this was headed. As far as he was concerned, between his grandmother and Edna, there was no way Jayden couldn't know he was leaving today. If she wanted to speak to him, she'd call. Daniel's father came to the door to help him with the bags.

"I hate good-byes, so you get on out of here." Molly started dabbing at her eyes.

Daniel blew her a kiss and picked up his luggage.

"Where do you think you're going? You come on back here."

"But you said…" Daniel never intended on walking out without giving his grandmother a hug and kiss. He knew she'd never let him get away with that.

"Don't pay any attention to me. I'm an old woman."

Daniel stood outside the house and took one last look. He had to fight the urge to go by Mr. Weiskopf's store, pick Jayden up in his arms, and try to make it all right again. But he was convinced more than ever that she didn't want him in her life.

"You know, Son, you don't have to do this if you're not ready to go back. I'm sure Doc and Rachel will be able to find a replacement for you."

His apprehension must have showed on his face. "I want to go, really. It's just that maybe I'm not as ready to leave as I was a year ago, but nonetheless, I told them I'd come."

"Okay. You know what you want more than I do, but it seems to me you may not be listening to what that little voice inside you is saying."

"I appreciate your concern, Dad. I don't want to be disrespectful, but I've had a lot of people giving out unsolicited advice."

"They're not trying to be in your business, Son. They really do care."

"I know. I'm just a little edgy and didn't sleep."

"I have one more thing to add," his father said.

"What's that?"

"Did you pack enough writing paper and stamps? You know your mother and grandmother. They'll want a blow-by-blow account of what you're doing."

"I'll keep a journal for them." Daniel laughed and then stared out the window. Tomorrow there would be a continent between him and the woman he loved. Time and distance. That was what the doctor ordered to heal his mind and spirit.

Twenty-six

"You need to slow down; I can't write that fast."

"Repeat it back to me, so I'll know you wrote it down correctly." With something this important, Edna wanted him to get every detail right.

"No time. I see her coming now. Let me hang up before she suspects we've been talking."

Mr. Weiskopf fumbled with the phone; he dropped the receiver. He didn't want to appear too conspicuous. For the last month, he'd watched as the generally happy-go-lucky Jayden gradually sank into depression, going through the motions of living. To him, she had become a shell of a person.

"What on earth you doing here, missy?" Mr. Weiskopf asked, as Jayden walked through the door.

"Why wouldn't I be here?"

"Maybe because if I'm not mistaken, you should be at the airport seeing off your friend before he leaves the country. Isn't that today?"

"I suppose he's leaving unless his plans have changed." Jayden was nonchalant as she hung up her sweater.

Mr. Weiskopf followed directly behind her, firing one question after another at her. "Maybe he has changed his plans."

"I wouldn't know," she said quietly.

"I don't understand young people. This is craziness. These games your generation plays. In my time, when you liked someone, you wanted everyone to know it. Mark my words, young lady, if you don't resolve this before he leaves, you will live to regret it."

Jayden said nothing. It had been the same for the last few mornings when Mr. Weiskopf had tried making conversation. Jayden seemed so distracted, and answered only—if she answered at all—with a quick yes or no. He looked at his watch. How was he going to get Jayden out of the store and to the airport in time?

"How many times are you going to dust those shelves and rearrange the display cases in one day?" He scowled at her. "Besides, it's past noon. When do you plan to eat lunch? I can't have my employees taking lunch at all hours, you know. What would I do if I had a mad rush of customers in the store? Do you expect me to handle everything myself? No, I can't have this. I have a business to run. You must go in the back now and at least take a break."

Jayden didn't really know why it would matter to him when she ate lunch or took a break; he'd never made an issue out of it before. And a mad rush of people? What was he talking about?

"I think you're right. I'll go have a bite to eat over at Burger and More. The fresh air will do me good."

"You never go out to eat. Didn't you bring your lunch today?"

"No, I didn't even think about making my lunch. It doesn't matter. I'll grab a burger and come back and eat it here."

"Nah, that makes no difference to me."

"I'll see you in a few minutes." Jayden had just managed to get out the front door when he called after her.

"Aren't you forgetting something? Like your sweater? It looks pretty chilly out to me."

"Chilly? It's 72 degrees outside. I'll be just fine," Jayden said.

Mr. Weiskopf didn't have any other option. Time was almost out. "Wait right here."

He came back with her sweater in his hand. "You're going to make me old before my time. There's no time to waste asking all these questions." He reached inside the pocket of her sweater and handed her a handwritten paper.

"What's this?"

"Read! You read it now."

"American Airlines Flight 4672 to Dallas at 3:15 p.m. Did you put this in my sweater?"

Mr. Weiskopf shrugged, looking like the cat that ate the canary. "Are you going to stand around all day, or are you going to get to the airport?"

"Edna put you up to this, didn't she?"

"You are going to be the death of me," he said. "Yes, yes, if you must know, Edna called me and I jotted down the information. Are you going to get out of here or what?"

Jayden leaned over and kissed him on the cheek.

"I don't understand women. Go now before I change my mind and make you stay till closing time."

"I'm gone." Jayden bolted out the door.

Mr. Weiskopf picked up the phone as soon as Jayden was completely out of sight.

"Edna, it worked like a charm. She should be home soon."

⊱⊰

It was 2:15 p.m. Jayden was at a dead run, racing up the front steps. To her surprise, Edna was already waiting for her with car keys in hand. "Turn right back around, young lady. There's no time to waste! I'll drive to the airport and let you off in front and then I'll park the car."

Jayden started to say she wanted to change clothes quickly, but Edna pulled the front door closed, locking it.

"How did you know I was coming home?" Jayden asked.

"I just know these things," Edna said slyly.

Jayden jumped in the car. "All right, 'fess up, Edna. It was you that called Mr. Weiskopf and gave him Daniel's flight information. And how did you...wait a minute! This was all a scheme between you, Molly, and Mr. Weiskopf, wasn't it?"

"Moie?" Edna said putting on her innocent face.

"You can't pretend you didn't know a thing about it. I can see right through you. I know good and well the three of you were in on this, and furthermore—" Jayden paused for effect—"I don't know how I will ever thank you."

"You can thank us by the two of you stopping being so prideful; it's one of the sins, you know."

There wasn't an adequate response to that. Jayden knew Edna was right. And now she would pay the price of pride.

The twenty-minute ride to the airport seemed endless. Ordinarily, she'd be able to make at least one green light but not on this trip. Edna hit every red light imaginable. And to make matters worse, traffic was merging into one lane because of road construction.

Once at the airport, Jayden watched the signs overhead. "There it is." She pointed at the American Airline sign. "Terminal one. Hurry!" For a moment, Jayden felt queasy from the rush of adrenaline through her veins.

"Hey, now wait a minute! The car is still moving," Edna hollered after Jayden, but she was already entering into the turnstile to go inside the airport.

"Okay, guess I'll park the car and meet you inside," Edna laughed. "Kids."

Dashing in and out of crowds, Jayden searched the overhead monitors for Daniel's departure gate. Flight 4672 Gate B-13.

"Excuse me, Miss, is that flight 4672?" Jayden asked. She tried to catch her breath. The young woman at the ticket counter latched the door leading to the jet bridge. "Yes, ma'am."

"You can't shut the door! I need to speak to someone on that plane."

"I'm sorry." The ticket agent was snippy. "But once the doors shut, we don't open them so you can speak to someone on the plane. After all, there are schedules to keep."

"But you can't…you can't…" Jayden could see the woman wasn't about to budge. She walked over to the full window glancing out at the plane. Maybe Daniel would at least see she tried to make it before he left. Jayden kissed her hand and pressed it against the cool glass.

"I love you, Daniel."

"He knows you do." Jayden turned to find Daniel's father standing behind her. "I can speak for my son when I say he loves you very much."

Jayden's knees started to buckle. She felt as though she might faint.

"Sit down right here."

"I'll be okay. I just got a little dizzy."

Daniel's father sat down next to her. "He wanted me to give this to you when I saw you next." He handed a picture album to her. She recalled the day Daniel told her he was putting all of their memories together in an album.

"Isn't that something a girl might do?" she remembered teasing him about it.

"Are you saying that girls have a market on being sentimental?"

She looked at Mr. Taylor. "Are you sure he wanted me to have this?"

"Those were my instructions."

"Mr. Taylor, I really wanted to see Daniel before he left."

"I believe you did, honey, but sometimes things work out the way they're meant to even if we don't understand it at the time. I hope you won't be a stranger. Come by for a visit with the family from time to time. You're like a daughter to me and the Mrs." He kissed her on the forehead. "Did you come here alone?"

"No, Edna's parking the car."

"Good. I wouldn't feel right about leaving you here."

Jayden hugged Daniel's father. "I promise I'll come around. Will you let me know when you hear from Daniel?"

"I surely will. But if I know him, you're going to be the first one to hear from him."

"I wish I could be as sure of that."

She waited until he left the gate area, then flipped open the first page of the photo album. There was an envelope taped inside the cover of the album. It was addressed to her. Her hands were starting to tremble as she read the letter.

> Jayden:
> It's 3:00 a.m. as I sit down to write. I'm not able to sleep. The proverbial counting sheep isn't working. One might think it's the excitement of returning to a continent I find absolutely fascinating or that I'm excited to see Doc and Rachel; and while all of that's true, it's not the root of my anxiety. I feel like leaving you tomorrow makes our parting final. For all I know, it was final for you the day we left the cabin.
> What I've put myself through this last month has been strictly my fault. You've been completely honest from the start about not wanting a serious relationship. Either I didn't pay attention or just plain didn't want

to hear it.

I wish you could have shared what has happened to you with me. That you trusted others more is what is so hurtful.

I will be gone for at least a year or until Doc and Rachel come back to the States. The time away will help put my life back on track. I want us to remain friends. I can't imagine what life would be like if you weren't in it.

I've prayed for God to be with you on your journey.

Please tell Edna and Mr. Weiskopf good-bye for me. I will write to you from time to time and hope to hear from you as well.

My prayers are with you.

Love always,

Daniel

She flipped through the photo album. The entire book was filled with the pictures they had taken together. Each one had a special memory attached to it. Her eyes filled with tears when she saw the last of the pictures taken the weekend in Ruidoso.

Jayden closed the book and walked back to the window, peering out over the runway. A light drizzle of rain left a zigzag pattern down the glass. *It's going to be better this way. What did we really have in common, Daniel? I don't think I would have fit in with the fairy tale life you had planned for us. Even our religious beliefs, or lack of, would have been a problem.*

She sat down, covering her eyes with her hands. *You're not kidding anyone but yourself, Jayden Arman. You have made a terrible mistake.*

Edna was out of breath by the time she reached Daniel's departure gate. "Land's sake, I had to park clear out in the boon docks."

"He's gone," Jayden said in a quivering voice.

"I know, hon, I saw his father as I was coming in. Are you going to be okay?"

"When I see Daniel again, then I'll be okay. Edna, you were right."

"About?"

"About a lot of things, but when you said my pride would end up causing me pain, you were right. What have I done?"

"It isn't going to help if you beat yourself up, you know. That's just a waste of time."

"I think when we get home I'll change my clothes and do some work in the garden," Jayden said.

"Needing some old-fashioned therapy, are you?"

"You might say that... Why don't I go pull the car around for you?" Jayden offered.

Minutes later, she stood outside in the parking area, watching the sky as a 747 came in for a landing. "I'll wait for you, Daniel."

Twenty-seven

The seat belt sign remained lit, but most of the passengers were already starting to unbuckle to be the first one to jump to their feet and grab their carry-on in the overhead compartment. This was the first time Jayden had ever been on an airplane, so she wasn't quite sure of airplane etiquette. However, it did seem futile to just stand in the aisle waiting for the doors to open. She and Edna remained seated.

Her emotions were on a roller coaster. She was excited but at the same time scared. "Edna, what if Emma isn't happy to see me or she has forgotten me?"

"I doubt either will happen, but you'll know soon enough." Edna motioned for Jayden to get up. Jayden rounded the last turn of the walkway when she saw the crowd of people standing by the gate waiting for their friends and family. She and Edna moved to the side so people could pass.

"Do you see her?" Edna asked.

"No…oh yes, I do. There she is."

Emma was standing next to her new family and waving at Jayden.

Jayden left Edna and ran to Emma. She picked her up and held onto her. "I missed you so much, baby girl."

"Me too, Jay."

"It's a real pleasure to finally meet you. You're a household name, you know." Emma's mother walked up to the girls and put her arms around both of them. "Emma talks about you all the time. We feel like we already know you. I'm Diane Kirkpatrick, and this is Emma's father, Henry."

A big burly man approached her. He wasn't exactly how Jayden pictured him when she'd spoken to him on the phone. He stepped forward and patted her arm. "It's so nice to meet you. We've been anxious for this day to get here."

"And these are Emma's brothers, Stephen and Larry."

"Hello." Stephen's contorted body was supported by pillows strapped inside his wheelchair. His face was emotionless. Every now and then he would let out a disturbing sound. Mrs. Kirkpatrick was so attentive, staying by his side and stroking the side of his face, which seemed to calm him.

Larry, on the other hand, was standing behind Henry, making silly faces. He looked to be a year or two younger than Emma.

"Hi, Larry. Come over here so I can see you," Jayden said. His features were like that of Emma, but most children with Down Syndrome had similar features. Emma wriggled around so Jayden would put her down. Immediately, she went over to Larry and grabbed his hand.

"This is my brother," Emma said with pride. Then she walked over to Stephen and kissed his cheek. It was amazing. His expression immediately changed when Emma kissed him. A smile parted his lips.

"It's the craziest thing. Stephen just knows when Emma's in the room. He doesn't react that way with anyone else."

"What's wrong with Stephen?" Jayden didn't want to be rude but she was curious.

"Cerebral Palsy and he's visually impaired. He's such a courageous little boy," Diane said.

"Oh my gosh, I almost forgot about Edna." Jayden glanced back at the gate where she'd left her friend, but Edna was already coming down the hallway.

"Goodness me, how the airport can call that a bathroom, I'll never know. It's a crackerjack box. Sorry, were you looking for me? I had to visit the little girl's room."

"Mr. and Mrs. Kirkpatrick, I'd like you to meet my family, Edna Sullivan."

After Edna greeted everyone, her attention went to Emma. "You are such a big girl, Emma. Jayden has told me so many wonderful things about you."

Emma had her hands clasped behind her back, swaying from side to side, a big grin showing off her two missing front teeth.

"Well, why we don't go down to baggage claim so we can get home. I'm sure you are probably hungry and tired after the trip," Henry said.

"Oh, Jayden, Emma has already informed us that you would be staying in her room. Is that all right with you?"

"Of course," Jayden didn't want to miss a moment with Emma. The girls chatted for the entire two hours back to their home.

"This is it, the old homestead." Mr. Kirkpatrick pulled the van down a winding road.

Jayden was surprised when they pulled up in front of a large white two-story house with colonial columns in the front. Two golden retrievers chased the van as they turned the corner. Emma bounced up and down in her seat. Jayden was so glad to see how happy and well-adjusted she was.

"Now who has to mow all this?" Edna teased as she commented on the acreage the home sat on.

"Henry does it, with a little help from some neighborhood boys, that is," Diane said nudging her husband in the arm.

"I have my own house," Emma said.

"You sure do." Jayden had only seen homes that magnificent in magazines.

"No, not that house—*my* house."

"What Emma is trying to say is that she has her own special place in the back of the house. Henry built her a little playhouse. It's her castle." Diane patted Emma's leg.

"No, Mama, not a castle. It's a house."

"Just a figure of speech, sweetie."

Mama. It was strange to hear Emma call someone mama. Jayden was glad, of course, that Emma finally had a mother and a father. On the other hand, she was sad. Sad because she felt as though she no longer played a vital role in Emma's life, as though she wasn't needed any longer. Henry took the wheelchair out of the back of the van and gently put Stephen in it.

"Diane, if you get everyone inside, I'll get Stevie and the luggage."

"Come to my house first, Jay." Emma pulled her by the hand and led her to the backyard.

"We should probably go inside first, Emma." Then Diane laughed. "Go ahead; she's been so anxious to show it off to you."

Edna motioned for her to go on with Emma. "I'll be fine; you just go."

"All right, let's go see your playhouse."

Manicured foliage lined the walkway to the back. A staggered tri-level cedar deck, large enough for patio furniture and barbecue pit, extended from the patio door out into the yard. Emma and her brothers had their own entertainment center. A covered sandbox was positioned next to a swing set and teeter totter. Emma's playhouse sat under a large oak tree. It was a miniature version of a regular house. Jayden couldn't get over it. Henry put a lot of time and effort into making sure Emma had the best.

"Wipe your feet," Emma said, pointing to the door mat. "I'll go in first, and then you ring the bell."

"You have your own doorbell?" Jayden said.

"Ring it, hurry, so you can come in," Emma squealed from the other side of the door with enthusiasm and excitement. "Come in." Emma held the door open. Jayden had to bend down so she wouldn't hit her head on the doorframe.

Jayden couldn't believe the fine details, right down to shag carpeting, curtains for the windows, and wallpaper. Emma took a seat in her rocking chair, pretending to feed her doll. The furnishings were ideal for a little girl, with a small plastic oven and matching refrigerator, play dishes with food, dolls, and a baby cradle and stroller. Henry had spared no expense.

"Did you do this?" Jayden asked, pointing to a crayon drawing of two stick figures.

"Yes. That's you and that's me. Mommy hung it on the wall." *Mommy.*

"Emma, you're a lucky little girl. Have you been happy?"

"Yes, and I like to play with my friends, too," Emma said.

"Where do you play with your friends?"

"School. We play games."

"That's great, honey! Your mommy and daddy are very nice. They sure do love you, Emma."

"My brothers are nice, too."

"Yes, they are very nice. Do you know how much I love you?"

Emma's eyes lit up. She stretched out her arms. "This big?"

"Bigger than that."

"Bigger than the whole world?"

"Bigger than life itself." Jayden was touched Emma remembered.

Diane poked her head inside the door. "You girls ready for dinner?"

Emma ran to her mother and jumped in her arms. Diane kissed Emma's cheek. Jayden was happy that Emma was cherished. It was all she ever wanted for her.

≼⥈≽

"That was a wonderful dinner," Edna said. "If you don't mind I'd like to get the recipe for this chicken."

"No problem. Why don't we move into the living room and relax? Does anyone have room for dessert?"

Everyone moaned.

"I couldn't eat another thing," Jayden said.

"I'll second that. But I'll help you do the dishes," Edna offered.

"Leave the dishes. I'd rather spend time talking," Diane said.

"I brought some of Emma's baby pictures with me if you'd like to see them," Jayden offered.

"There you go! That's much more fun than doing dishes." Diane and Henry gathered around Edna and Jayden.

"You were sure good with Emma, Jayden. How can we ever thank you for all the care you gave our little girl?"

"You've thanked me already. I can't tell you how at peace I feel now that she has both of you. That's all the thanks I need."

Diane dabbed at her eyes. "Emma, why don't we show Jayden where she will sleep tonight?"

"Okay."

They first showed Edna to a guest bedroom. "See you all in the morning," she said before turning in for the night.

Then they headed for Emma's bedroom. Jayden thought Emma's

playhouse was sweet, but the bedroom was made for a princess. There were twin canopy beds with matching lilac comforters. The white built-in bookshelf held row after row of children's books supported by animal book ends.

Emma got into her pajamas and knelt beside her bed. "You too, Jay," Emma said. Jayden knelt down beside her. "You do it like this, Jay." Emma put her hands together and bowed her head. Jayden put her hands together. "What do we do next, Emma?"

"You talk to God. He likes that," she said.

"What do you talk to him about?" Jayden asked.

"Just listen to me. Dear Jesus, thank you for Mommy, Daddy, Stevie, and Larry. Thank you for letting Jay come to visit me."

"And Edna too," Jayden added.

"Edna, too." Emma opened one eye and looked over at Jayden.

"What?" Jayden asked.

"God told me He wanted you to talk to Him."

"I don't know how."

"It's easy. You just start to talk and He listens."

"How do you know?"

"My heart tells me," Emma said with all the innocence and sincerity of a child.

"I think you're right, Emma. I'm starting to believe He does listen." So Jayden quietly began to talk to God.

Twenty-eight

Jayden glanced over at the twin bed where Emma slept. It was empty. She could hear Emma's laughter coming from downstairs. Jayden lay in bed for a few more minutes to collect her thoughts. A huge weight had been lifted from her. Life was starting to work out. Maybe, eventually, everything else would fall into place as well.

Jayden thought she would write Tilly a letter when she got back home. It was time to let go of the hurt and anger. If she hadn't sent Emma to another foster home, the adoption by the Kirkpatricks would never have taken place. Emma had more people in her life to love and protect her now.

With Emma's safety reassured, she could now turn her attention towards finding her family. Unfortunately, that would be like looking for a needle in a haystack.

"Well, good morning, sleepyhead." Edna sat at the kitchen nook, sipping coffee with Diane.

"Sleepyhead," Emma echoed, sitting next to Edna, eating a piece of toast and jam.

"You shouldn't have let me sleep so long," Jayden said.

"We were just talking about waking you up in a few minutes. I'd like to show you around town some. There's a beautiful little park not too far from here where Emma attends school," Diane suggested.

"I'd love that."

"If ya'll don't mind, I think I'll stay here and rest," Edna said.

Jayden was worried. Edna hadn't been acting herself since they arrived at the Kirkpatricks'. She seemed more fatigued than usual. With the least bit of exertion, she became short of breath.

"Are you all right?" Jayden and Diane both asked.

"Just tired. Nothing a little rest won't take care of."

"I don't want to leave you here by yourself while we're out

running around town."

"Now, don't you think twice about that. I'll be just fine."

"I'm not sure…," Jayden started to say.

"Well, I'm sure. Now you get ready and go have a good time. I'll bet Emma can show you all kinds of interesting places to see," Edna said.

"Then I'll call you when we stop for lunch and check on you."

"That will be fine."

Maybe the timing wasn't the best for Edna to come along on the trip. As soon as they got back home, Jayden was going to make sure she made an appointment for Edna to see the doctor for a checkup.

"If you'd like, Jayden, I thought we could pick up a couple of sandwiches and go over to the Towne Lake Park for lunch," Diane suggested. "Emma just loves it there. I just need to take Stevie over to the sitter's house. It's difficult to take him places that aren't wheelchair accessible."

"We can always go somewhere else if you'd like," Jayden offered.

"No, no! Stevie loves Maureen; that's his sitter. She is such a blessing. Her background is in physical therapy, so she usually works a little with him, trying to exercise and limber up his muscles."

"Give me a minute to get ready then. I'm definitely looking forward to it."

❧❦

When they arrived at the park, the women spread out a blanket while Emma and Larry ran around playing chase.

"Jayden, I'm glad I can talk to you alone. There are no words for me to express what a blessing Emma is in our lives. I don't know anything about your situation except that you were in foster care with Emma. From what I've found out, you are the sole reason our little girl is so happy and emotionally healthy. It couldn't have been easy on you."

"Emma and I were a team," Jayden said. "I did take care of her, but I'm not sure I'm the reason she's such an incredible kid. But thank you."

"Henry and I were talking last night. I know you're on your own, well, that is, with the exception of Edna. It's plain to see that woman adores you, but if there is anything we can do for you, please never hesitate to contact us. We'd like it very much if you'd consider us your family too."

Jayden didn't know what to say. It was so generous of her. Diane wanted to give some background information about her and Henry. Jayden learned they were both attorneys and had their own law practice up until three years ago. That's when they decided they wanted to start a family.

"I always believed that when we were ready to start a family that would be all there was to it. Not in our case. After a couple of years trekking to a fertility specialist and going through the hormonal mood swings of the fertility drugs, we reconciled ourselves to the fact we were not meant to have a biological child. That's when we started looking into adoption. What we learned was that there are many older children as well as handicapped children who needed a home.

"We didn't need an infant. We just wanted a child to love. Now we have three wonderful children. They are perfect in every way, even though they come with their own challenges. We need them as much as they need us. Our lives are complete."

There was no question about her sincerity. Jayden and Edna would be able to leave Maine knowing Emma would grow up in a home full of love.

"How did you find Emma, I mean, with you living here in Maine while she was in Texas?"

"A lot of people were integral in our search. All it takes is knowing the right people in the field. To make a long story short, we knew of a person that knew of a person, and that person eventually linked us up with a representative from the foster care agency where Emma was. And the rest is history."

"God works in mysterious ways." Jayden couldn't believe she had just said that out loud. *What's happening to me?*

"That He does," Diane answered. "That He does."

The week had finally come to an end, and Edna and Jayden were packed and ready to leave.

"I can't believe the week's flown by so fast," Jayden said an hour or later as she hugged Diane and Henry good-bye at the airport.

"Now don't be a stranger. We're family now. You and Edna are welcome anytime."

"Thank you. That means a lot."

Jayden took Emma by the hand and led her to a row of seats where they would wait for the flight to be announced.

"Sweetie, do you understand why Jay is leaving?"

"Uh huh. You're going home."

"Yes, I'm going home. I want you to remember how much I love you even if I can't always be right here with you. One day I hope you will be able to come out and see me."

"When you get married?" Emma asked, as though there was something she already knew…but of course she couldn't know that.

"Married." Jayden laughed. "I don't know about that. I hope you can come out a lot sooner than that. I have something to give you." She handed Emma the stuffed dog she'd left behind. Emma's face lit up. "I'm not alone anymore, Emma."

Edna was hugging everyone good-bye. She was just as emotional as Jayden. "It's been such a joy meeting all of you. Emma, come over here."

Minutes after the boarding call, Jayden took one last look before turning the corner in the jet bridge where she'd no longer be able to see them.

Emma waved and blew her kisses. "I love you, Jay."

Jayden stood there for a second taking it all in. Emma was hand in hand with her parents. There were no tearful cries or begging for her not to leave; nothing like the last time they were together. It was all going to be fine now. Emma finally belonged somewhere.

Jayden pointed at the blonde child and then touched her heart. Emma grinned, pointing at her heart. It was their secret language, understood only between the two of them. They knew it meant, *You live in my heart.*

Edna tugged at her hand. "Come on, honey. We don't want the

plane to leave without us."

Jayden stared out of the plane window as they waited for takeoff, hoping to catch a glimpse of Emma. People were lined up against the window, but she couldn't make out if Emma was there.

Jayden closed her eyes. A tear rolled down her face. "And life goes on," she murmured.

"What did you say? I didn't hear you," Edna asked.

"Oh, just commenting on how life keeps moving forward even if you don't."

"It surely does that. Are you sure Jonathan is going to pick us up at the airport? For the life of me, I can't understand why he'd be coming all the way from Odessa to do that."

"He said he had some business in San Antonio. Don't ask me what it is, but the timing couldn't be more perfect. I'll be glad to see him. I need to ask his advice," Jayden said.

"Advice?"

"I made a terrible mistake with Daniel, and I need another man's opinion on how I can make it all right with him again."

"Do you think Jonathan is the right person to talk to about that?"

"Of course. He's my friend and a minister."

"He's also a man—a man who is in love with you."

"Will you stop saying that? Jonathan does love me, but his kind of love is the 'love thy neighbor' love."

"It must be easier for you to pretend. You don't see the way he looks at you."

"Nonsense. Let's change the subject. A couple of times back at Diane and Henry's you weren't feeling very well. I noticed it was hard for you to breathe. What's going on?"

"All the excitement, I suppose. Don't worry so much."

"I don't buy that." Jayden wasn't going to let Edna brush this off easily.

"Everyone goes through periods of time when they're out of sync. I'm not as young as I used to be, but I can tell you this: seeing you and Emma together made the trip all worthwhile. So I guess it's my turn to ask you a question. How are you doing with all of this?" Edna patted Jayden's arm.

"Funny—on the one hand, I feel so complete. On the other, there's almost an empty feeling."

"That's to be expected," Edna said.

"What do you mean?"

"For starters, there's no doubt in my mind that you're glad Emma has found a home and family of her own, yet there's the side of you that feels maybe like you've been replaced."

Jayden exhaled. "Edna, you know me so well."

"I can tell you this: that little girl loves you so much. You'll always be her Jay, and she'll always be your Emma."

Jayden leaned over and rested her head on Edna's shoulder. "I don't know what I would have done all this time if it wasn't for you."

"Now you stop that, you hear. We've shed enough tears today, so don't get me started."

"There's one other thing I'd like to talk to Jonathan about, but I can share it with you, too" Jayden said.

"Go on, honey, ask me anything."

"I prayed with Emma the other night."

"Okay…"

"No, I mean I *prayed.* I got down on my knees and did something I've never done before."

"Tell me about it, hon."

"This may sound ridiculous, but when I got down on my knees with Emma and talked to God alongside her, I actually felt He heard me. I didn't know how to pray, and I didn't even know what kind of words to say, but I had the strangest feeling it didn't matter what I said…just that I talked to Him. I'm sure it was only my imagination. Oh, this is crazy sounding. Maybe it's the high altitude that's making me feel strange."

When Edna spoke, her words quivered with emotion. "The altitude doesn't have one thing to do with it. The Bible tells us that if we call to Him, He will answer. He can hear even the smallest whisper. You see, Jayden, He listens to your heart, not just to your words."

Jayden grinned sheepishly. *How could my heart have changed so much?* She didn't want to put up defenses anymore. "I have so many questions. I want to talk to Jonathan about what all this means."

"Oh, Jayden, that's a wonderful idea."

As Edna lay her head against the back of the airplane seat, she knew that this was not the time to share any more information—just to be quiet and let Jayden reflect.

But in Edna's heart, she knew that, for Jayden, there would be no turning back now.

Twenty-nine

Jonathan arrived at the airport an hour before Jayden's flight was due in. He couldn't wait to see her and tell her the news about the job he was offered starting in one month right there in San Antonio.

Jayden saw him first. "Jonathan!" she called out, dancing from foot to foot in excitement.

He moved towards her. "I'm so glad to see you. How was the trip, and how's Emma?"

"I'll tell you everything as soon as we get our luggage and get Edna home. I don't think she's feeling well."

"I heard that," Edna said.

"Well, you haven't been well." Jayden looked back at her.

"Nothing a good hot bath and a decent night's sleep won't cure," Edna spit back.

Jonathan looked at Jayden as though trying to decide if he should say anything at all. He knew better than to argue with a woman…or to get between two arguing women.

"Honey, I can't tell you how nice it is to be on the ground. If God intended for us to fly, he'd have given us wings." Edna gave him a hug.

Jonathan winked at Jayden. "I'm glad to see you, Edna."

"If you don't mind, just get me home. I know Jayden has a lot to tell you, but for me I only want to be in my own bed tonight."

"You sure you don't want to stop for a bite to eat?" Jonathan said.

"Not me, but don't let that stop the two of you."

"Okay, so we'll take you home first, then go back out," Jayden said, eyeing Edna as if she were worried. "On my way home, I'll have Jonathan stop by the store so I can pick up some bread and milk for us."

"Sounds good to me." Edna yawned.

"Where would you like to have dinner?" Jonathan asked Jayden.

"You pick. I'm not all that hungry. I just wanted to spend some time alone with you and talk."

"Really?" He hoped his voice didn't sound too anxious.

"I have some things I want to share, but let's get somewhere quiet where we won't be interrupted."

Jonathan's interest was piqued. He couldn't wait to tell her his news as well. He would be the new pastor at a church only a few blocks from where she lived. He had looked for an opportunity to move closer to her, so when this had come up, he'd immediately applied. It wasn't a sure thing until two days before Jayden and Edna were due home.

His age was his biggest obstacle. The deacons believed wisdom could only come with years of experience, and he was still new in the ministry, but they did like his style and thought he held a lot of promise. For the last several years the church had become stagnant. Many of the young adults were moving to more progressive churches. They saw an opportunity for growth if they brought in new blood. Someone with new ideas and energy. Someone like Jonathan.

After they dropped Edna off, they drove to Edna's church. There it was quiet and they could talk. "Is this okay with you?" Jonathan said.

"It's great."

"You start," Jonathan said. "Tell me how Emma is doing, and don't leave out any details."

"She's incredible. She doesn't look like the same little girl. I believe she's grown at least a foot, not to mention she's missing her front baby teeth. But most importantly, she's with a wonderful family. I really like them. When Emma and I were alone it was as though nothing had changed, but that's not really true. Everything is changing, especially with me."

"What do you mean?"

"It was like a lightning bolt going off in my head. All these years, I've been fighting the One who loves me the most."

Jonathan couldn't bear the suspense. "What are you saying?"

"I have so many questions to ask you, but I don't really know where to begin. Basically, I want to know about God. I want to know how to be like you and Edna. I've watched you all these months and you have such a peace about you. How do I get that?"

Jonathan was ecstatic. He had prayed for this moment. Now it was here. He silently sent up a "'thank you" prayer and asked for wisdom in this conversation. He didn't want to overwhelm Jayden with the magnitude of what she was doing.

"I can't tell you how happy I am that you are asking these questions," he said. "Your decision to follow the Lord is the wisest decision you will ever make. It's simple enough for even a child to understand. We big people are the ones who sometimes make it complicated."

Jayden smiled sheepishly and nodded. She continued to listen very quietly.

"You see, God has waited for you to reach this moment. He's very patient and kind…a real gentleman. He never forces anyone to follow Him, but He loves you more than you can imagine."

"But how can He accept me? I've never believed that God even existed. I pushed Him away."

Jonathan just smiled. "He knows you! And He knows all that defensiveness was just self-defense. He can instantly bring down any barriers left standing. You don't need all the answers up front. He will be your Teacher right when you need Him."

"Jonathan, I don't even know how to pray. What do I say?"

"Just tell Him what's on your heart; that's what He really wants…your heart. You see, what Jesus did for you and for me is beyond comprehension. Think about it like this. Imagine yourself locked in a prison cell, overcome with grief and buried with guilt for all the wrong things in your life, things you can't change. The judge has sentenced you to be executed, and you know that death is what you deserve. You weep uncontrollably, wishing you could undo all those wrongs, but you know you can't. You can't change the past.

"Then a Gentleman comes to your cell, unlocks the door, and says, 'You are free! You no longer have to be punished for your sins. Someone is being executed in your place!' You wonder, *How can that be? Who would do such a thing? I don't believe it!*

"Well, believe it, Jayden. God saw all our sin—past, present, and future. He was saddened but sent His only Son into the world to take on our sin and die in our place. Because Jesus died on the cross, we are free from all our sin, even when we don't deserve it.

"We can accept that gift or reject it. It's up to each person. When you accept the gift, you accept Jesus as your Lord and Savior and, believe me, your life will take on new meaning. You will never be the same."

Jayden was quiet and thoughtful for a few minutes. She had never heard such talk. If only it could be true. Jonathan sat still, letting the Good News sink in.

Jonathan took Jayden's hand, and they both bowed their heads reverently.

Jayden spoke. "Dear Lord, Jonathan tells me You already know me. Thank You for loving me. I've really been wrong about You, and I want to change. I want to give You my whole heart. Please forgive me for all my sins and wrong thinking. Teach me how You want me to be. And thank You so much for taking care of Emma. You have kept her safe and given her a good life. I love you, God. Amen." Tears ran down Jayden's face.

Jayden looked at Jonathan with such joy in her face. She practically beamed. Jonathan laughed aloud with happiness that his dear, sweet friend was now in the family of God.

"Jayden, God is so much bigger than we think. He is bigger than any problem we can imagine. Trust Him for everything, grab on, and get ready for the ride of your life. You are never going to be the same!"

After a few moments of basking in the sunlight shining through the stained glass windows, Jayden turned to Jonathan. "I've spent the last couple of years feeling sorry for myself. I was paralyzed with fear. I remembered something you said."

"Oh?"

"You said, 'Jayden you can't move on with the future until you resolve the past.' You're so right. I can't shut people out of my life and wait for the day everything falls into place."

"It wouldn't be healthy," Jonathan added.

"I want you to know how much I appreciate your friendship. I'm ashamed of myself for not telling you sooner how much you mean to me."

"I care a lot about you too." Jonathan touched her hand.

"I know you do, and that's why I've shared so many things with you. Of course, Daniel wasn't real thrilled that I did that with you but not with him."

"Daniel. What does Daniel have to do with this?"

"This is just a little of what I want to talk to you about. There's something more."

Something told Jonathan the less said at this very moment the better.

"The weekend Daniel and I went with his family to the cabin, he asked me to be his wife."

Jonathan bit his bottom lip the way he did when he got nervous. "Are congratulations in order?"

She hesitated. "Well, I wanted to say yes, but instead I said no."

"Now you've lost me," Jonathan said.

"I want to enter a marriage with a clean past."

"Clean past? Well, I would hardly consider you as having a tarnished past. Circumstances beyond your control led you to where you are today, and I happen to think you're doing very well."

"I am starting to believe that, too. It's just that I've lived most of my life hiding in the shadows of shame. I didn't trust Daniel enough to share my life with him. To make matters worse, I told him I didn't need to tell him. I had already shared that with you."

"Ouch."

"'Ouch' is right. I feel horrible. You're my pastor and friend but I think he could also see you as a threat. I want a second chance with Daniel, and I don't know how to do that."

Jonathan tried not to show any emotion other than concern for her. The knot in his stomach tightened. The human side, the selfish side, wanted to look her straight in the eye and say, "I love you." But in his heart, Jonathan always knew they would just be friends. And if he had to lose out to anyone, he was glad it was a man like Daniel, someone who would always love and cherish Jayden.

"I'm sure he wouldn't hesitate to give you a second chance—" Jonathan's voice cracked—"if he felt you wanted one."

"I'd like to think that, too, but it may be too late for that."

"How's that?"

"There's another woman in the picture."

Jonathan shook his head slightly. "I can't believe that. What would lead you to that conclusion?"

"He wrote to me right before I left for Maine. I received the letter yesterday. He didn't actually say there was another woman, but he did talk about some woman named Catherine and he did seem fond of her."

"So it's speculation on your part?"

"Yes, I guess, but a woman just knows this stuff. Trust me."

"I wouldn't jump to conclusions; you need to come right out and ask him," Jonathan said.

There was a moment of silence between them before Jonathan spoke again. "Jayden there's one more thing you must do for a life of renewal."

"What?"

"Baptism."

"You mean where people are put under water?"

"It's called a public profession of faith, and it signifies the important step you have just taken. Jesus Himself was baptized and instructed us to do this same, to let the world know that you have decided to follow Christ."

"I feel awkward in front of a crowd."

"Are you serious about your decision?"

Jayden nodded vigorously.

"Then this is the way. I can arrange it for a couple of Sundays from now."

"Okay. I feel so at peace. I've never felt so happy! Here I go again always talking about myself. You had something you wanted to share with me, right?"

"Right. But it's nothing really."

"Don't you dare do that to me. I shared, and now you have to."

"Remember the position I told you about that I looked into about a year or so ago?"

"And you said it probably had already been filled."

"Seems like they never found the right person."

"Are you saying what I think you're saying?"

"Yes, I applied and was accepted. I start next week."

Jayden's delight was obvious.

"I'm glad you're happy about it."

"Happy? That's putting it mildly. I'm ecstatic! My best friend right here in town with me."

"I'm pleased about it as well," Jonathan said.

"Things keep looking up, Jonathan. Since meeting you things just keep getting better."

"Now imagine how much better you'll feel now that you're a part of the family of God."

Jonathan was thrilled about Jayden's decision. He just wished that the human side of his heart felt better about the rest of their conversation.

Thirty

There was a knock on the dressing room door. Jayden was adjusting her robe.

"Be right there." The door was partially opened.

"Don't worry, hon, it's just me." Edna stood in the entryway dabbing at her eyes with a tissue and then alternately blowing her nose.

Jayden smiled. "Now don't you start that, or you'll get me started."

"I'm so very proud of you, sweetheart. I was thinking earlier, you know, that the church family will be your witness, and I can picture my Willum, my Mary Beth, and your mother watching over you from above. I had a little talk with them last night."

Jayden embraced Edna. "I couldn't love you more if I was your real daughter."

"You *are* my real daughter. I didn't need to give birth to you for you to earn that title. Now I'll go out front and wait."

Jayden took one final look in the mirror and walked out into the hallway. Jonathan was already coming down the corridor for her.

"Not exactly a fashion statement." Jayden laughed, gesturing toward her plain white robe.

"You look just fine. Are you ready to get this show on the road?"

"I've waited a long time for this. I'm looking forward to a return to innocence."

"Our Heavenly Father has been patiently waiting for you, too." Jonathan walked into the baptismal, extending his hand for Jayden to join him.

This was a very important day in Jayden's life. Months ago, she had prayed the prayer of accepting Jesus as her Savior. It was the first step toward a new and wonderful life of faith. She then spent hours talking with Jonathan and Edna as a new believer.

She soaked up this new life of freedom and the knowledge that she now had a Heavenly Father who loved her very much. Today, she was telling the world of this new walk as she responded to Christ's teaching of baptism. After praying with Edna and Jonathan in his study, Jayden went to the beautiful chapel where the small congregation looked on with happiness as their new little sister in Christ stepped forward to the baptistery.

Jonathan took her hand as she smiled and stepped into the warm water. She looked up at him as he began to speak. He considered her with such pride and affection—as her good friend and big brother. "I'm very proud of my friend today," he said. "She has overcome huge obstacles to come to this place. I pray that someday she will tell you her story, for it is hers to tell, not mine." Then he looked over at Jayden. "Jayden, have you accepted the Lord as your personal Savior?"

She smiled sweetly but spoke in a very firm voice. "Yes, I have."

Jonathan smiled into her hazel eyes. Slowly he lowered her into the water, leaving her burdens and sinful nature to lie at the bottom. "Jayden, I baptize you in the name of the Father and the Son and the Holy Ghost." As he brought her up out of the water, he repeated the familiar words, "Rise to walk in newness of life."

As Jayden came up out of the water, a cleansing, spiritual tide washd over her. She knew the baptismal waters hadn't cleansed her but rather the promise of the Lord Himself that her sins would become white as snow and be remembered no more.

She looked at Jonathan. Tears of joy streamed down his face.

Then she looked out into the faces of her new family. She belonged.

"Welcome, my little sister," Jonathan said, "to your new life in Christ."

My dear Daniel,

I had a dream last night. You were taking pictures while I read. But when I woke, a sadness overcame me. There are no words to tell you how much you are missed by all, but especially by me. Whenever you return home, I hope you find it in your heart to spend some time with me to talk about our relationship. I was completely at fault about how I handled the situation when all you wanted to do was be a part of my life.

Edna and I took the trip to Maine and visited with Emma and her family. It was so wonderful to see her again. At least that part of the uncertainty in my life is a closed chapter.

There is something I have been so excited to share with you. Are you sitting down? Remember the old me and how I used to scoff at religion? Much less anyone who was a believer? Well, I've joined the ranks of Christians. I can't stop telling everyone I meet. The old Jayden Arman no longer exists. I feel such freedom. Shame from my past and fear of the future have been replaced with a new life. I actually followed through with my public profession of faith. Me, who is terrified of being in crowds, stood in the baptismal and told everyone I had accepted Jesus Christ as my personal Lord and Savior. Today I turned my worry and sorrow over to the Lord and just let His will be done. Thank you for being such an inspiration and witness for Christ. Thank you for never giving up on me, and most of all, thank you for being my friend.

With all love,
Jayden

Thirty-one

Jayden stood outside the bedroom door listening to Edna's labored breathing. Why was Edna being so stubborn about making an appointment to see her doctor? "Maybe all you need is a simple antibiotic to get rid of whatever is causing you to feel bad," Jayden would try to reason with Edna.

"Mercy me, child, all it amounts to is a little seasonal allergies."

But Jayden knew different. Something was wrong—very wrong.

Jayden tried to be careful when she opened the back screen door, but the screech of rusted metal on metal echoed in the quiet. She glanced up at Edna's bedroom window and hoped the noise hadn't disturbed her. The dim glow from Edna's bedside lamp sifted through the curtain sheers.

I need to remember to grease those hinges in the morning.

A thin streak of silvery moonlight lit her path to the garden—the place Jayden could often be found spending hours alone in blissful solitude. She felt the damp ground on the soles of her feet. Her warm breath was suspended like a cloud in the crisp night air. With a quick swipe on the wrought-iron bench, she brushed away the puddle of water that had collected during the night.

It was the one time of day when the sun peeked over the mountain landscape, resuming dominance in the sky—a time for the unveiling of the heavens in an orchestrated display of magnificence.

Jayden reflected over the last year, a year of firsts. It was her first year as a Christ-follower, her first time belonging to a church family, the first time since losing her family that she had been called someone's daughter, *and* her first year without Daniel. There was no doubt Jayden had come a long way, but her hunger and desire to grow spiritually was evident. Her former self no longer existed, and for that she was grateful. God was in charge of her life now.

And it showed. Jayden was a shining example of a true believer placing her trust in Christ. With a little help from Jonathan and very little coaxing, he helped Jayden find her niche in the church.

"I've assessed the needs of the community primarily among the young people," he said.

Jayden knew somehow she was going to be a part of whatever he was about to say.

"Some of our families in the community are in trouble, and the children will ultimately be the ones to pay for it."

"Go on," Jayden said.

"I was thinking about starting a group here at the church where children in crisis could come," Jonathan said.

"You mean like a refuge, a safe place?" Jayden asked.

"Yes, exactly. I know you may not be comfortable with the idea and it could bring back some unpleasant memories when you see the pain on their faces or hear the stories, but I couldn't think of anyone better to listen with an understanding and open heart."

Jayden thought for a moment before she answered. "I see," she said, visualizing how meaningful that would be.

"I know it's a lot to ask, but—"

Jayden interrupted him. "I'm thrilled you thought of me, that you would have that kind of trust in me. Thank you, Jonathan. It would be a privilege and honor to help you bring together a group for the kids."

Over the next several weeks, Jonathan and Jayden worked feverishly to start a special place in the church for troubled kids, which they called Kids for Him. It was a huge success, but it came with a price. Both of them were on 24/7 call to comfort and support a child in need, but Jayden believed God had called her to do this and she couldn't think of any way she would rather spend her time and energy.

It was during this time that Jonathan confided in Jayden about the grief he had experienced in life with the loss of his parents and the death of Gina. She was surprised to learn Jonathan had been married and had been expecting a child.

"Why didn't you tell me before?" she had asked him.

"It wasn't the right time."

She knew him well enough by now to know what he meant was

that her pain took precedence over his. Jonathan Baxter was a walking testament to faith, and she thanked God daily for bringing him into her life. Their relationship was priceless, as was her growing relationship with her Creator. Her walk with God had opened up a whole new world—a world free from fear, shame, and loneliness. For once she understood that she would never face another day without her Heavenly Father by her side. He lifted her burdens and cleansed her spirit.

⌘

Dear Jayden,

I hoped to get a letter out sooner, but it has been a particularly hectic time. First and foremost let me ask how you and Edna are faring. I pray this letter finds you both well. I can't tell you how happy I am for your decision to become a born-again Christian. It's a choice you'll never regret.

On a more solemn note, our village has been placed under quarantine. I'm fine; well, that is if you're asking how I am physically. Emotionally is another story. It seems as though many of the village people were stricken with polio.

Jayden lay the letter down on her lap and said a silent prayer before she continued to read.

Most of the children were vaccinated but many of the elderly and a few of the younger adults were overcome with the virus. To date the total death toll has been 78.

The devastation of this virus is incomprehensible. Many of the village children were left orphaned. Rachel and Catherine have served as surrogate mothers. The family members left have taken in as many of the children as they can.

We worked from sunup to sundown in heat above 100 degrees disposing of the bodies before decay set in. There was little time to think. We were running on automatic.

This is the first time I've had time to sit, and I'm in a dark place right now alone with my thoughts. I tried to find an out-of-the-way place to release my anger and frustration. I'm not ashamed to tell you I broke down. My screams must have frightened something lurking in the brush because all I heard was the sound of hoofs running away, stirring up the dust. Suddenly I looked up because I thought I saw a figure standing in the shadows. It was a small child from the village. His name is Jakaal. He is around two years old. His parents and older sister died in the first wave. The boy's maternal aunt survived and took him in, yet she has too many children to care for. I didn't make any sudden movements towards him, afraid I would frighten him, so we just sat and watched one another for the longest time. Tears left zigzag streaks down his dirty face. I picked him up in my arms and we clung to each other. At that very moment, I don't know who needed who more.

I took him back to my hut and bathed and fed him. He's taken over my bed and that's fine. I'm comfortable sleeping on a pallet on the floor. There's a special bond growing between us. I've tried taking him back to his aunt, but she doesn't want him there, and I get the distinct feeling that Jakaal doesn't want to be there either. At first, I said, 'I can't take care of him; what do I know about watching a child?' but it seems to be going all right. God set examples of how we should love and care for one another. How can I argue with that?

Life is so precious, Jayden. I don't want another day to go by without telling you how very much I love you.

God Bless

Jayden's heart ached for him. Why had she been so shallow, so dedicated to wallowing in her small world of self-pity? Daniel had sacrificed so much. He was truly a living example of what God intended his people to do—to love one another.

As she watched the sun rise, Jayden often wondered whether Daniel were watching the sun set over the African desert. He wrote weekly, yet she felt an emotional distance. That was harder to handle than the fact they lived on two separate continents. It wasn't so much what he said in his letters; it was what he didn't say.

The subject of Catherine was never approached by either one of them. He was probably trying to spare her the details of the other woman. "I'm so sorry, Daniel. Please forgive me," she said aloud. "I'm so sorry my pride came between us. Good night, my love."

Jayden was awakened by the chirping of birds in the distance. She went inside to start the morning coffee as she always did and then upstairs to dress for church.

She stopped again by Edna's door and listened, then tapped. "Edna, do you need anything before I get ready for church?" There was no answer. Jayden opened the door partially, enough to see Edna resting comfortably. She quietly closed the door and tiptoed out.

Thirty-two

As usual, Jonathan was greeting the congregation at the front door when Jayden arrived.

"Hello!"

"Good morning!"

"What?" Jayden knew by the look on his face that Jonathan was up to something.

"You're so suspicious!" He laughed.

"Are you going to tell me, or do I have to guess?"

"Would you be willing to help out with the youth group this morning?"

"I can, but I'll be leaving directly after church today."

"That's not a problem. Is everything okay?"

"It's Edna; she's not well."

"I have noticed that she doesn't seem to be her spry, chipper self lately. Is there anything I can do?" Jonathan asked.

"She won't let me do anything for her, but I'm going home to look after her anyway."

"Would you like me to go along?"

"No…well, actually yes. I'd appreciate that. I hope I'm not making a mountain out of a molehill." Jayden couldn't shake the uneasy feeling that sat like a rock in the pit of her stomach. Maybe Jonathan would be able to see for himself what she feared.

❧☙

When the service was over, Jonathan pulled the car around front. "Do we have time to stop off at the bread store and pick up one of her favorite muffins?" he asked.

"No, let's just hurry. I'm not going to feel good until I see if she's all right."

The two blocks to Edna's house seemed more like two miles. Before Jonathan could put the car brake on, Jayden fled up the front steps and fumbled with her house key.

A minute later, Jonathan stood inside the front door. "Hello, Jayden…Edna…"

A scream came from upstairs. It sent the hair on the back of Jonathan's neck on end. It was Jayden who was screaming.

As he climbed the stairs two at a time, Jonathan yelled, "Jayden, where are you?"

"In here!"

He found Jayden in Edna's room kneeling on the floor. Edna's bleeding head was cradled in Jayden's lap. The nightstand was flipped over on its side, and the glass lamp was shattered across the wooden floor. The telephone receiver was still clutched tightly in Edna's hand.

"Jonathan, please help her," Jayden cried.

"Put the phone back on the hook so I can call for an ambulance." He took over calmly, trying to show a confidence he didn't really feel.

※※

The ER personnel greeted the ambulance once it reached the hospital. Everything happened quickly. Medical staff wheeled Edna's gurney down the corridor, disappearing around the corner.

"Are you the daughter?" the admitting clerk asked as she smacked her bubblegum and then popped a bubble.

"Daughter, yes. I'm her daughter."

"Insurance card."

"Insurance, I don't know."

"You don't know?" The woman didn't even look up to see if she was speaking to a real person.

"No."

The exasperated clerk rolled her eyes. "Figures."

"Excuse me?" This was the last thing Jayden needed now, a surly clerk.

"Have a seat out in the lobby." The woman slapped a no-pay

sticker on Edna's chart before tossing it into a bin.

As infuriated as the clerk's indifferent attitude made her, Jayden was going to pick her battles. "When can I see her?" she asked.

"Just have a seat." The clerk started to slide the window closed.

"Look, I'm sorry if you're having a bad day, but I asked when I can see Mrs. Sullivan." The bored look on the clerk's face said it all. She could care less if and when Jayden saw Edna. The clerk pursed her lips, forming another bubble with the gum. It popped unexpectedly, leaving a sticky residue in the woman's hair.

Sweet justice.

The woman was annoyed. "When the docs know something, they'll come out and get you, and not before that." The glass window shut, preventing Jayden from saying another word to her. She felt her cheeks flush. Jayden had started to reopen the window when she saw Jonathan.

"How is she?" he asked.

"I don't know. They took her into a room."

"How are you?" he said, leading Jayden into a chair in the waiting area.

"What will I do if something happens to her?" She felt a wave of impending disaster. "I should call Molly." Her voice quivered.

"Do you want me to do that for you?"

"Yes, thank you. I'm not sure I'm up to dealing with any more drama today."

When he returned, Jayden was pacing the corridor. "Did you get in touch with Molly?" she asked Jonathan.

"Yes, and as in true form, she fell apart. I asked her not to come to the hospital; I didn't think you needed anyone else to worry over."

"No! No! I know exactly what you mean, and I appreciate your foresight."

The wait was unbearable. Jayden started to go ask someone if there was any word when Molly made a grand entrance holding onto the handrails as though she was about to faint.

It wasn't a godly response, Jayden knew, but the moment she saw Molly, all Jayden could think of was finding a place to hide. She loved Molly, but the woman had a knack for always needing to be the center of attention, and today Edna was the focus.

"Oh, Jayden, how dreadful." Molly ran her hand alongside the tiled wall to steady herself. "How's poor Edna?" Molly's voice was cracked with emotion.

"We don't know anything yet."

"Well, that's inexcusable. I'll find out what's going on this instant," Molly said.

"No, Molly." Jayden didn't want to push her luck. "Let's just let the doctors do their jobs."

"I can't stand this." Molly collapsed onto a bench.

Jayden was feeling physically drained but had to keep going.

"Here comes one of the doctors." Jonathan helped Jayden to her feet.

"Are you Mrs. Sullivan's family?" he said.

"We're her family," the three of them spoke at once.

"My name is Dr. Patel. Mrs. Sullivan is stabilized, but we haven't received the results of some of the blood tests and x-rays as of yet."

"What did I tell you? I knew she'd be fine." Molly was indignant.

"I didn't say that." The doctor looked directly at Jayden.

"Go on, and please be truthful with us. We can take it no matter what it is," Jayden said.

"All right. I felt it necessary to vent Ms. Sullivan. She has fluid on the lungs due to her congestive heart failure, and her body is worn out from trying to maintain respirations on her own."

Jayden turned pale. "Congestive heart failure? Vent?"

"I thought you might know that," the physician said.

"It doesn't matter. What will happen now?"

"It's not as bad as it sounds. Vent, or more precisely, the ventilator will help her breathe. This will allow her body to rest."

Molly groaned. "Oh, I've seen those contraptions on one of my soaps. It's horrible."

Jonathan gave Molly a disgruntled look.

"I promise," the doctor said, "it's what she needs right now."

Molly collapsed in the chair.

"May I see her?" Jayden said.

"Yes, but only for a few minutes and one person at a time in the room. You need to be aware that Edna hasn't regained consciousness."

"Why's that?" Jayden asked.

"I shouldn't say anything until all the tests are in, but I have a hunch, and it's only a hunch, that Mrs. Sullivan may have had a stroke."

Molly gasped and started fanning herself.

"A stroke?" Every muscle in Jayden's body was so tense she ached all over.

"We will know more when we get the results of the brain scan."

"You need to go see Edna now, Jayden," Jonathan said. "We'll wait right here for you."

Jayden wasn't prepared to see Edna lying on a gurney, her head extended backwards and a plastic tube jutting from her throat. It was frightening. The mechanical sound of the ventilator sent shudders down her spine. IVs ran in both of her arms. Her skin was pale and clammy to the touch. Jayden leaned close to Edna's ear.

"Edna, it's me, Jayden. I'm here with you." There was no acknowledgement. Jayden brushed Edna's hair back, kissing her forehead.

Jonathan was out of his seat the moment Jayden walked out of Edna's room. She burst into tears. Fearing the worst he asked, "How is she?"

"It's horrible, Jonathan. It doesn't even look like her. What will I do if she doesn't pull through this?"

Memories of Gina's final days flooded Jonathan. There were no life support machines, no heroic measures. He'd never forget how beautiful, how fragile she appeared.

Gina had touched the side of Jonathan's face. She didn't speak. "What is it, Gina?" he had said. But he already knew; he saw it in her eyes. For the first time in months, she was at peace. There was no more pain.

A tear ran down the side of her face. "You are my prince," she said.

Jonathan lay on the bed next to her. "I love you," he said.

Then Gina closed her eyes and entered the kingdom of heaven.

When Jayden got home after a long night, there was a letter from Daniel.

> Dear Jayden:
>
> I'm sure by now you know what has happened. The Red Cross contacted my family to inform them I am fine. I know my family probably called you right away. The mail was prohibited from coming in or going out of the camp. Many of our supplies have been dropped by plane. While the virus has run its course and there haven't been any new cases, there is still fear among the villagers.
>
> Once delivery started again I received all your letters at once; it was a bright spot in my evening. I sat down and read them all. I wrote you every night as well and sent them in a bundle. That should make the mailman happy.
>
> Life here is slowly returning to normal. Jakaal is quite the little man. I have to tell you this has been an experience, but I wouldn't trade it for anything in the world.
>
> I have one regret…the time I wasted while I was still at home before I left for Africa. We should have been together talking and working out any issues we have. Pride and ego have a way of tearing down relationships. I hope we can talk more about this at some point.
>
> Love,
> Daniel

Jayden was thrilled to hear that he wanted to talk about their relationship. Obviously, he wasn't completely over her. That was a relief.

Thirty-three

Three weeks had passed with Edna on life support, and Jayden hadn't considered disconnecting the life support until now. Jayden recalled a conversation she'd had with Edna. "Don't you let them hook me up to no machines to keep me alive, promise? If the good Lord wants me home, then that's what will happen." She didn't think, of course, that she would ever need to make that decision for Edna, but now Jayden felt she hadn't abided by Edna's wishes. It was a decision that tore at her heart.

"If you're not 100 percent sure about this…," Jonathan said.

"One hundred percent sure? How can I be 100 percent sure of something like this!" Jayden snapped at him.

"All I'm saying is, don't let anyone pressure you into making a quick decision."

"It's what Edna would want. She didn't want to have machines keep her alive. I've prayed about this. I have to trust in God."

Jayden, Jonathan, and Molly circled around Edna's bedside holding hands, each taking turns praying for Edna. The nurse handed Jayden a consent form to sign. It seemed surreal. The nurse took a final reading off a strip and then shut down the ventilator. A paralyzing silence followed.

Jayden was terrified to open her eyes and look at Edna, afraid she was gone. The nurse at the head of the bed took her blood pressure while another listened for lung sounds.

"I'll tell the doctor," one of the nurses commented before leaving the room.

"Is she gone?" Jayden said.

"No, she's maintaining a blood pressure and breathing on her own." The nurse didn't appear too surprised. Perhaps to her it was commonplace, but to the three waiting friends in the room, it was a miracle.

Molly let out a loud cry, "Praise the Lord!"

Jayden's legs felt numb. The three of them hugged and praised God for allowing Edna to remain on earth a little longer. The physician walked in and assessed Edna one more time.

"Will someone kindly tell me what all of this means? She's breathing on her own; isn't that a good sign?" Jayden said.

"Well, yes, it's good, really good, but there's still the question of the coma she's in. As we discussed before, the brain scan results are indicative of a stroke."

"That's all medical mumbo jumbo," Molly said between sobs.

"That may be, but it has definitely caused some problems. It's all a 'wait and see' game now," he said before walking out of the room.

"What do they know? She'll show them," Molly said. "You just wait and see."

For the first time, Jayden hoped Molly was right.

※

Daniel,

I can't imagine how you came through the ordeal of the polio virus with the quarantine. You must have felt like a leper. I put you and your group on the prayer chain at church.

There have been so many thoughts going through my mind. Here I sit day after day in the comfort of a home with heat and air conditioning. I can walk about without fear and the dread of some disease devastating our community.

A third-world country is hard for one to wrap her mind around. You are so brave and dedicated to give of yourself like that. I wish I had your courage.

Daniel, I think of you often. I do miss the times we had together. Please take care of yourself, and remember you are in the thoughts and prayers of many.

I'm sure by now you have received my letters telling you about Edna's condition. She's still in the hospital and remains in a coma.

Wish you were here with us. Please pray for her.

Love,

Jayden

Thirty-four

The best you can do is prepare for the worst, but hope for the best. That message played over and over in Jayden's mind. At first, all she wanted was for Edna to sit up in bed and scold her for making such a fuss. Now she would settle for Edna showing some kind of sign that she knew Jayden was in the room. Jayden set a daily routine. She was intent on keeping things operating as close to normal as possible. Jayden arrived first thing in the morning and stayed throughout the day. She talked and read to Edna as though the older woman could hear every word. Jayden felt very fortunate that Mr. Weiskopf had given her an indefinite time to be off work.

"Good morning," the clerk said when she saw Jayden. Everyone on the floor had become acquainted with Jayden, Jonathan, and Molly. "How did she do last night?" Jayden said to one of the nurses.

"She's a peach. Not a peep out of her." The nurse laughed.

To an outsider, the nurse's comment might appear cold and callous, but Jayden understood there had to be some humor and lightheartedness; otherwise the seriousness of the situation would take its toll. Jayden plopped down a canvas bag on Edna's bedside table.

"Need a little help?" Jayden said to the aide who was repositioning Edna single-handedly.

"My back would thank you," the woman said.

"Has she been talking your ear off?" Jayden teased.

"You know Edna. There's never a lull in the conversation."

"Edna, guess what I brought? Go ahead, guess." Jayden combed Edna's hair away from her face with her fingers. "I brought a dozen get-well cards from your friends at church. My goodness, we could wallpaper an entire living room wall with all the cards you've received."

The nursing assistant patted Jayden's hand. "You keep up the good work. What you're doing is excellent stimulation for her. We still don't know what the comatose patient may hear."

"I have to keep her up to date on everything." Jayden smiled.

"She's very lucky to have you, hon."

"Edna would tell you luck has nothing to do with it."

"Maybe so. But not too many young people would be as committed as you are to Ms. Sullivan. I only hope my own daughter will be that dedicated to me when I need help."

"She's my Edna."

"Well, use the call light if you need anything." The aide walked out and pulled the door closed.

"Oh Edna, you should open your eyes and look at this beautiful card from Betty Rogers. Isn't she that woman who works in the infant's room in the church nursery? The front of the card is beautiful. It's a picture of a babbling brook. It says:

> Our Lord formed the universe.
> He is strong enough to hold and heal you.
> May you rest your spirit and
> heal in the comfort of your Father's arms.
> "He shall feed His flock like a shepherd;
> he shall gather the lambs in his arms
> and carry them in His bosom."
>   Isaiah 40:11

Engrossed in reading the get-well card, she was startled when a man's voice said, "Jayden."

She stopped reading and put the card on the bed. There was no reason to turn around to see who was standing inside the doorway. She knew by the sound of his voice that it was Daniel.

He walked up behind her, touched her on the shoulder, and gently kissed her neck. "I've missed you," he whispered.

The sound of his voice and his touch made her want to turn around and hug him. Instead she moved out from under his embrace. There was still the lingering doubt of his relationship with Catherine.

"I'm so glad you're here," she said.

"How is she?" Daniel moved closer to Edna.

"There's been no change."

Daniel picked up Edna's hand and kissed it. "Grandmother has filled me in on everything. I tried to get home sooner but…"

"You're here now. That's all that matters." The words slipped off her tongue before she realized how transparent she must alppear. She quickly changed the subject. "The doctors didn't think she'd pull through once the life support was removed, but she proved them wrong. Now her greatest challenge is the stroke."

Daniel looked pensive. "I've been praying for her. In fact, my entire village is praying for her. How are you doing with all of this? You must be exhausted."

"I'll be fine whenever Edna gets better. How long can you stay?"

"I don't know…until visiting hours are over."

"That's not what I meant. How long will you be in the States?" Jayden wanted to hold onto him and his strength forever.

"I told Doc and Rachel that I am on an indefinite leave of absence."

That pleased her. Daniel had an air of confidence about him. With him here, everything would be all right.

Her hand slipped into his. "I've missed you too," she whispered.

Thirty-five

Jonathan stepped off of the elevator.

"Oh, Reverend Baxter," the unit clerk called. She always seemed to perk right up when she saw him. "How are you doing today?"

"Never better—and you?"

"I'm fine." She stretched her neck over the counter to see what he had in his hand. "Look how beautiful those flowers are. A dozen long-stemmed roses? I'm sure Ms. Sullivan will love them."

"These aren't for Ms. Sullivan this time."

The woman smiled. "I see."

He headed for Room 212. The door was slightly ajar. He started to go inside when he heard a man's voice. When he peered into the room, he saw Jayden hand in hand with Daniel.

Cautiously, Jonathan backed away, leaning against a wall in the hallway. He was angry with himself for feeling jealous. Reason told him Jayden had always belonged with Daniel, but his heart said something different.

Jonathan walked to the nurses' station before Jayden and Daniel had an opportunity to see him. He handed the roses to the clerk.

"Is everything all right?" the young woman asked with a puzzled expression.

"Fine. I just changed my mind. I thought the staff might enjoy the flowers."

"Thank you so much! I'll find a vase to put them in."

As soon as the clerk left, Jonathan walked swiftly toward the elevator. He had to get out of the hospital as soon as possible. "Why are you acting like a child?" he mumbled.

But he knew why. *Jayden is in love, but not with you, my friend.*

One morning each week, Molly relieved Jayden at the hospital so she could get a little rest. All in a fluster as usual, Molly literally felt her way into Edna's room since her vision was obstructed with all the items she was carrying.

"Edna girl, I'm back." Molly put everything on the counter when she saw the image in the mirror. Edna was staring directly at her. "Please, dear Lord, don't let my eyes deceive me!" Molly cried.

Edna looked dazed and disoriented, but she was awake.

Molly rushed over and came within inches of her face, looking directly into her eyes. "Edna, can you see me?" Molly's voice was loud enough to be heard in the next room. "Can I get you something?"

Edna closed her eyes as if in pain.

A nurse walked in. "Everything all right in here?"

"I think she's hurting somewhere," Molly said to the nurse.

"It might keep her calm if you talk in a low voice," the nurse suggested. "But I don't think she's in pain. I assessed her not more than an hour ago; she may be a little overstimulated."

"And how do you figure that? I haven't seen her do anything and, goodness knows, she hasn't talked in weeks." Molly was smug.

"No, she may not be talking, but we've tried another form of communication with her."

"Well, how else can one communicate if she can't talk?" Molly knew she had the nurse now.

"For example, we asked her to blink once for 'no' and twice for 'yes.' As of right now, that's how she communicates with us."

"I can't imagine why Jayden didn't call me and let me know." Molly was hurt.

"She doesn't know yet," the nurse said.

Molly was pleased she was the first to know Edna was conscious.

"At first we thought it was a reflex, when she opened her eyes, so we didn't get too excited," the nurse said. "But then she followed commands. We wanted the doctor to check her out first before we called Jayden."

"And what did the doctor say?" Molly said.

"Just what we suspected: neurological damage has affected her ability to speak."

"I'll call Jayden." Molly picked up the phone when Edna let out a loud moan. She moved her head slowly from side to side.

"I think she wants to surprise Jayden herself," the nurse said.

Molly sat next to Edna. "Oh, that's silly. We don't know that's what Edna's trying to say." She picked up the phone and tried to dial again when Edna groaned even louder. "All right, all right!" Molly put the phone back in the cradle and pouted. "Go ahead and spoil my fun."

For the next five minutes, Molly didn't take a breath as she talked.

The nurse reached down to take Edna's pulse. "You know," the nurse said firmly, "I think all of this may be a bit overwhelming for Edna. We should let her rest."

"Rest?" Molly scowled. "That's all she's been doing."

But the nurse ignored her comment and scooted Molly out of the room.

∽⋄∾

Later in the evening, Daniel and Molly sat on the front porch enjoying each other's company. "Thanks, Grandmother, for the lemonade. It's exactly what I needed."

"You're a good boy—oh my, I apologize…a good man. And I'm glad you're home."

"I do hope Edna is okay. I suppose at a time like this you don't really know what to say." Daniel leaned his head back.

Molly patted his knee. "You're home now, and that means a lot." She headed into the house. "You can stay out here as long as you like, but these old bones are going to bed."

Daniel remained on the porch swing enjoying the cool night breeze. He thought of Jayden and the last time they were together.

Then Jakaal entered his thoughts. He recalled the day Doc and Rachel had brought the boy to the airfield to see Daniel off. There was such sadness in his eyes. After the child lost his entire family, how could Daniel make him understand that he would return? Seeing the little boy standing there while the plane took off broke his heart. He took a picture of Jakaal out of his wallet and stared at it.

Thirty-six

The moment the two of them came onto the unit, Jayden had a sense something was wrong by the reaction of the staff nurse.

"Did something happen?" Jayden started to panic.

"Something wonderful," one of the nurses said.

"You can see for yourself," another nurse said, "but before you do, there's something I need to tell you…."

But Jayden was already on her way to Edna's room. To her amazement, Edna was sitting up in bed with virtually little support. The moment she saw Jayden, she tried to reach out to her.

"I've waited so long for this day!" Jayden cried, laying her head across Edna's lap.

With great difficulty, Edna tried to talk, but her words came out slurred and garbled.

Jayden was alarmed. "Edna?"

Daniel walked in at that precise moment.

Jayden looked at him, wondering why he had lagged behind. "Daniel?"

"I stopped to find out what the nurse was trying to tell you. She said the stroke left Edna partially paralyzed and affected her speech. It will take physical therapy for her to relearn to speak and gain strength in her extremities."

Daniel reached to hold Edna's hand. With great effort, Edna moved his hand over to Jayden's hand, removing her own. Daniel and Jayden smiled at one another.

"You always were the matchmaker. But you don't need to worry; I'm here now, and I don't plan on leaving anytime soon," Daniel promised.

Jayden hoped that Daniel could see in her eyes how glad she was that he was back.

As each day passed, Edna's strength gradually returned. Her speech improved, so at least the ones closest to her understood what she was saying. Trying times still lay ahead, but for Jayden, having Edna coherent was enough.

Of late, what concerned Jayden was Jonathan. He always used to visit when he knew she was at the hospital. Now he came after she had already left for the day. If Jayden didn't know better, she would think he was trying to avoid her.

"Are you going to be okay, Edna, if I run along? I promised to make dinner for Daniel tonight. I was thinking meatloaf?"

Edna nodded in agreement.

"Good. Meatloaf it is." Jayden kissed Edna and started to leave when Edna cleared her throat to get Jayden's attention. She motioned for the chalk and the chalk board to write a message: *What about Jonathan?*

"I'm sure he's fine, just busy."

Edna erased her question and wrote: *Busy or excluded?*

"I'm assuming busy. Why on earth would he feel excluded? You worry too much, Edna. I love you. If you need anything, be sure and tell one of the nurses to call me."

Excluded? Jayden thought about what Edna asked on the way home. *Have I somehow hurt Jonathan's feelings?*

Thirty-seven

Doc and Rachel,

I made it back in one piece. The jet lag is a killer. Thank you for your love and concern for Edna. While she's not fully recovered, I believe, with prayer, we will see the old Edna back in no time.

How's Jakaal? Still getting into everything? You have no idea how relieved I was when you decided to open your home for him until I return. I know it's a lot since you're expecting your new addition any day. I'm not sure how long I'll be gone, Doc. As you know from our past discussions, I need this time to resolve my relationship with Jayden no matter which way it should go.

I don't know how you and Rachel have been able to stand me going on like I did over Jayden, but once you meet and get to know her you'll understand. I have no doubt you will come to love her. If I have my way, she will be with me when I return.

I made a cassette tape for Jakaal. I want him to know I'm thinking of him. It's a tape of his favorite story. Hopefully he'll enjoy hearing me read it to him even if I can't be there.

Let me know as soon as the baby is born. I think the name *Elizabeth* for a girl is nice and for a boy, I love the name *Isaac Daniel*. What's wrong with *Daniel Isaac?* Just kidding.

Your brother in Christ,
Daniel

Thirty-eight

"If you'll tell me where the potholder is, I'll take the meatloaf out of the oven," Daniel said.

"In the top right-hand drawer. Everything else is ready if you are." Jayden poured the tea.

"Almost ready; just a couple of minor touches." Daniel went into the living room and came back with a brown grocery bag.

"I hope dessert is in there!".

Daniel reached into the bag and brought out two tapered candles and a vinyl record. "Do you think Edna would mind if I used her stereo?"

"I don't think she'd mind at all. What are you doing?"

"It's called ambiance," he teased.

"You're a true romantic."

"Shh, don't tell anyone. It's our secret." He smiled mischievously.

After dinner, the two sat across from one another listening to the music in the background. Jayden blew out the candles and started to clear the table. He reached out and pulled her down on his lap.

"I should get the dishes done," she said, but she didn't try too hard to stand.

"What you need to do is talk to me."

"I don't know what you mean. I've been talking."

"Yeah, for the last several weeks you've talked, but I get a sense there's something on your mind you haven't said." Daniel held her gaze.

"Okay. When were you going to tell me about your relationship with Catherine?"

Daniel knit his eyebrows. "My relationship with Catherine?"

"Yeah."

"What relationship?" Daniel was completely stunned by the question.

"See—that's why I never mentioned it. I didn't think you'd want to discuss it with me." Jayden looked down.

"I would talk about it if I knew what you meant."

"All right, let me see if this will jog your memory. The two of you sitting around in the evening telling stories. She makes you laugh. You said you really liked her and enjoyed her company."

Daniel winced. He'd meant to plant a seed of doubt to evoke some jealousy, but he didn't recall talking about Catherine like that to her. "If you say I said those things then I guess I did, but for the life of me I don't recall it."

"To be perfectly honest," Jayden said, "you didn't say those exact words. I just used my imagination to fill in the blanks."

By the wounded way in which she said the words, Daniel knew he needed to clear the air of this quickly. "Catherine is a sixty-five-year-old retired school teacher. She taught anthropology at Berkley. She is a wonderful woman and yes, her stories are inspirational. I would like to think we had a good friendship, but it was a mother-son relationship more than anything else."

Jayden turned to face him. "So you tried to make me jealous?"

"I suppose that was the intent. I'm sorry. It was immature on my part."

"All of these months I thought…"

Daniel took her by the hand. "Come into the living room with me." He flipped the record over and led her into the middle of the room. His arms went around her waist as their feet kept time with the beat of the music. There was no doubt in his mind that tonight was the night. He would again ask her to marry him.

Once the song ended without warning he plunged her into a dip. He liked the idea that he could be spontaneous with her.

She laughed. "You're crazy, you know that?"

"Crazy about you."

"Like that's an original line."

"The truth is I love everything about you, our friendship, and the way we can talk and be ourselves, and I like who I am when I'm with you," he said. His heart was so full of love for her. He was startled when, an instant later, she pulled away. "What's the matter, Jayden? Don't you want this?"

"I do, but I have to be honest with you first. I've never shared this with anyone. I was so ashamed."

He looked straight into her eyes. "You can tell me anything."

"I can tell you now because I'm free from the sins of my past. I turned everything over to God, but I need you to know why I've been so hesitant to commit to a relationship with you."

At that moment, Daniel made up his mind. No matter what she said, he would always love her.

"Douglas Jenson, my foster father—" Jayden paused and looked down again—"he did things no man should do to a little girl."

Daniel put his arms around her. Now he understood. How his heart ached for her! "I need you to understand this, Jayden," he said quietly. "I hate what that man did to you. It was so wrong. But *you* are not wrong. It wasn't your fault." He hugged her more tightly. "I can't make up for the past, but I want to be part of your future. I promise I will do whatever it takes to make a good life for you…for us."

Daniel and Jayden clung to one another and cried. He blotted her eyes with his handkerchief.

"I must look a mess," she said between sniffles.

"You're breathtaking. This last year without you has been hard, but it has also opened my eyes. Jayden, I want more than anything for you to be my wife, to have children and grandchildren one day." He took a ring box out of his pocket and opened it. Inside was the same beautiful engagement ring he had proposed with a year earlier.

"Jayden Arman, you would make me the happiest man in the world if you would be my wife." He slipped the ring on her finger.

Jayden threw her arms around him. "There's nothing more I want at this very moment than to be Mrs. Daniel Taylor."

Thirty-nine

Jayden couldn't wait to share the news with Jonathan. She'd all but given up on calling him since he never seemed to be at home, so she took it upon herself to go over to his church office and wait for him.

❧❦

Jonathan was standing at his office window looking out when there was a tap on the door. Thinking it was probably his secretary, he said, "You can leave the forms on my desk, Mary."

"It's not Mary," Jayden said, closing the door behind her.

Surprised and yet pleased to see her, Jonathan shook her hand as though they were casual acquaintances.

"Are you all right?" Jayden asked, appearing puzzled.

"Yes, why do you ask?"

"I don't know. You just seem very businesslike today."

"Today? No, not especially. I dictated a sermon to Mary, and when I heard the knock on the door I expected it was her with the finished product."

"Can I sit, or are you busy?"

"Where are my manners? Of course, have a seat." Jonathan positioned himself on the corner of the desk close to Jayden. "Now, to what do I owe this special occasion? Is Edna all right?"

"She's improving every day. We had a coming home party for her. I tried to call you—several times, in fact—but for some reason we never connected."

"I took a few days off and went back to visit my sister. I wish I'd been here for that. Please send Edna my regards." He purposely kept his voice, distant, formal.

"That's okay. It was kind of spur-of-the-moment anyway. The

reason I came out today was to ask you a question. "What's on your calendar for January?"

"January, let me see…" Jonathan picked up his yearly planner and flipped to January. "Looks pretty open for now. December is the busy month. Why?"

Jayden held out her ring finger.

"An engagement ring?"

"Daniel proposed the other night. I wanted to call my best friend immediately, but you never answer your phone."

He wasn't quite sure what to say, but "congratulations" just didn't come to his mind. His reaction must have surprised her.

"You are happy for me, aren't you?"

Jonathan paused. "Happy? Of course. I'm happy for you both. I guess I was just surprised."

"Imagine how I felt. I didn't expect him to pop the question quite so soon after returning home."

"Come here, you." Jonathan pulled Jayden to her feet and hugged her. He wanted to be excited for her, but his heart ached. "January, huh? I see no reason why I couldn't attend."

"Attend? Well, I hope you can attend. After all, Daniel and I want you to perform the ceremony."

Jonathan stood back. He hoped his expression didn't reveal how he felt inside.

"Did I say something wrong?" she asked. "If you don't want to officiate, that's okay. I just want you to be a part of it."

Think before you speak. "It would be an honor to marry you and Daniel." Jonathan was honest about his feelings. He knew Daniel was a wonderful person and that he would love and cherish Jayden.

"Oh, Jonathan, I want the three of us to be so close. One day you'll find the perfect girl and marry. I can imagine the four of us going on vacations together, and our children will be best friends."

How could she not see the pain in his eyes? In so many ways, she was naïve. That was one of her charms. "You always were the big planner," he said, and smiled.

"Oh my goodness, you should see how excited Edna is! Against doctor's orders, she climbed into the attic, can you believe it? Well, she dug out her wedding gown that she had preserved for her daughter. She wants me to wear it!"

"That must be very special to Edna."

"My, yes. It bothered me that my own mother would never see me walk down the aisle, but with Edna helping, all my dreams are coming true. Guess I'd better run. We're having dinner with Daniel's parents tonight. It will be weird in a way to call them Mom and Dad. I love you, dear friend."

"I love you." Jonathan walked her to the door and watched as she drove off.

If eyes are the window to the soul, Jayden, then why can't you see how deeply in love I am with you?

Forty

Jayden rolled over and looked at the alarm clock. *2:00 a.m.* Twelve hours to go before the big day. Her eyes ached from lack of sleep, but her anxiety level was at an all-time high, so sleep was out of the question.

She tossed the covers back, slipped on her robe, and made her way downstairs to make Edna's remedy for a good night's sleep: a scoop of cocoa, three teaspoons of sugar, and a cup of warm milk.

Just then the grandfather clock gave its deep reverberating bong on the quarter hour. Jayden started back upstairs when out of the corner of her eye something caught her attention. She flipped on the light switch in the entryway. The wooden frame of the picture window was caked with snow. Not just a light dusting either. She opened the front door as though she couldn't believe her eyes and needed more proof. Edna always said snow was a rarity in San Antonio.

"Not on my wedding day," she mumbled under her breath. A drift of snow blew inside before she could shut the door. "Guess the weatherman didn't see that coming." She let out a sigh and sat on the window seat looking out.

The steam from her mug fogged the inside of the frosty window pane. She drew her legs under her flannel robe and covered her shivering legs. The antiquated gas heater sputtered and clanked, making a valiant effort to warm the house, but it never seemed to be enough to break the chill. Watching the snow fall lent an air of tranquility; a hint of pine from the tree lingered in the air. Tinsel and strings of tree lights lay scattered about, ready to be boxed and stored until next year.

"Best laid plans." Jayden had had every intention of putting all the decorations away so Edna wouldn't get a bee in her bonnet and climb the attic stairs to do it herself. Now it would just have to wait until she and Daniel returned from their honeymoon.

The felt-lined box that held the glass ornament Jonathan had given her for Christmas was on the floor with the rest of the ornaments. She carefully removed it, holding it between two fingers and watching it twirl. The artist had painted a snow sled with "Christmas 1979" etched across it. This would be the first ornament on hers and Daniel's Christmas tree.

Jayden picked up the framed picture on the window ledge taken a couple of days before Christmas. She was standing between Daniel and Jonathan. It was the coldest day recorded in twenty years, and the temperature had dropped below zero. Most of the group had grumbled when Jayden came up with the idea to go Christmas caroling on the back of a hay wagon. The picture had been taken as the three of them had just come inside to get warm. They looked silly with their stocking caps, beet-red noses, and chapped cheeks, but it was a precious moment.

In fact, it was just one of many precious moments she'd had since she had become a Christian. Her life had all new meaning. She didn't think or act the same. In fact, it was hard to recall the old Jayden.

No longer did she carry around the pain of her childhood or mourn what might have been. Growing in God's Word, she relinquished all control. She had the kind of peace she never knew was possible. It didn't mean she was giving up the dream of reuniting with her father or finding her brothers, but she believed God had a plan.

And it became quite clear one of His plans was for her to continue with the group Kids for Him. In the beginning, Jonathan had a hard time trying to keep the small group together. Now the classrooms were busting at the seams. The growth was amazing. Additional rooms were added so staff could accommodate the varying ages of the kids. Jonathan was elated when Daniel offered to volunteer his time in the role of a big brother for the troubled older boys. He was a natural. Kids for Him had received the 1979 Mayor's Award for service to a community of children in need.

Jayden was startled by the creak of dry wood. Someone was coming down the stairway. The entryway light went on.

"Edna, did I wake you?"

"Goodness no, but why aren't you asleep? Did you forget you're getting married today?"

"I couldn't sleep, so I made a cup of hot cocoa and decided to sit here and watch it snow."

Edna went to the window and looked out. "Snow?"

"Will you sit with me for awhile?" Jayden patted the spot next to her.

"Look how tranquil and pristine." Edna looked through the snow-laden pane. She sighed.

Both of the women sat side by side. Jayden laid her head on Edna's shoulder.

Forty-one

Emma looked adorable in her long white lace dress with the satin bow tied in the back. A ring of flowers lay on top of her blonde tresses. "Every since she found out she was going to be the flower girl, we've been practicing her walk and how to gently toss the rose petals from the basket," Emma's mother said.

"Are you excited, Emma?" Cynthia said.

"Hmm hum." Emma was watching as guests arrived.

Cynthia was focused on the last-minute details. "Now let's see, we still need something borrowed."

"The wedding dress is borrowed." Jayden smiled at Edna.

"Check." You could see the wheels turning in Cynthia's mind as though she was mentally crossing off the items on the must do list.

"Something blue?" Edna said.

"I can help out there." Cynthia pulled out a gift wrapped in tissue from her purse and handed it to Jayden.

"What's this?"

"Open it." Everyone gathered around to get a better look.

Jayden smiled in approval.

"I take it you like it," Cynthia said.

"I really do but…"

"But nothing. Jonathan and I talked it over and we agreed. The sapphire bracelet has been collecting dust in our mother's jewelry box. I couldn't think of a better occasion to see it worn again."

"Your mother's?"

"There's a matching necklace too, but since you always wear your pendant, I know it must hold some real significance for you."

"I've never taken it off; it was my mother's," Jayden said.

"All right, let's move on. We don't have a lot of time. What about something new?" Cynthia asked.

"I have something new…these." Jayden pulled her hair back showing off a pair of ecru stud earrings. "This is a gift from Molly."

"Goodness," Edna said, "I have to admit those are very nice. One thing about ol' Mol, she has good taste."

"How do I look?" Jayden turned around for approval.

"Absolutely stunning," Emma's mother said.

Emma giggled, "You're pretty."

"So are you, Emma," Jayden teased.

Cynthia wasn't one for all the small talk; she got right to the point. "You do look nice. Now bend down so I can pin on the veil and don't forget to pull it over your face before you enter the chapel."

Edna touched Jayden's cheek. "There are no words…"

Jayden put her arms around Edna. "I love you…" She hesitated, then decided it was, after all, how she felt. "I…I love you, Mom."

That was all it took. Edna started to sob. Emma's mother understood the importance of what Jayden had said to Edna, and she started to cry as well. Emma looked confused. She tried to comfort her mother and Edna at the same time.

Jayden's eyes welled up with tears. Everyone searched the room for tissues. "Now don't you dare," Cynthia said to Jayden, "not after my expert makeup job. Do you want to have red eyes?"

A knock interrupted the moment. "It's only me, Jonathan."

"You can't come in! Everyone's crying!" Emma said.

The women broke out in laughter, lightening the mood.

"Go away, little brother; you can't see the bride just yet."

"It's the groom who can't see the bride," Jonathan corrected her.

"Come on—" Edna motioned for everyone to leave—"let Jonathan have a last word with our girl. We'll be waiting out front. God bless you, sweetheart." She kissed Jayden.

"Come on, Emma, you and I will take one more bathroom break before the ceremony begins," Cynthia said.

Jonathan stood before Jayden. There were several seconds of silence between the two of them.

"Well, do I look all right?" she asked.

Why does she have to look so breathtaking? "Look," Jonathan said with a glint of humor, "I found a way you can escape if you're having second thoughts."

"Let me think about this. No, I'm going to go through with it."

"In all honesty, you look very nice," Jonathan said.

"Nice? After hours of work, that's all you can say?" Jayden stuck out her bottom lip in a pout.

"Women. Okay, okay, you look ravishing."

"Maybe that's a little much, but I'll take it. Thanks."

His intentions were to come in and give her some profound bit of advice, but the words were wedged in his throat. *It's too late now to be honest and tell her how you feel.*

"Was there something you wanted to say?" Jayden's eyes sparkled with love and anticipation.

He extended an arm. "Are you ready to get this show on the road?"

She walked over and kissed him on the cheek. "You're one in a million, Jonathan Baxter."

Daniel's father paced back and forth, mumbling his lines. He waited in the front lobby for the wedding party to show. As flower girl, Emma would go in first, followed by the bridesmaid, and then the bride and him. It seemed as though the girls were taking too long, but he had two women in his life and knew how long the primping could go on.

Every now and then, he stole a glance inside the chapel to see the rows of seats filling with guests. In the front sat Mr. Taylor's bride of twenty-nine years and his daughter. Daniel stood at the front talking to people. He looked handsome, dressed to the tee in a three-piece black suit. Mr. Taylor was so proud of the man his son had become.

Cynthia caught Mr. Taylor peeking through the gap in the doors. "My wife is concerned I won't remember my one liner," he told Cynthia.

"Emma, you look like a little princess," Mr. Taylor said.

Emma blushed and swished her dress from side to side.

Jayden and Jonathan walked in next. Jonathan handed Jayden over to Mr. Taylor. "My dear, it has been a pleasure. See you down front." Jonathan left through the side door, taking his position in the chapel.

Mr. Taylor recalled the night Jayden asked if he would walk her down the aisle. It was a request he didn't need to think twice about. As far as he was concerned, she was his daughter. Mr. Taylor held her at arm's length. "I'm sure you've been told over and over today how gorgeous you look. We're honored to have you as part of our family."

"Thank you." Jayden hugged him.

The wedding march played.

Cynthia positioned Emma in the front. "Go ahead, honey, just like your mama showed you."

Emma started—one step, then feet together, then another, reaching into the basket to toss a few petals to one side and then the other. Cynthia followed close behind, holding a bouquet in front of her.

"Ready to follow this parade?" Mr. Taylor pulled the veil down over her face.

"I've never been more ready." Jayden grabbed his hand and gave it a light squeeze.

The moment Jayden stood at the top of the aisle, all eyes were on her. She was pleased at the way Edna and Molly had decorated the pews in blushing pink flowers and dusky rose satin fabric. Two sets of candelabra, one on each side of a floral arrangement, burned brightly.

Daniel's face glowed when he saw her. His love was evident. Jayden's heart had never been fuller. God continued to answer her prayers. While there were still so many uncertainties in her life, she knew now she would never be alone. Her Heavenly Father promised to travel the road with her. And she believed it was no accident that she had met and fallen in love with Daniel. He was a man who put God above all others and loved her with such depth and purity.

Jonathan took a couple of steps down to be at the same level as Daniel. "Today is the beginning of a new life together for Daniel and Jayden. It marks the commencement of new relationships with their families, their friends, and principally with each other. We have come today, in the presence of God, to join Daniel and Jayden in holy marriage.

"Daniel and Jayden, it is my special privilege and delight to participate in your wedding. Thank you for asking me to be a part of your special day. Next to your personal decisions to trust in Jesus Christ to forgive you and give you eternal life, this is the most important day of your lives. When you trusted in Jesus, you began a new life; you were born again. Now, as you join yourselves together in marriage, you are starting a new life as a couple.

"Daniel and Jayden, as you step into this new life together, what a comfort it is to know that God knew each of your exact needs when He brought you together. He knew what each of you needed to be a full reflection of His image. Together, as you commit yourselves to each other, completing each other, you will be a fuller image of the unity and love of God. You have asked to speak to one another in front of these witnesses…."

As Jonathan spoke, Edna thought back a couple of years earlier to the day a frightened, wide-eyed girl stood on her front porch looking for a place to live. She marveled at how far Jayden had come in her spiritual life. Edna was certain God sent Jayden to her to love and to guide. They were a family.

Mrs. Taylor watched her only son as he exchanged vows with the woman he loved. Tears rolled down her face as the different stages of his life flashed through her mind…his first step…first day of school…summer camp…Little League…it all seemed just like yesterday. Now he was taking a wife.

"Let us pray," Jonathan said. "Now may the God of patience and comfort grant you to be like-minded to one another in Jesus Christ, that you may with one heart and with one mind glorify God. Gracious Father, make the inward aspirations of their hearts the outward reality of their home. Make their home a place of light and truth, a place of beauty, a place of joy and ministry all the days of their life. In the name of the Father, Son, and Holy Spirit, Amen.

"Daniel, you may now kiss your bride."

There was a hush as their lips met, then an audible sigh.

"Ladies and gentlemen, it is now my privilege to present to you Mr. and Mrs. Daniel Taylor."

Forty-two

At first Edna didn't understand why Jayden wanted the reception held at the park pavilion when there were so many nice places to rent for this sort of thing. But when she saw it, she knew why. The rustic log cabin nestled amongst the trees held all the charm of days gone by. A set of wooden stairs, one on each side of the stone fireplace, led to an upstairs landing.

It was perfect. Magnolia white paper wedding bells hung from the eaves. A large banner with *Congratulations, Daniel and Jayden* was strung from one front porch post to the other.

The real challenge, however, was to get the seventy-five helium-filled balloons in the car and back to the pavilion without losing one. Edna thought it would be a nice touch to have everyone release a balloon to the heavens in Daniel's and Jayden's honor, but it was Jonathan's idea to order the balloons with a preprinted message on them. He and Edna decided on *A Love for Eternity*.

Molly was on cloud nine when Jayden asked her to be reception coordinator. One would have thought she had been knighted. But it was fine with Edna. That left her more time to spend with the actual wedding plans.

Daniel's mother was in charge of the music, which disgruntled Rebecca. She found every opportunity she could to switch out the "old people's music," as she called it, to a more "with it" beat.

The limo pulled up into the snow-covered circular driveway.

"Here they are," some of the guests announced.

"Put my coat around your shoulders so you won't catch cold." Daniel took off his jacket and wrapped Jayden in it. "Well, Mrs. Taylor, are you ready?"

"I surely am, Mr. Taylor."

He loved it when she fell into her Scarlett O'Hara Southern drawl.

"Dear family and friends, today you shared with me and my family the exchange of wedding vows between my son, Daniel, and the love of his life, Jayden. I remember when Daniel first came to me and told me he had asked Jayden to marry him and that she had accepted. Of course, my wife and I were thrilled. You see, as far as we're concerned, Jayden was a part of our family already.

"As a father, I felt it my duty to ask my son, 'What is your concept of marriage?' Daniel replied appropriately that he believes it's a covenant that should not be entered on impulse. That it's a commitment to one another and a lifetime of faithfulness and devotion.

"Daniel asked me, 'What is that has made yours and Mom's marriage successful?' It was a question that I really didn't need to give much thought to. I told him that, after God, we make one another a priority. It's easy to stay in love when you're in the good times. But when the bad times get us down, I always remember when my wife made me laugh and the times she encouraged me or nursed me back to health when I was ill. To this day, my beautiful bride can walk into a room and I still get goose bumps.

"Daniel thought about what I said for a moment, and I can tell you he paid me the highest honor when he said, 'Dad, if Jayden and I can achieve in marriage what you and Mom have, I will consider our union a complete success.' I ask you, what else can a parent hope for?...except a lot of grandkids! So, to my son and daughter-in-law, may Almighty God pour His blessings on you; may He grant you wisdom and peace and a home filled with love and laughter."

All the guests said, "Amen!" then raised their goblets in the air. "To Daniel and Jayden Taylor!"

With the endless stream of people hugging and congratulating the couple, Jayden was relieved when it came time for the bride and groom to cut the cake. Daniel held his hand on top of Jayden's as they made the first slice. Following tradition, they fed each other a big bite of cake and then Daniel kissed Jayden.

Rebecca hollered, "Yuk!" which in turn received a harsh glare from her mother. Everyone clapped and cheered for the newlyweds.

Daniel led his bride to the center of the room, and everyone formed a circle around them. The music started. Jayden picked up her long train in one arm. When the song ended, Daniel's father danced with his new daughter-in-law while Daniel danced with his mother.

Finally Jonathan stepped in. "May I have the next dance?"

"It would be my pleasure." Jayden did a slight curtsy.

"You know, I hope you find a woman who treasures you and realizes how special of a man you are," Jayden said to Jonathan.

"It's hard. Once the women find out how much money a pastor makes I don't know if it's me they want or my money." He laughed.

"Seriously."

"I'm taking a break from seriousness today."

"Yes, but all I'm saying is that…"

"All I'm saying is today is a day of celebration. Tomorrow I'll be serious."

Jayden detected aloofness in his voice. The last several months had been spent planning the wedding; there had been little time left for socializing with friends.

When the song was over, Jonathan kissed Jayden's cheek. "Thank you for the dance," he said.

"Jonathan…"

He stopped and turned around to face her.

"As soon as we get back into town, let's plan to have lunch so we can catch up with one another."

"I'll look forward to it," he said.

"Come on, honey." Daniel took Jayden by the hand. "I think my sister is trying to get your attention."

"It's time." Cynthia waved her arms wildly in the air to get Jayden's attention.

Jayden leaned over the rail and searched the faces below. Jonathan stood apart from the others against the front door. He gave her a thumbs-up.

"Turn around and throw it!" one of the men bellowed. The bouquet sailed through the air. High-pitched squeals came from the rush of women scrambling for the bouquet.

Jennifer, one of Edna's nurses from the hospital, caught it. Jayden thought she was a very pretty girl with a great sense of humor. *Potential dating material for Jonathan.* Several of the kids walked around the room and handed out the helium balloons that were attached to a long ribbon.

"What does it say on the balloon, Mama?" Emma asked.

"A Love for Eternity, Daniel and Jayden."

Jayden snuggled into Daniel's warm embrace.

Molly started to orchestrate the guests to move outside. "Let's make it quick," she announced. "The sooner everyone gets out here the quicker we can release them altogether and get back inside where it's warm." One thing about it, Molly was good at keeping everything on task.

The crisp air was refreshing but a bit too cold to stay out too long. "Molly, you better hurry up," Edna ordered. "I can see teeth chattering."

"All right, all right," Molly said. "It's just these things take some time. Listen up! On the count of three everyone release the balloons." Edna tried to help Molly count but couldn't make herself heard over Molly's militaristic countdown.

"One, two, three, and release!" Dozens of colored balloons floated upward. A couple popped from the cold air.

"A Love for Eternity." Daniel kissed his bride.

Jayden leaned against him.

Jonathan stayed outside alone, watching the faint trail of the last balloon. The sound of laughter and music came from inside.

Jonathan didn't feel like joining the group. He needed some time alone. Time to reflect. Time to move on. He felt more fortunate than many others. It may have been short-lived, but he once had had the love and happiness Daniel and Jayden now shared. Maybe one day God would bless him again with "a love for eternity."

Forty-three

Jayden took a break from unpacking. They had been in their own place for over six months now, and there were still cardboard boxes that hadn't been unpacked. It was a joke between her and Daniel. She pulled out a lawn chair and sat on the balcony of their apartment sipping a beverage.

She opened her journal and started to write:

June12, 1980

So much has happened since I wrote last. Daniel and I were married, and it was an incredible wedding. For a wedding gift Daniel's family gave us a one week trip to Mexico. What a change from the cold January weather here! When we left, it was snowing in San Antonio, and when we landed in Mexico, the weather was 90 degrees; the sun never stopped shining. We met another couple who had just gotten married and the four of us snorkeled and tried surfing. I'm sorry to say that's not where my talent lies. In the evenings Daniel and I had the most romantic walks along the beach, the warm surf splashing against our tan legs.

But the best part was coming home to see Edna and moving into our own apartment. It's not too far from where Edna and Daniel's parents live but far enough for us to have our privacy and independence.

I'm also pleased to announce that my dear best friend Jonathan has recently started to date Jenny, one of the nurses from the hospital. She's a wonderful girl and seems to adore Jonathan. When Daniel and I came home from our honeymoon, we invited Jonathan and Jenny over for my first home-cooked meal. They seem to be hitting it off really well.

I no longer work at the pharmacy. It was never the same anyway after Mr. Weiskopf sold it. I work four days a week at the church. My title is Special Project Coordinator. Sounds fancy, huh? But in our wildest dreams I would have never imagined the Kids for Him group would become an example for other communities to follow. I spend a lot of my time going to different areas helping other churches start their own groups.

Lately, though, I haven't been feeling myself. I'm more tired than usual. Daniel worries I've been overdoing it. Edna says I've been looking a little under the weather and all I need to do is take vitamins. They both are probably right, but I've never been happier. Better close for now. Daniel's home and I need to give the appearance that I've been trying to unpack these boxes. Only joking.

Jayden opened the door before Daniel could get his key in. She met him with a hug and a long passionate kiss.

"Well, something tells me you're feeling better. Did you get some rest today?" he said.

"I did. In fact you'll notice by the look of things, I did quite a bit of that today." Jayden laughed.

Daniel looked around and shrugged. "The good thing about leaving everything in boxes is that if we decide to move to another apartment, it's ready to go."

"Talk about going, we're having dinner with your family tonight, remember?"

"Good thing you reminded me." Daniel said. "But first, there's something I want to talk to you about. Can we sit for a minute before we change clothes?" He led her out to the balcony.

"Are you all right?" she said, a bit worried.

"I'm good. No, great! And no, it's not the landscaping business. We got a large order at the new church across town. What I want to talk to you about is…" Daniel settled into a comfortable position.

Jayden could tell by the way he lowered his voice, it was something he was very serious about. "You can tell me anything, sweetheart."

"I like my job, but you know landscaping isn't my heart."

"What would make you happy? And remember, whatever it is I'll support you."

Daniel didn't know how she would receive what he was about to say. "I love you, Jayden, more every day but…"

A tension knotted inside Jayden.

Daniel continued, "My dream is to go back to Africa and work with the children there. Don't get me wrong. I enjoy working with the kids in the church group. I truly do."

"Africa?" she repeated for clarification.

"I want us to go back together. You would understand if you could see the villagers."

Jayden didn't hesitate. "I'll go wherever you go."

"You would love Doc and Rachel and..." Daniel stopped. "Did I hear you right?"

Jayden knelt before him. "You are my husband." She laid her head on his lap. "We are partners in this life. I'll support you wholeheartedly."

"Thank You, Jesus, for this precious woman."

Forty-four

The evening started out fine but fizzled the moment Daniel shared his plans with his parents about returning to Africa. His father looked sternly at him. "Boy, why can't you just be happy earning a living right here on this continent?"

"There was so much work to be done there…" Daniel always tried to rationalize this topic with his father.

"It's an uncivilized place—and not a place for Jayden, either."

Daniel's perception of a civilized people and his father's were quite different.

Daniel challenged, "What constitutes civilization? Is it modern conveniences or state-of-the-art technology? How about a large bank account or college degrees?" He used this as an argument in the debate. He knew at least Jayden was by his side on this; however, the topic usually ended poorly.

Daniel's mother was silent most of the evening. It was evident she wasn't thrilled about the idea of her son and new daughter-in-law leaving, but she knew her son well enough to know he was his own man.

On the drive back home, Jayden tried to make small talk with him, but Daniel would only answer with a yes or no. While Jayden dressed for bed, Daniel apologized for his behavior.

"There's no apology necessary, honey; your parents are just parents. They love you deeply, and I'm sure they don't want to see you move off again."

"It's not so much my mother as it is Dad. He has never trusted my judgment."

She knew when Daniel spoke of leaving in a roundabout way it destroyed his father's dreams of continuity.

"Well, first off, I believe that he trusts your judgment," Jayden said.

"I'm sure no matter how old a child is there is always worry and concern for them."

Daniel walked over and put his arms around her. "How did you get so smart?"

"Isn't that why you married me?" she teased.

Daniel kissed her. "I noticed you didn't eat much at dinner."

"The heat's been bothering me lately," she reasoned.

"Dad said we can use one of their fans if we want. I'll go over there tomorrow and pick it up, but why don't we camp out tonight on the balcony? It's a cool enough night."

"Sleeping bags and all?" she asked, halfway kidding.

"Sleeping bags and all. In fact, I've been known to tell some pretty good stories on camping trips. Why don't I run to the store and pick up a snack for us?"

"Not for me. I don't feel quite right."

It was well into the night when Daniel rolled over to pull Jayden close to him, but she was gone. He saw her walking down the hallway, her hair matted with perspiration. She was trembling.

"Honey?"

"I'll be fine, I just need to…"

Daniel's quick reflexes caught Jayden before she fainted.

When she woke, she was lying on the couch with a wet washcloth on her forehead. The look in Daniel's eyes was that of sheer terror.

"You scared the dickens out of me," he said.

"I don't know what happened. I started to come back to bed when the room started to spin. That's the last I remember."

"Promise me tomorrow you'll call your doctor and get in to see him. I'll have Mom drive you to the appointment."

"You shouldn't worry; it's probably just a virus or something."

But Daniel did worry. If she didn't call the doctor, he was going to.

Forty-five

"Hand me that 3/4 wrench over there." His father held out his hand. Daniel picked up something entirely different without looking and placed it in his hand.

"A 3/4 wrench, Dan." His father only called him Dan when he was getting aggravated.

"Sorry, Dad. I guess my mind is a hundred other places right now."

"I know where your mind is right now. Why don't you get out of here and go check on your wife?"

"I can't leave till we finish up," Daniel said.

"You can't stay here either. You're no good to me like this; now go on."

Daniel didn't need to be told twice. Before his father could say another word, Daniel was gone.

❦

Jayden and Mrs. Taylor finally arrived home. Daniel was standing on the balcony, watching for them.

"Good luck, honey. Call me tomorrow and let me know how it went," Mrs. Taylor said.

Jayden started up the apartment stairs when Daniel met her at the landing. "What are you doing home so early?" she said.

"I wasn't a lot of help to Dad. All I could think about was you. Well, what did the doctor say?" Daniel said.

"Let's talk upstairs."

Jayden had never seen Daniel so antsy.

"I wanted to prepare a nice dinner over candlelight and tell you, but you're not going to give me a chance to do that," Jayden said.

"Don't keep me in suspense."

"Daniel, you're going to be a daddy."

"Yes! Yes!" he said, raising his arms overhead as though he had just scored a touchdown. He grabbed her in his arms, lifting her feet off the ground. "You've made me the happiest man on earth!"

I hope so, Daniel. But she knew this could put a kink in his plans to return to Africa anytime soon.

That night Daniel fell asleep before she did. She watched him for a while, then decided to go out on the balcony, catch the cool night air, and write in her journal.

> *July 5, 1980*
>
> What a glorious day. I found out what I had been suspecting for a couple of weeks: Daniel and I are going to be parents. As thrilled as I am, I'm also scared. God is entrusting us with one of His precious children. That's a pretty awesome responsibility. There are so many things I need to learn, but I'm fortunate to have such wonderful family and friends to seek advice from.
>
> I do have an immediate concern. Daniel wants to finish his mission trip, and I was to go along. I don't see why this should stop us. After all, Doc and Rachel had a child there and are doing fine. I know Daniel misses Jakaal even if he is reassured the child is well taken care of. But Daniel yearns to go back. I want that for him and for us.
>
> God has been so good to us. I know if we continue to seek His guidance, everything will turn out according to his plans.

With all the responsibilities Jayden held at the church, there was little time to enjoy the summer. Daniel worked from sunup until sundown in the sweltering heat to save money for the baby.

Summer and autumn passed, and the Thanksgiving season was soon upon them.

> *Nov. 16, 1980*
>
> Today I felt the baby move. I'm carrying a human life! True, I've heard the heartbeat, but now it seems more real. There's not a lot of

movement, or at least it's not strong enough to feel every time he or she wiggles about, but I'm sure with each passing day, there will be more activity.

Daniel is so cute. Together with his father, he has been working Saturday afternoons on a cradle for the baby.

✥

"Good morning, sunshine." Daniel opened the Venetian blinds.

Jayden rolled away from the light.

"Now, now, rise and shine. There's a lot to do today." How he could always sound so cheery in the morning baffled her.

"I'm getting up," she said, pulling the covers over her head.

"Come on. I need to leave and help Dad with a couple of finishing touches on the cradle, and you have a breakfast date with Jonathan in an hour."

"All right…all right." She swung her legs over the side of the bed.

Daniel helped her get her robe and slippers on. He kissed her good-bye. "Have a nice time with Jonathan. I'll pick you and Edna up afterwards."

Jonathan arrived at the door just as Jayden was about to pick up the telephone to see where he was.

"Hi, it's so good to see you," she said, letting him inside.

"You look great!" he said, exaggerating as he tried to put his arms around her for a hug.

"Very funny." She couldn't help but laugh.

A short while later Jonathan led her to a back room of the restaurant.

"Why don't we sit up front?" she asked. "There are plenty of tables there."

"I thought it would be more private, you know, where we can talk."

When he opened the café doors that separated the banquet room from the main dining area, several children from Kids for Him jumped out and screamed, "Surprise!"

Jayden was overwhelmed. She couldn't believe her eyes. The table was decorated in pink and blue with a large glass punch bowl full of orange juice in the center. There were homemade gifts for the baby scattered about.

"All right, you guys, I said not to startle Mrs. Taylor."

"Sorry." The kids giggled.

Jayden was speechless.

After the shower and breakfast was over, Jayden sat back in her chair, too uncomfortable to move. "I shouldn't have eaten so many pancakes." She patted her swollen belly.

The kids helped clean up while Jonathan pulled a chair over to Jayden so they could have their chat.

"How are you feeling?" Jonathan asked.

"I feel like a whale, and I can't even see my feet," Jayden responded. "But I don't want to talk about me; I want to talk about you. So tell me, how's Jennifer these days?"

"Nothing much to tell. We've gone on a few dates."

"Men! Why do women jump on the phone to tell about their dates? But men just say, 'It went fine.'"

December 1980

Daniel is doing what I wish I could do...sleep. There's never a comfortable position to get in. But that will soon resolve. Today I was surprised with a lovely baby shower, and we received so many nice gifts. But I have to say the most precious gift of all came from Daniel and his father's own hands, the most beautiful handcrafted cradle. What an incredible keepsake. I believe with all my heart Daniel and I will be good parents. I've been reading in the Bible where it says, "Raise up a child in the way he should go...he will not depart from it." We have so many plans to do just that. We want to pray with our baby every night and read Bible stories to him from the very beginning. I want him to have all the opportunities I didn't have for a good life.

The Christmas season was always Jayden's favorite time of year with all the festivities, but at eight months she tired easily. This season she did more observation than participation. Daniel suggested Jayden cut back on her hours at the church, which she enthusiastically did, yet she felt guilty knowing Jonathan would take on her work load.

Edna and Daniel's mother were taking out the last batch of Christmas cookies, while Daniel and his father had several strings of tree lights spread out across the floor, plugging in one at a time to determine which bulb was keeping the lights from working. The men had it down to a fine science. It was a sight to see.

Rebecca Taylor couldn't care less what was going on around her. She lay on her back, one leg crossed in the air over the other, the phone glued to her ear while she talked a mile a minute to her friends. It irritated her mother, but Jayden found it humorous. She enjoyed watching the different stages of the teenage years Rebecca went through.

The subject of moving to Africa never came up between Daniel and his father again. It was a moot point; however, the topic of Jakaal was brought up by his parents quite often. They sent gifts to him often, always signing them "Grandma and Grandpa."

"I'll get it." Rebecca rushed to the door as though she was expecting someone.

Jonathan stood there stomping the slush off his boots. "Am I interrupting anything?"

"Not at all, come on in," Daniel said as he helped Jayden to her feet.

"No, no, you stay put. I can't stay. Jennifer baked a little something and wanted me to drop it off to you. She's in the car waiting; we're having dinner with some of her friends." Jonathan handed a platter wrapped in aluminum foil to Edna.

Jayden smiled at Jonathan. "Jennifer...hmm...seems to me, you two have been seeing a lot of one another."

All eyes were on Jonathan, waiting for him to say something.

Daniel came to his rescue. "Sorry if we're making you uncomfortable; it's really none of our business," he said, glancing back at everyone.

"How do you feel, kiddo?" Jonathan asked Jayden, shifting the attention to her.

"Tired, but otherwise, I'm fine."

"Well, if I don't see you all before then, have a wonderful Christmas."

Jayden watched as he left, got into the driver's side of his car, and pulled away. Fresh tire tracks were left in the snow. Life had become so hectic, she felt as though she had lost contact with him and that saddened her.

"I have an announcement to make," Daniel said, getting everyone's attention.

Everyone gathered around. "Here's the moment you've all been waiting for." With that, he turned out the lights and plugged in the tree lights. There was a flicker and then suddenly the entire tree sparkled with greens, blues, and reds. The lights cast shadows on the walls, creating a kaleidoscope effect. It was mesmerizing.

"Groovy," Rebecca said quickly before returning to her phone conversation.

"You two did a nice job," Jayden said.

"Cookies, anyone?" Edna looked like Betty Crocker with a hand mitt on each hand and an apron tied around her waist as she balanced a cookie sheet. It was a memorable evening—family, *her* family, gathered together sharing in the holiday. A new tradition was created with her included.

The evening came to a close with everyone in the living room. Daniel sat at Jayden's feet and Edna was in her favorite recliner while Rebecca snuggled against her mother. Mr. Taylor sat on the sofa reading the Christmas story: "And the shepherds returned, glorifying and praising God for all the things they had heard and seen, which were just as they had been told."

"I don't think I will ever tire of that story." Rebecca stretched her arms out and yawned.

Mr. Taylor rose to his feet and reached his hand out to take hold of the person's hand to his left and to his right. Each person followed suit until they formed an unbroken circle. Every head was bowed.

"Lord, we praise your name. You are the almighty Lord of the heavens and the earth. Lord, You are the one in charge of our future. Each and every one of us here this evening has a personal relationship with You that is unlike any other. We are not just mere extensions of someone else. I pray that You will help us to grow in our desire to study Your word. Help us to trust in You at all times. Navigate our hearts. May the truth of Your word be firmly established in us."

Edna was the last to leave. Daniel helped her to her car while Jayden readied herself for bed. She brought out her journal and made a cup of warm cocoa.

"Goodness, the snow's really coming down," Daniel said, shaking the snow from his hair. "I told Edna and my parents as soon as they get home to give us a call so we know they made it okay."

"I'm glad you asked them to do that," she said, pulling her journal out of the desk drawer.

"Are you going to sit up and write at this hour? Aren't you tired?" he said.

"I think taking that nap today did me more harm than good. Besides, I seem to only be able to sleep when I sit up. At least I breathe easier when I do."

Daniel sat down next to her and rubbed her feet. "It's hard to imagine in just a few short weeks, we're going to be parents. Are you a little nervous?" he asked.

"You could say that. I just want everything to be perfect."

"Are you worried about labor?" Daniel was concerned enough, she knew, for the both of them. "The doctor said if you need pain relief don't think you have to be a martyr and go through natural childbirth."

"I don't fear anything about the birth," Jayden said. "I'm more anxious about getting things in order to join Doc, Rachel, and Jakaal as soon as possible. You've already been separated from Jakaal for over a year now, and I don't want anything to stand in your way of fulfilling your dream...*our* dream."

He pulled her legs across his lap and gently laid his head on her belly, feeling their unborn child move. "I have everything I could possibly want right here. But yes, I look forward to the day the three of us will travel together and join Jakaal; but you have to understand, you and our child have to be my main priority. I won't jeopardize either one of you. Jakaal is in good hands, and for that I'm thankful. If it's in God's plans for us to return, then that door will open." Daniel turned out the kitchen light and locked the door. "Please don't stay up too late."

"I won't." Jayden blew him a kiss.

The sky was a mottled gray, yet it was absolutely awe-inspiring. Jayden pulled the curtains back far enough so she could look out. Outside it was blissfully quiet. The bedroom phone rang once when Daniel answered. She heard him say, "Thanks for calling and letting us know you got home safely."

Dec. 22, 1980

    Sometimes I have to pinch myself to make sure I'm not dreaming. I'd never have guessed a couple of years ago I'd be sitting in my own place, my husband asleep in the next room, and our unborn child slumbering in my womb. Tonight, Daniel's father read the Christmas Story. I've read it in the past to Emma, but this time, I envisioned the emotions Mary and Joseph must have endured as they journeyed through the night looking for a place to rest, a place for her to give birth. What a story of incredible faith and trust in the Lord. How I pray one day to achieve such unshakeable faith.

    Our time on this earth is limited, yet there is so much I want to accomplish—but only if it serves God's purpose for me. Thoughts of my brothers and my father lay heavy on my heart. I pray if it's God's will, we will soon be reunited. As for my father, a miracle has happened. Last week I received a letter from him. He seems happy for me that I'm married now and having a child, his grandchild. He was moved a year ago to another maximum security prison which is a good two-day drive from here. It is with God's divine intervention that my father has agreed to visit with me but not until after the baby is born. He would like to see his grandchild, and he doesn't want me to make the journey this far along in my pregnancy. I can't begin to put into words how I feel. Daniel has agreed he will think about leaving for Africa when our child is about one year old. But I must remember that it's all in the Lord's time frame, not ours.

Forty-six

"What in the world?" Daniel looked up when he heard the skidding of tires across the slick pavement.

Jonathan threw the car in park and left the car running. He cupped his hands around his mouth and yelled at Daniel and his father, trying not to slip on the ice as he walked towards them.

Mr. Taylor stepped down from the back of his truck.

"Hurry! It's Jayden," Jonathan said. "Get in the truck, I'll drive."

The men were out of breath by the time they reached the hospital registration desk. "I'm looking for Jayden Taylor; I'm her husband."

"Daniel!"

He whirled around to see his mother standing behind him.

"Mom, have you seen her?" Daniel said.

"Yes, they just took her into the labor and delivery room."

"But the baby isn't due for another month," Daniel worried.

"It will be fine," his mother tried to calm him.

"But the doctor said if the baby is early, there's a possibility the lungs may not be fully developed," he said.

His mother put her arm around his shoulder. "Don't let Jayden see that you're concerned. She needs you now. You'd better go to her, Daniel. The doctor said she's dilated to four, so this is it."

"Are you Dad?" A short pudgy nurse stood before him, holding a cap and gown in her hand.

"Yes, I am." Daniel stepped forward.

"Come on, then, I'll show you where you can scrub. The rest of you can wait out here. Someone will come out to let you know how Mom and baby are doing."

Edna opened a big canvas bag. "I've prepared a care package for everyone." She handed Jonathan and Daniel's father a deck of cards and crossword puzzles for the women.

"Do you have any food in there?" Rebecca asked.

"As a matter of fact, I do." Edna tossed her a pack of crackers. "My motto is to always be prepared."

Jayden smiled when Daniel walked into the room. "You look like a masked bandit."

"How can you make jokes at a time like this?"

"Because it's at times like this when humor is needed the most...."

"Will you sit down, Grandpa?" Mrs. Taylor scolded her husband. "You're going to wear a hole in the carpet."

"This whole thing is making me a nervous wreck," Mr. Taylor said. "When you were giving birth to Daniel and Rebecca, men weren't allowed in the delivery room. We paced just like this, and when it was over, we passed out cigars."

Once again, Rebecca announced the time as though that would move things along faster.

"Yes, Rebecca, we all know what time it is." Mrs. Taylor was perturbed over her daughter's impatience.

"Sorry, Mom, it's just we've been here for almost four hours."

About that time, Daniel walked into the waiting area, removing his cap. Everyone stood.

"Well?" his mother said.

"Grandmas and Grandpa," Daniel said, since he and Jayden considered Edna the baby's grandmother as well, "you have a grandson."

"Praise the Lord!" Edna shouted.

Daniel's father, not one for public displays of affection, gave Daniel a hug.

"Congratulations." Jonathan crossed the room and shook Daniel's hand.

"Did you finally settle on a name?" Daniel's mother asked.

"Yes. Daniel Jonathan Taylor."

All eyes were on Jonathan, waiting for his reaction.

Jonathan never imagined they would honor him in such a way to name their firstborn after him. "I don't know what to say."

"When can we see him?" Both grandmothers were very anxious.

"The nurses are cleaning him up now. Give it a few more minutes and we'll go down to the nursery."

Twenty minutes later, each face was pressed up against the glass. Rebecca started to read the names on the blue tags at the end of the bassinets aloud, "…Rogers, Williams, Taylor, that's him!" she said, excited.

Daniel pointed to his son, and a nurse walked over, picked up the swaddled infant, and held him up to the window for everyone to see. Edna and Daniel's mother held hands and cried.

Mr. Taylor stood straight and tall, an expression of total satisfaction on his face. "Looks like a future linebacker if you ask me."

Rebecca made faces and cooed at him.

Jonathan didn't generally make a fuss over babies. He liked it better when they could talk and tell someone what was wrong. But there was no denying it: baby Daniel was the most adorable infant he had ever seen.

Forty-seven

The weeks that followed were hectic but sweet. Jayden found herself standing over the crib just staring in amazement at the miracle of their newborn baby. She rocked and fed the baby with gratitude for each little act of love that she could give her child.

Often memories of her days with Emma came to mind and how much she loved that little girl when they were in the foster home. Jayden never dreamed that she would have an even deeper love for this child.

Jonathan had encouraged Daniel and Jayden to be a part of the Baby Dedication at the church. It was always such a special occasion for all the families bringing their little ones. Today was the day as Daniel, Jayden, Daniel's parents, and Edna surrounded Daniel Jonathan Taylor as he was being dedicated. Jonathan spoke to the group gathered.

"We read in the New Testament how Jesus loved the little children. He wanted them to be around Him. He told the disciples to let the little children come to Him. I can imagine that He would play with them, maybe even toss them in the air, laughing at their delight. Jesus told us that we must have the faith as a little child as we come to Him. He wants us to trust Him like a little child would.

"We have instructions from the Bible to bring up a little child in the way he should go and he will not depart from it. Parents have a heavy responsibility to talk to the children about God and His love for us.

"In Deuteronomy, we are told that we are to impress the Lord's commandments on our children. 'Talk about them when you sit at home and when you walk along the road, when you lie down and when you get up. Tie them as symbols on your hands and bind them on your foreheads. Write them on the doorframes of your houses and on your gates.'

"The Lord has given you these precious children as a gift to love and cherish and bring up loving the Lord and His ways. Let me encourage you, parents and grandparents, to take your responsibility seriously. And may He bless you and give you wisdom throughout all the days ahead as these children look to you for guidance and security in the home. Let us pray.

"Father in heaven, we come to You today bringing this precious child before You to bless and keep him safe in your care. Bless these parents and grandparents as they seek to bring him up in the fear and admonition of the Lord. Thank You for Your gift to Daniel and Jayden. May You strengthen them in the days and years ahead to seek Your will in all things. In Jesus' name. Amen."

March 5, 1981

Where did the month go? It's certainly been a huge adjustment, but I think the three of us are finally settling into a routine. It's quiet at this moment. Little Danny is nestled inside the safety of his father's arms. This afternoon, Danny was dedicated to the Lord. It was such a nice ceremony. All our family was there to rejoice with us. Danny is changing daily. He has my auburn hair and his father's piercing blue eyes. I thank the Lord everyday for His incredible gift to us.

Tomorrow morning marks another important event. The three of us will be making the trip to Huntsville State Penitentiary. It will be the first time I've seen my father in thirteen years. If I'm this nervous, I can only imagine how he must feel. Finally, after a long wait, I will get answers to my questions.

Forty-eight

"Are you sure it's a good idea to be on the roads with a cold front heading this way? The weatherman's saying five to six inches of snow," Daniel's father said as he handed his son the keys to his car. He felt better knowing they'd be in a vehicle with new tires and a recent tune up.

"I'm sure it will be fine. Jayden has already cancelled the trip twice because of the weather. I don't think I can convince her to cancel again."

"There's not a cloud in the sky," Jayden said reassuringly. "We'll be fine, Dad. We'll drive safely and not too fast."

He waved at them as they pulled away.

⊰⊱

As they entered the front gates of the prison, Jayden was struck by the towering stone walls that ran the length of the compound. There was barbed wire secured on top of the massive fence. The authoritative prison guards with guns strapped to their hips emptied Jayden's purse and diaper bag on the table while Daniel put his keys, wallet, and loose change in a tray.

"Do you understand the rules?" It was obvious the guard enjoyed intimidating visitors.

"Yes, sir."

Jayden was repulsed by the demoralizing environment. A door automatically opened as they approached.

The guard grunted at Daniel. "In here," he said.

It was Jayden's decision to have Daniel and the baby wait in the front lobby until she met with her father first. Jayden was led into a cement block room with only a table and two chairs in the middle.

"You've been granted forty-five minutes in which to visit, and I'll be in the room at all times. If there is any behavior I deem unacceptable, I will call the visit over. Any questions?"

"No questions."

Jayden felt panicky, almost nauseous. She bowed her head and prayed silently, *Lord I come to You with a clean heart and confess the sins of my family even if I don't know what they are, but You in your infinite wisdom know them all. I pray our child will not inherit the sins of the family but will inherit the riches of the kingdom You have prepared him. Please help me be strong. Amen.*

Within minutes, a metal door opened. A man wearing an orange jumpsuit entered. Jayden stood to greet him. His hands were cuffed in front of him, leg chains around each ankle. *This can't be my father.* She remembered him as a strong heroic type. The man that stood before her was an old, downtrodden man who wouldn't look her in the eyes.

"Arman, have a seat."

It was him. Her eyes filled with tears as she searched her father's face.

"Dad, it's me...Jayden," she said gently, looking for any signs of recognition.

He slowly lifted his head, looking at her with haunting eyes, and his lips trembled. Tears rolled down his face. "My little girl."

She reached across the table and held his hand. The guard moved around so he could get a closer look at them.

"Daddy, I've missed you so very much."

Memories began to flood over Jeffrey Arman as he thought back to the days they were together. Good days, but mixed with sadness, for now he didn't even know his own daughter. Yet the resemblance to her mother was uncanny.

"This probably wasn't a good idea," he said.

"Don't say that, please. I've written so many letters begging for you to see me. I need you in my life."

"I don't see the point. What good am I?"

"You are my father. I need your help."

"Help?" What can I do?" The pain he saw in her face was

unbearable. He wanted to hold her in his arms.

"You're the only one who holds the key to the answers I so desperately need."

"About your mother?"

"Yes, please, Dad. Help me put it to rest once and for all."

He wiped the beads of sweat off of his forehead. "I'm guessing you want to know if I killed her. Well, the answer is yes, I killed your mother."

Jayden wasn't expecting that answer. Absolute despair tore at her heart. *Years of defending his honor, and for what?* "How?" She just had to know. Nausea rose to her throat.

"What difference can that make now?" he said, trying to spare her the details.

"Please, I need to know."

He weighed each word carefully, not wanting to paint her mother in a bad light. "I never loved anyone the way I loved her, but it wasn't enough. She was a tortured soul. She carried the burden of shame and guilt, shunned by her family."

"When we married and then you came along, I thought she was doing better. But I watched as she slowly spiraled into deep depressions sometimes lasting for weeks on end." He felt no need to tell Jayden details of her mother's psychiatric hospitalizations or when she would leave them alone for days with no contact.

"I read the report, Dad. She was stabbed with a pair of scissors. When you were arrested, there were slash marks across your arm. It was as though she fought her attacker."

"The day of your birthday, your mother sat at her dressing table staring into the mirror, almost in a catatonic state. It worried me; for all I knew she had taken too many of her antidepressants. She grabbed a hair brush and scraped the nylon bristles against her skin. She thought bugs were crawling on her. I tried to console her, to bring her back to reality, but she became combative.

"Before I knew it, she lunged at a pair of scissors sticking out of her sewing basket. I pleaded with her to hand them to me, but she was outraged. I went over to the bedroom door. I wanted to call for help but…" He looked away. "She didn't know what she was doing, I'm sure of that, but in one swift movement I pushed her away with my foot and she lost her balance and fell on the scissors." He sobbed uncontrollably.

"You didn't kill her; you were only defending yourself." She reached over and took her father's hands into hers. "Dad, we can get another attorney and have the case reopened. I know of one I can call."

"Let it go, Jayden. I may not have killed her with the scissors, but I knew how ill she was, how desolate, and I ignored it. I managed to maintain our perfect image but in reality, we were falling apart. I deserted her the way her family had. When she called out for help, I didn't want to hear her desperation. It was all too foreign to me, too uncomfortable."

"I can't let you sit in here when you're innocent. I won't," she said with an urgency in her voice.

"Go on with your life. You have a husband and son to concentrate on."

Initially, Jayden had intended to ask her father if he also had any information on her brothers. But it wasn't the right time. A lot of progress had been made already. Even though it wasn't an ideal situation, Jayden was just thrilled to be having a conversation with her father. One thing was for sure, when she left today she would contact Emma's father and seek his advice on how to reopen her father's case.

Every time the guard looked at the clock, she was reminded of how little time they had together. And every now and then, he would clear his throat to remind them he was still in the room.

"Dad, I have a gift for you."

"But I have nothing for you."

"You've given me exactly what I needed: the truth. Would you like to meet your son-in-law and your grandson?" Jayden asked the guard to bring in Daniel and the baby.

His eyes lit up. "Are they here?" When Daniel walked in carrying their infant, her father stood ready to greet them. "Dad, I'd like you to meet my husband." The men exchanged polite greetings, but when he looked into the eyes of his grandson, it was sheer joy.

"Would you like to hold him?" she asked, ignoring the glare and grunt coming from the guard.

"With these on?"

"I'll help you; it will be fine." Jayden placed the baby in his arms, expecting the guard to stop them. Instead, in a moment of human kindness, he turned away, allowing them to have this time together. Danny looked up at his grandfather with his big round eyes.

"I'm at a total loss for words," her father said. "It brings back memories of when I held you as a baby."

"I think he knows you're his grandfather." She put her arms around her father and kissed his cheek.

"Time's up." The guard tapped at his watch.

"I'll be back, Dad. I promise." She handed the baby to Daniel. "Would you be offended if we prayed together?"

"I'd like that."

They stood close together, forming a circle. Jayden held tightly onto her father's hand, not wanting to ever let go.

"Dear heavenly Father, please keep my father safe from harm and give him guidance and let him know You are his refuge. Help us through whatever actions we need to take to clear my father's name and bring him home."

"Thank you," he said with tears in his eyes.

"For the prayer?"

"For never losing faith in me."

Forty-nine

"Are you all right?" Daniel looked over at Jayden. She hadn't spoken since they left the prison.

"Just thinking."

"Do you feel like sharing?"

"It was so freeing to hear his side of the story. I always knew he was innocent, but I needed for him to look me in the eyes and say it."

Daniel peeked in the rearview mirror. Danny was snuggled inside a fleece snow suit, secured in his infant seat. Daniel stroked the side of Jayden's cheek. She kissed the back of his hand.

"Why are you staring at me?" Jayden said.

"Until today, I guess I didn't fully understand the significance of this visit with your father. Jayden, today you gave him hope where there was none. You gave him the kindness and love we are supposed to have for one another, no matter what the circumstances. Today, I witnessed forgiveness at its highest. I'm so proud of you."

She smiled.

Fifty miles out, their visibility was quickly diminishing. The wind gusts were creating snowdrifts alongside the highway. Daniel slowed down considerably. The wiper blades couldn't clear the windshield fast enough.

"Daniel, should we pull over to the side of the road and wait it out?"

His father's voice resonated in his head. *"Daniel, it's better to be safe than sorry."* But he was anxious to get his family home safe and secure. "I think it'll be fine. I can still see the brake lights from the car in front of me. That will help me judge the distance."

Jayden turned around to check on Danny. The baby was fixated on his animal toy mobile. "Thank you for being such a good baby." She patted his foot.

Once they arrived in town, the worst of the storm appeared to be over. Daniel pulled into the garage. "Okay, little guy," he said as he placed a receiving blanket over his face to keep him warm, "let's make a run for it."

"You going to be all right?" he asked Jayden as he continued up the staircase to get the baby inside.

"I'll be up shortly."

She stood in the yard, her face lifted to the sky, catching snowflakes on her tongue. "Thank You for today, Father."

Daniel put the baby, who was now asleep, in his cradle and then went to look for Jayden. He saw her from the balcony. She was lying on her back in the snow, her arms and legs moving up and out.

"Jayden Taylor, what are you doing?" he called. "You're going to get sick!"

"Come out here with me for just a minute."

"But Danny's in his cradle."

"We'll listen for him."

Daniel put his heavy coat on and gloves on and joined Jayden in the yard. "I left the patio door open so we can hear him," he said.

"Lie down next to me." Jayden smoothed a mound of snow for him.

"I don't think so." Daniel gave her a funny look.

"Come on, pull the hood up on your coat, and your head won't get wet."

"I wonder about you sometimes," he said lying next to her in the snow.

"Now, do like I do," she said, demonstrating how she synchronized her arms and legs in a sweeping motion.

"Stand up and look," she said proudly. "We made snow angels."

"You amaze me." He laughed.

"Well, I've never made one." That was part of her charm he loved. At the top of the snow angels she drew a heart in the snow with an arrow through it.

"Let's go upstairs and get an aerial view of our art." She hurried up the stairs, with Daniel quickly following. They flung their jackets off, then walked to the rail.

Jayden pointed at their artwork. "Look how perfect."

"So are you," he said giving her a hug and a kiss.

"I didn't plan for dinner since I wasn't sure when we'd be home."

"Forget cooking. Why don't I go to the Chinese Palace and pick up a dinner for two?"

"And I'll set out the candles and play some romantic music."

"Then I'll definitely hurry back," he teased.

"Just take your time. I'll be here."

Daniel already had his jacket back on.

"Don't forget this," Jayden said to Daniel, handing him the scarf she made for him at Christmas.

A minute later, she turned around to find him still standing at the door, watching her.

"Anything wrong?" she said.

"I just like looking at you."

Jayden walked over and gave him a light kiss on the cheek. He held her tightly in his arms.

Jayden felt his intensity. "Are you all right, sweetheart?"

"I am just a man in love," he said. Then he turned and ran down the steps toward the car.

Jayden grabbed her sweater and watched as he drove away.

Fifty

At the age of fifteen, the young man was well aware it was against the law to drive without an adult. But his parents would be late anyway, and he was only going a couple blocks from his house. Besides, he wanted to show off the restored Mustang he had worked on every weekend with his father.

The trucker barreled down the street. He glanced at his watch, checking it against the clipboard on the visor. "No bonus for this load, it looks like," he grumbled to himself. Sixty-five miles per hour in a 35 m.p.h. zone was not good, but he hadn't seen any cops, and there wasn't any traffic on the road.

"White Fox to Mad Dog," the voice crackled over the radio.

Daniel jumped in the car and put the bag of Chinese food on the seat next to him. The VW backfired as it commonly did when it was first cranked. A glance in the side mirror. All clear.

Daniel put on the turn signal.

"Go ahead, White Fox," the trucker said, "Mad Dog here."

The boy swerved the Mustang, just missing a dog who was running across the street. It was difficult for an inexperienced driver to regain control. The Mustang did a complete 360 before ramming the front end into the sign post.

Daniel's attention was drawn to the wrecked Mustang—and the smoldering fire pouring out from under its hood. The teenager sat on the street curb, his hands covering his face.

Poor kid. Daniel cringed at the very thought of his son behind the wheel of a car one day.

"Mad Dog, you there?" The truck driver dropped the receiver on the floor. He came upon the intersection so quickly that he didn't notice the four-way flashing red light. "Mad Dog, come in."

Daniel rolled through the intersection without stopping. Even though he was very familiar with the intersection, he was distracted. The screeching of rubber on asphalt jolted Daniel back to reality. In a split second he looked over his shoulder. A flash of silver brilliance was only feet from him. Panic welled in his throat as his foot hit the clutch trying to shift to a higher gear. It was inescapable.

"Jayden!" he said in a broken whisper.

∽∽

Jonathan had just taken a seat in the back of the diner when he heard the crash. "My goodness, that sounded like some accident."

The waitress peered out the window. "Are you ready to order?" she said to Jonathan.

"No, I'm going to see what happened." Jonathan stood on the sidewalk next to a couple of elderly men. There was already a crowd forming, but from where Jonathan stood, all he could see was a big diesel jack-knifed in the middle of the intersection.

"Did you see the way that diesel split that car? Must have knocked it a good thirty feet. I'd hate to be the guy driving that Volkswagen. Don't see how anyone could survive an impact like that," one of the men commented to the other.

Volkswagen. Daniel and Jayden drive a Volkswagen. The thought crossed Jonathan's mind as he made his way toward the scene of the accident. As he got closer, he could see a yellow VW on its top with most of the back end missing. Jonathan pushed his way through the crowd. There was no driver inside, but when he saw a picture of Jayden and Danny still on the rearview mirror, his heart raced.

"Where's the driver of the car?" Jonathan asked wildly. He ran to several different people before someone answered him.

"Over here," someone in the crowd yelled back. Jonathan gasped when he saw Daniel lying on the ground. He didn't look conscious. Several people surrounded him. A young woman took off her coat and covered Daniel to keep him from going into shock.

"You'll need more pressure on that leg, or he'll bleed to death," someone said to a man applying pressure to a large wound on Daniel's leg.

"Hey buddy, you need to stand back; there's nothing to see here." A burly bouncer-type blocked Jonathan.

"I know him. He's my friend. Please let me go to him," Jonathan said.

"All right, let him through."

Jonathan fell to his knees by Daniel's side.

"I'm a nurse, and I told those men over there not to move him in case he has a neck injury," a woman told Jonathan.

Daniel tried to open his eyes.

"Hey buddy," Jonathan said softly, "you just hang on, do you hear me?" Then he turned and yelled, "Who called for an ambulance?"

Daniel coughed up blood.

"Help is on the way, Daniel. Just a little longer." Jonathan tried to remain calm for Daniel, but he himself was terrified.

Daniel tried to speak. Jonathan leaned close to hear him.

"Take care of her," Daniel gasped and his voice trailed off. Warmth filled his eyes. The intense pain and fear in them were replaced with an expression of peace. He was free to let go.

"Open your eyes, Daniel. Please open your eyes." Jonathan's voice broke. He searched the faces in the crowd, pleading for help. There was none. "No! No!" Jonathan screamed. His body trembled with grief.

"Get out of the way," two men said as they squeezed in between people. "Move, sir, we're paramedics."

Jonathan sat off to one side, praying. "Not now, dear Lord, not now."

The paramedics implemented life-saving techniques, administering five chest compressions to one breath and checking for a pulse for several attempts. They looked at Jonathan. "Sorry, sir. There's nothing more we can do."

"Don't stop trying. Please, you've got to help him."

The crowd was silent.

Jonathan crawled over to Daniel, tears streaming down his face. He placed the picture of Jayden and Danny on his chest, and his heartfelt sobs echoed throughout the square.

Fifty-one

It was five minutes later than the last time she looked at the clock. *Knowing Daniel, if he saw someone he knew in town, he was chatting and just lost track of time.* With her ear to the door, Jayden listened for Danny. He was beginning to fidget.

She went into the room and gently rocked his cradle. "Shh, be a good boy and go back to sleep." She marveled at his perfection. They were truly blessed parents to have such a healthy son.

Headlights beamed through the bedroom curtains as a car turned into the driveway.

"Finally," she murmured, "your daddy's home."

Jayden crept to the door, closing it behind her. The table was prepared with tapered candles in the center, crystal wine glasses from their wedding, and two china dinner plates. *A romantic evening for the two of us.*

The knock on the door was unexpected. Why didn't Daniel just use his keys to get in?

She glanced through the door's peephole. "Jonathan?"

She was puzzled. He didn't usually show up without calling first. She was horrified when she opened the door. Jonathan's condition was appalling. There he stood, his clothes and shoes wet and muddy, his eyes raw and reddened. She reached for his trembling hand; his flesh was ice cold.

"Come in."

There was a chilling silence between them. Jayden helped him slip out of his coat. "I'll get something warm to cover you."

Jonathan sat at the breakfast nook, his head in his hands. Jayden returned with a throw and wrapped it around his shoulders. She looked at him with pleading eyes. "What's happened?"

"It's Daniel." He choked on his words.

"What about him?"

Fresh tears stung his sore eyes. "There's been an accident."

"Is he all right?" Jayden said with half-anticipation and half-dread.

Jonathan shook his head. "No," he whispered.

Jayden's anxiety mounted. *Daniel will be here soon. We're going to have a romantic dinner together and spend some time alone.*

"He's gone." Jonathan's voice was breaking.

"What are you talking about?" Jayden didn't try to hide her frustration.

Jonathan repeated, "He's gone, Jayden."

Jayden took a step back. Her mind reeled with confusion. "I have to go to him. Stay with the baby."

Jonathan wrapped his arms around her to calm her and keep her from running off. "Jayden, listen to me, Daniel is gone."

"I don't believe you…I don't believe you."

Sheer black fright shot through her. Jayden's fist beat against Jonathan's chest. She struggled to free herself, crying out for Daniel, but Jonathan held her close. After several minutes the physical and emotional exertions exhausted her. Finally, she fell silent.

"I'm so very sorry, Jayden…so very, very sorry."

"Please, just let me go."

Jonathan released his hold on her.

Jayden walked into the living room. She stared back at him in disbelief. Suddenly, she didn't know where she was. Everything looked odd, as though she were looking through one of the distorted mirrors at a carnival. She heard her own heart pounding in her ears.

The front door opened, and Mr. Taylor walked in with a police officer. Jayden was baffled.

"Jayden."

Her father-in-law held her in his arms. She could feel his tears against her flesh. Jayden felt as though she had stepped outside and now watched the events unfold. The police officer sat next to Jonathan, his hand on his shoulder. It appeared as though the officer was asking questions and taking notes.

None of it seemed real. The room started to spin and grow dim.

Her knees buckled. Mr. Taylor caught her as she started to fall. Out of the corner of her eye, she saw Jonathan leap to his feet and move towards her.

"Daniel." His name escaped her lips before she lost consciousness.

Fifty-two

Jayden's eyes fluttered and she moaned. "She's coming around, Doctor." The sound of Edna's voice reassured Jayden.

"Let's see." The doctor checked Jayden's pupil response. "Good thing someone was there when she fainted; otherwise she might have gotten one heck of a concussion."

"Daniel." Jayden's voice was barely above a whisper.

"Doctor?" Edna said.

"I've given her an injection. It will keep her calm for several hours. I'm also writing a prescription for some Valium to take as needed."

Jayden tried to raise her head, but it felt heavy. Edna sat next to her. "You just rest, honey. We're all here."

"Daniel?" Jayden cried, then rolled over, turning her back to everyone.

Edna wiped Jayden's face with a cool washcloth. "Just rest..." Her heartfelt cries broke Edna's heart and brought back memories of her own personal sorrow....

With the help of the medication and sheer exhaustion, Jayden succumbed to a deep sleep.

What? Jayden thought she heard a voice whispering to her... *"Jayden, come with me."*

She looked over at Edna. It was obvious that Edna didn't hear the voice; she remained in her rocker reading her Bible. Jonathan stood at the bedroom window looking out. Jayden wondered why she was the only one that heard the voice.

She slid out of bed and walked past Edna and Jonathan. They didn't notice her when she opened the bedroom door. Jayden stepped onto a desolate stretch of sandy beach. A cool breeze carried the scent of salt plumes from the ocean. The brackish water moved in and out, sending white-tipped waves smashing against the rocks. Thunder rumbled in the sky.

"Come with me," she heard the voice say again.

Jayden saw the figure of a man standing in the distance. Her pace quickened until she reached him.

"Daniel," she said.

She could feel tears on her cheeks. He smiled and offered his hand, drawing her close to him. She laid her head against his chest and suddenly was lifted into the cradle of his embrace. A warm glow of peace filled her. Music from their special song echoed in the air.

"May I have this dance?" Daniel placed one hand in the hollow of her back and held her hand close to his face. Their bare feet shifted in the sand as the waves splashed against their legs. His eyes were gentle and full of love. At the end of the song, Daniel leaned her backwards in a dip and held her there for a minute. A bright light surrounded Daniel. He backed toward it.

Jayden called out, "Take me with you!"

Daniel answered, *"It's not your time. Take care of our son."*

As the light diminished, so did Daniel. But somehow now, in Jayden's heart, she knew that she would be all right.

Jayden repeated over and over in her sleep, *"Daniel,"* as perspiration beaded on her forehead....

"Jonathan, I think she's coming around." Edna and Jonathan were frightened for her.

"Honey, it's Edna," she said, patting Jayden's hand. Her eyes barely opened.

"He came for me," Jayden said in a soft whisper.

"You've been dreaming, honey." Edna patted her hand.

"No, he was with me; we even danced."

Edna looked over at Jonathan. "Get me another cool washcloth; she's warm."

The bathroom faucet ran cold. Jonathan dipped the washcloth in the water and then stared at his reflection in the mirror. "Why, Father?" Jonathan banged his fist on the bathroom sink. "Why now?" A minute later, he composed himself and handed the cool cloth to Edna.

"She's fallen back to sleep. I'll stay with her," Edna said. "Danny will be staying with the Taylors for awhile, so why don't you go home and get some rest?"

"Do you mind if I stay with you? I can sleep on the couch."

Edna nodded. "Thank you; that would be nice. It's important for us to keep a close eye on her. I called her doctor earlier today. He said if she doesn't improve and start eating and drinking, he'll hospitalize her. Sorrow is a powerful thing, Jonathan. It comes at you when you least expect it. You're battered down to your very soul. Then you're tossed aside and left to pick up the pieces and move on. One thing's for certain: if you survive, you're a changed person."

Fifty-three

Jayden lay awake staring at the ceiling. Emptiness gripped her. She buried her face in Daniel's pillow, drinking in his scent. "I don't know if I can do this, dear God. I don't know if I can do this." Her cries were muffled by the pillow.

Edna and Jonathan were awakened by Jayden's sobs. There was nothing they could do but listen and be there if she needed them. Jonathan's heart ached for her. He knelt beside the couch and prayed for the Lord to give her strength.

"Dear Father, hear my prayer. Place Your loving arms around Jayden and protect her. In her eyes, her world is falling apart, but You have told us You will allow no suffering without a purpose. Please help her see that purpose. Help her to find strength and encouragement in Your word. In your name, I ask. Amen."

⁕⁕

The last three days had been a blur to Jayden. She had lost all track of time and she was glad. Maybe none of this was true, and it would turn out to be a bad dream. Jayden managed to dress herself and sit in the chair by her bedroom window. Her body ached. Feelings of isolation overwhelmed her. The sky was rainbow-colored as a thick haze slowly burned off. Moisture lay in dew drops on the ground below.

First day of spring, new life. "You promised, Daniel," she said. "You promised never to leave me."

Moving forward without Daniel was hard to imagine, and then there was Danny. *How will he ever know how wonderful his father was?* She thought of the numerous talks they had well into the night, planning their life, planning their family.

She could only imagine how her own father dealt with the loss of his wife and his child. His spirit must have died on that day as did hers. But she was glad that she had opened her heart and fallen in love, if only for a short time.

⊰⊱

"The family car is here," Edna said to Jonathan.

"Let me tell her," Jonathan said. Edna nodded in agreement. Jonathan knew he had to share with Jayden the last few minutes of Daniel's life. She needed to know. He tapped on the door before entering.

Jayden didn't respond when Jonathan came into the room. She was staring out the window, watching the birds.

"Daniel loved taking pictures of nature," she murmured.

Jonathan moved to stand beside her. "Jayden, before we leave, there is something I need to tell you." He pulled up a chair and sat in front of her. Tears bordered his eyes. "I was with Daniel until he…passed on."

She saw the emotion in his face, and the quiver in his lip. "What did you say?" she asked.

Jonathan looked thoughtful. "I came upon the scene of the accident just moments after it happened. There was nothing anyone could do. I went to him and held him in my arms. His last words were of you."

Jayden reached across and took Jonathan's hand. The dark shadow of grief started to lift from her heart. "Thank you for telling me that, Jonathan." She stood and embraced him. "Thank you, my friend."

⊰⊱

The ride to the church was completely silent. Danny cooed and gurgled as Jayden stared out of the car window.

Jayden took her place alongside the family at the front of the church. Edna and Mrs. Taylor were on either side of her. A young boy from the Kids for Him group walked to the front and stood by Daniel's casket. He pulled a harmonica out of his pocket and played a beautiful piece.

"Look, honey." Edna was looking at the back of the church. Jayden turned around. There wasn't a vacant seat inside the chapel. People were lined up against the wall. It was a wonderful sight. Daniel had touched the lives of so many. She started to turn around and face the front again when she noticed a man holding a small boy. Somehow the small boy looked familiar. *It couldn't be.*

Several of the children from the boys group Daniel worked with at the church made their way to the front next. One of the older boys passed out a candle in a holder to the others and then lit it. They sang "Amazing Grace." There wasn't a dry eye in the place.

Jayden closed her eyes. She felt Daniel's presence. His comforting arms embraced her as he whispered in her spirit, *"I will always be with you, now and forever; that is my promise to you."*

"Now and forever," she repeated under her breath.

Edna looked over at her and brushed the hair from her face. "Did you say something?" she asked. A smile parted Jayden's lips. "Nothing."

The pastor began to speak. "We've spent time today celebrating the life of Daniel Taylor. Daniel lived a life honoring God in his work, in his relationships, and in his mission. He loved his work in Africa and had plans to go back there very soon. He loved his family and friends and took great pride in his wife, Jayden, and their new baby, Danny.

"But most of all he loved the Lord and His word. Daniel spent hours reading his Bible and mentoring young people. He instilled in others the unique thought of living in the light of eternity. That meant doing everything you do with all the fervor and dedication that you could give to the glory of God.

"Daniel believed the Bible. He believed what Jesus said in John 14, 'Don't let your hearts be troubled. Trust in God, and trust also in me. There is more than enough room in my Father's home. If this were not so, would I have told you that I am going to prepare a place for you? When everything is ready, I will come and get you, so that you will always be with me where I am. And you know the way to where I am going.' Daniel knew the way. He knew that when his time on earth was finished, he would be with the Lord. And we must trust that we, too, will be there with him.

"This is a sad day because we will miss Daniel, but we must not despair because we will see him again when Jesus comes back to get us! That's His promise! So, let not your hearts be troubled. Jesus will walk with you every step of the way through this valley. Look to Him for comfort. Claim His promise that He will never leave you nor forsake you. As Daniel did, we must all learn to live in light of eternity. Let us pray."

It was time to go. The pallbearers carried Daniel's casket. Row by row, the family rose from the pew and made their way to the waiting cars. All heads were bowed as they passed.

"It was a beautiful service," Jonathan said.

Jayden managed a smile. *How can anyone understand? When everyone leaves today, they'll have their lives to live, but Danny's and my life has changed forever.*

As the cars entered through the large wrought-iron gate, Jayden looked over at Jonathan…their eyes locked. She could tell his heart went out to her.

Edna and Jonathan had their arms around Jayden as they walked behind the pallbearers.

The pastor looked over at Daniel's family. "God does not will the suffering of mankind. He is the first to cry when we cry."

Jayden turned a deaf ear. She couldn't bear to hear any more praises of God when He allowed such evil in the world. He robbed a family of their son, a wife of her husband, and a child of his father. *What kind of loving God would do this?*

Fifty-five

As the last car drove away, Mr. Taylor walked over to Jayden. He held her sleeping son in his arms. "I'd better get this little one home."

She touched Danny's leg and nodded. "Thank you."

Jonathan reached out for Jayden's hand to help her to her feet. "I'm not ready to leave yet," she said.

"I'll wait over by the car for you." Jonathan knew she needed to say her good-bye in private.

Two cemetery workers stood in the distance, waiting for her to leave so they could finish their job. She stood next to the coffin and picked up the framed picture of Daniel that was on top. "I don't know if I can do this, God. You've won! Do you hear me, Father? You've won!" she cried out. "Your wrath has fallen upon me once again. You are a jealous God. What else do You want from me?" Jayden doubled over in agony. "I trusted in You. Why do You take away everything I love and hold dear? You dangle happiness in front of me and then take it away at a whim.

"I remember the days when I didn't know You. Not like I know You now. I remember when I ridiculed anyone who had faith in You because I thought their belief was just a crutch. I thought I was so tough and independent. I bowed my back every time your name was mentioned. I even scoffed at You.

"Then I met Daniel and Jonathan and loved the kind of men they were. They showed me that You have a plan for my life, a plan to give me hope and a future. I began to see that plan unfold as You allowed me to see Emma again and You gave me Daniel, the man I wanted to spend the rest of my life with. Then we had Danny, a precious little boy who will grow up without his father. Why, when everything was so perfect, did You take Daniel? We need him! I can't do this alone!"

"Daughter, I will walk with you through this valley. I will never leave you."

Jayden turned around to see who might have been speaking to her, but no one was there. It wasn't an audible voice, but it was so strong in her spirit. Could it be that God was listening to her and answering her even when she was so angry?

"I have read in the Bible how you experienced sorrow when you were here on earth. Could it be that you understand this sadness? This loss? I feel like my heart has been ripped out of my body. How will I walk through all the lonely days ahead?

"Come to me, all you who are weary and burdened, and I will give you rest."

Jayden sat still for a few minutes pondering the realization all over again that the Lord is always with us when we cry out to Him. That He does understand sorrow and loneliness. That we can trust Him to take care of us, even when we can't see the way clearly. He will go before us and smooth the path.

She felt a strange sense of peace and comfort that she could not explain. No doubt, the days ahead would be difficult and the tears would come, but she would not have to walk this road alone. The Lord would walk with her, and He would bring people into her life to make her life easier.

Jayden kissed the casket. She stood up and looked back at Jonathan when she noticed a man walking towards her, holding the hand of a boy. She remembered them from the church. She straightened her dress and wiped the tears from her face. The closer they came, the more nervous she was. Jonathan sensed it as well and started to walk towards her.

They stood face to face. She couldn't take her eyes off of the child.

His large, brown eyes stared at the picture of Daniel. The young boy pointed. "Daniel."

The man extended his hand. "I guess I should introduce myself. I'm Jake, and this is Jakaal."

"Doc?" Jayden said.

Jake smiled at her "Yes, Daniel always called me 'Doc.'

"Jakaal!" Jayden kneeled down, eye level with the child. "I would know you anywhere. Daniel always had your picture with him." Her arms went around him and she kissed his cheek. She looked up at Doc. "Thank you so much for coming and bringing him."

Jakaal walked away and went over to the casket.

Doc and Jayden sat down and watched the child.

"I tried to get here sooner," Doc explained, "but it was so hard to get out of the country and there was no leaving Jakaal behind. My wife, Rachel, had to stay back with the baby. I'm so sorry for your loss. We loved Daniel dearly. He was like a brother to me."

"He felt the same about you. I was worried that you didn't know."

"Daniel's grandmother notified the Red Cross. The entire village is in mourning. His death is devastating to all of us. We don't always understand why these things happen," Doc said.

"Thank you for sharing that with me. Daniel loved you. How long will you be in town? I would love to spend some time with you and learn more about the village and the people Daniel loved. I'd like to be able to share that with our son one day."

"I'll be leaving in a few days and I consider it an honor to share with you what I know about Daniel." There was something about Doc that seemed familiar, as though she had always known him.

As Doc bent down and picked up Jakaal, she noticed he wore a gold pendant.

"I can't help but notice your necklace is half of a coin." Her quivering voice held a question and a sense of wonder all at the same time.

"This?" He held the medallion between his fingers. "It was my mother's. She gave it to me."

"When you were in Africa?" Jayden asked.

"No, I never knew my mother. After I was born she placed me in the care of my grandmother."

Jayden's pulse raced. "May I see it?" She reached up and held the medallion between her trembling fingers. It was half of a coin with a verse inscribed.

Jayden unfastened her necklace and held it up to his, the two halves forming one. The verse was completed. *Two Hearts Become*

One. Tears formed in her eyes. "Jacob?"

The shock of the discovery caused a momentary loss of his equilibrium. Jacob sank into one of the fold-out chairs. His eyes started to tear as he placed his head in his hands.

Both were astounded at the turn of events. Unspoken questions hung in the air. Jacob looked up at Jayden with an indefinable expression. "After all this time," he spoke in utter disbelief, "I can't believe I've found my sister I never knew I had. Why did Grandmother do this to me? Why?" Jacob's cry tore at her heart.

She knelt on the ground beside him. "I've prayed for this day to come," she said. "Daniel spoke of you so often; I felt I knew you."

Jacob said, "This is a miracle!" He touched the top of her head. Tears of joy streamed down his face.

They had so much to share...lost years, lost parents, a lost friend.

The three looked with love one last time at the casket laden with flowers. They knew that Daniel was in the arms of the God he loved and that, in time, they would laugh together again. Until then, Daniel would live in their hearts forever.

Hand in hand, the three of them walked toward Jonathan.

"There's someone very special I want you to meet," she said.

Epilogue

18 Months Later

"The whole thing is surreal." A question played over and over in her mind as she tried to listen to what her brother, Jacob, was saying.

A year and a half earlier, Jayden's world had come crashing down when the life of her Prince Charming tragically ended, leaving her a widow and their precious infant fatherless. Grasping God's promise to be with her through all the shock, anguish, and depression gave Jayden the strength to continue to live.

"Lord, am I doing the right thing? I know Daniel is with You and not buried in the earth, so why do I feel as though I'm deserting him?" Jayden mumbled under her breath.

"What did you say?" Jacob asked.

"I'm sorry. I was just thinking out loud," she said.

Jacob knew his sister was wrestling with her decision, yet he wanted desperately to have her and Danny join his family so he could take care of both of them. There had already been too many years that kept them apart, and he didn't want to waste any more time.

"I can't help feeling maybe this is all moving too fast," she said with a degree of hesitation.

Jacob took his sister's hand in his. "I want to take care of you and the baby. Please don't worry; you've done enough of that your entire life. Learn to lean on the love and support of others, Jayden. You can't always do everything alone."

She leaned her head on Jacob's shoulder. "I appreciate the offer you and Rachel have given me so graciously. I'm not backing out. It's just…" She stopped as she looked into his eyes. Something about his calming demeanor reminded her of Daniel. "Thank you, I can't think of any place Danny and I would rather be than with you and your family."

With that she stood and looked down the ramp, searching the faces in the crowd. Within the next hour she would be en route to the African continent to live for the next year. It concerned her greatly that Jonathan hadn't shown up to say good-bye.

"Where are you, Jonathan Baxter?" she said out loud, pacing back and forth. She turned around suddenly to the sound of Danny's high-pitched squeal as Edna pointed out the jets coming in for landing.

"Airp'ane!" Danny clapped his chubby little fists with glee.

"What a character." Jacob stood next to her, giving her shoulder a squeeze.

"Who, the baby?" Jayden asked.

"Well, him, too. But I was thinking more about Edna."

They laughed.

"I get a distinct feeling there's something more on your mind," Jacob probed.

"You're right, it's about Jonathan," Jayden immediately offered.

"Really, why?"

"It's not like him not to do what he says he will do." Jayden felt both concern and confusion.

"Maybe something came up. Besides, we still have another hour before we board."

Jayden was somewhat puzzled by Jacob's cavalier response, since he now knew how much she treasured her relationship with Jonathan.

"And there's something else," she continued.

He patiently listened.

"Our search for Joseph has been in vain. We're no closer now than we were a year ago." There was defeat in her voice.

"We will find him. Didn't we find each other?"

"That was sheer luck," she quipped.

"Luck has nothing to do with it. It was divine intervention."

"But there's so much we don't even know," she continued. "For instance, what do we know about his adoptive parents?"

There was a lull in the conversation before he responded. "I don't have all the answers, Sis. I just know we have to have faith and perseverance. All right! You've forced me to tell you a secret." A mischievous grin crossed his lips. "On this last trip back to the States to get you and Danny, I enlisted the aid of an investigator to find our brother. If Joseph is out there, we'll find him."

She smiled, watching as Edna headed toward them, balancing a sleepy Danny on her hip. "Mercy me, this little one is wearing me down!" Edna seemed winded.

"Well, it's that time," Jacob said as he took the toddler and diaper bag from Edna.

The announcement came over the loudspeaker for all families with children to board first. The elderly woman kissed the top of Danny's head.

"Take care of my family," she said, watching as they boarded the plane. Jayden didn't board right away.

"It's going to be all right, sweetheart. I will visit during Christmas," Edna said. "What a hoot that will be, searching for an evergreen tree in the middle of the jungle," she chided in her usual, jovial way.

"I will miss you so much," Jayden said with tears flowing down her face.

The two women held each other, neither wanting to be the first to let go.

"Edna, please tell Jonathan good-bye for me." Jayden tried to wipe the tears away, but they wouldn't stop.

"Yes, yes, now go on." Edna blew her nose in a hanky and went to the window to wave good-bye.

"Are you all right?" Jacob asked as he walked beside her down the concourse.

She smiled, marveling at her beautiful child sleeping soundly in his uncle's embrace.

"Looks like no one will be sitting next to you," he whispered with a sheepish grin.

Jayden leaned her head back against the headrest and said a silent prayer before takeoff when she thought she heard a man speaking to the stewardess. The voice was familiar. Her eyes remained closed.

"Sir, please take your seat," the flight attendant said.

"Excuse me, Miss, but I believe that's my seat." The voice was directed at her.

"It can't be!" Jayden opened her eyes to see Jonathan Baxter standing over her. "What on earth?" She glanced over at Jacob, whose expression looked like the cat that ate the canary.

Her heart raced.

"I said, I believe that's my seat."

Speechless, Jayden stood to let him pass.

"You should buckle up." Jonathan stifled a grin.

"What is going on? Why are you here?"

Jonathan turned to face her. His eyes held the answers to her questions. "Do you think I would let you and Danny leave without me?"

"I don't understand." Jayden wasn't able to think straight.

"Looks like I'm going to Africa, sweetheart," he said.

About the Author

JANICE BRASWELL enjoys creating characters and bringing them to life on paper or when performing on stage with the community theater. As a child growing up in El Paso, Texas, she witnessed daily the will of the human spirit of the people in Mexico crossed the border to achieve a better way of life. Janice admits she never realized the ramifications of poverty until her own family became a statistic. She knows all too well about stolen childhood innocence due to abandonment, homelessness, abuse, and alcoholism—and the lifelong struggle to regain a sense of worth as a result.

After many years as a stay-at-home mom, Janice raised her five children before returning to school to finish a bachelor's degree in nursing. For the last ten years, Janice has worked in the field of public health. She often sees the familiar look in her client's eyes of feeling "not worthy to be loved." Currently she is with a county health department in the beautiful state of Wisconsin.

Today, Janice, her husband of 28 years, their grown children and grandchildren, make their home in northern Illinois.

To write the author: **janicebraswell@gmail.com**

If you liked *A Love for Eternity*, you'll also like:

1885, Idaho Territory. A wounded heart. Desperate choices. Unfathomable love.

When Jemma meets Paul, a buckaroo lawyer, trouble is afoot.

Lonnie has dreamed of her own home and family, but not this soon. Not this way.

Maddie and Scott have the perfect life, but somehow they've lost their connection.

Who says love can't bloom at a Laundromat? *Set in the 1960s, inner-city Chicago.*

London, 1864. What if you were forced to marry someone you barely knew?

See these and other exciting OakTara novels at www.oaktara.com.

OakTara books are available through numerous national retailers such as **www.amazon.com**, **www.barnesandnoble.com**, and **www.christianbook.com**, and as ebooks through **www.amazonkindle.com**.

LaVergne, TN USA
26 October 2009
161990LV00003B/47/P